Wizards of the Apocalypse

Cover art by @enchantedinkpublishing and X Zombie
Interior design and typography by Catherine Kopf
Interior illustrations by X Zombie
Maps by X Zombie
ISBN: 979-8-218-03989-9

Wizards of the Apocalypse

THE FORGOTTEN PROPHECY

X. Zombie

HAUNTED LANDS

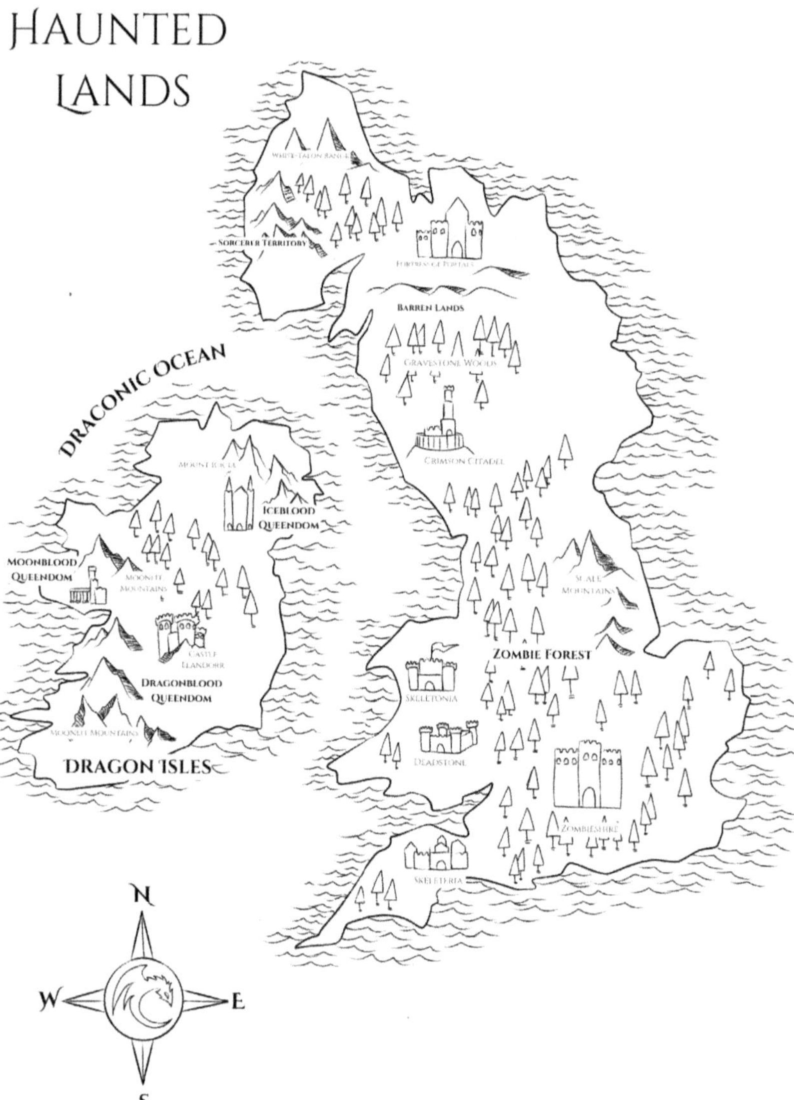

UNDERWORLD

OCEAN OF SOULS
BASALT WASTES
SHADOWBLOOD FORTRESS
HIGHBORN DEMON TERRITORY
WYVERN STABLES
MOUNT ONYX
MOUNT IGNEOUS
NOVA
SHADOWBLOOD OUTPOST
HALL OF BLACK MIRRORS
OBSIDIAN RANGE
LAKE MAGMA
GLASS BEACH
RIVER OF FIRE
SCARLET DUNES
INFERNO MOUNTAINS
BURNING PEAKS
SULFUR RIVER
LOWBORN DEMON TERRITORY
N
W E
S
SEARING PENINSULA
MOLTEN OCEAN

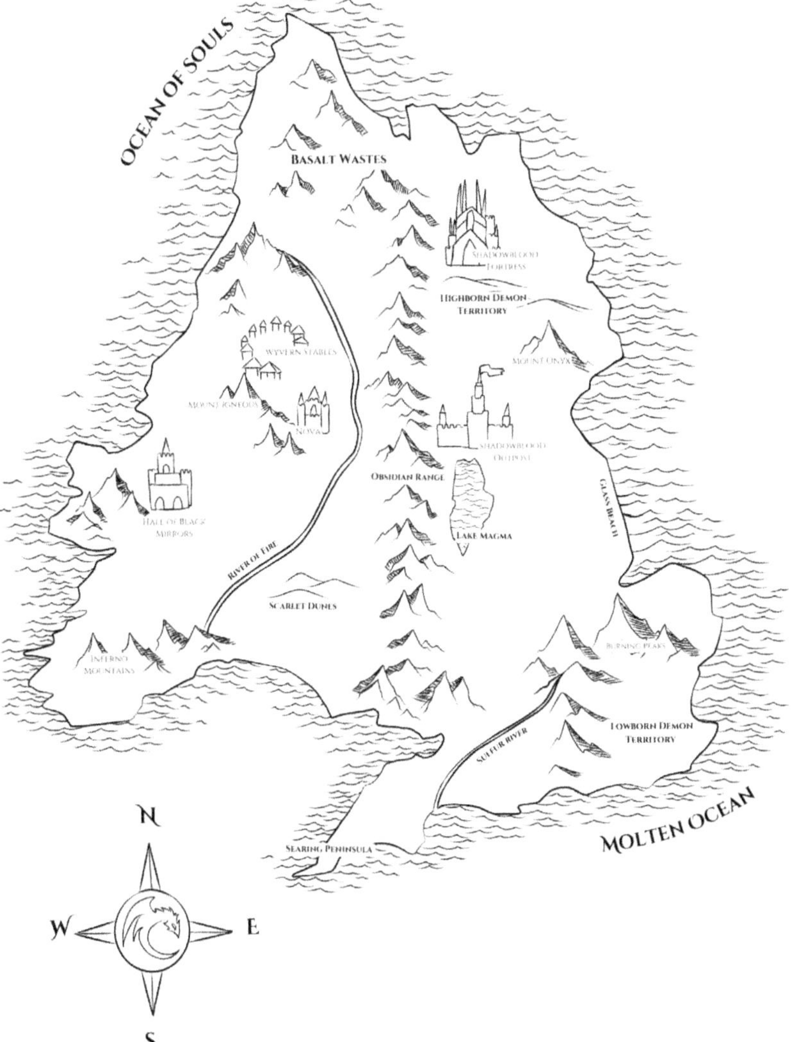

Chapter One

Tristan Skeleton slung his trusty quiver over his shoulder, then headed for the archery fields. The sun rose over the horizon, splashing rose-gold colors across the castle's towering spires and crenellations. A smile formed on Tristan's face as he watched the rolling hills sprout from beyond the castle walls; lush pine trees covered the land accentuating Earth's beauty.

Years had passed since the Zombie Apocalypse began—it was so long ago that no one could quite remember when it started. All they knew was that it left humanity teetering on the brink of extinction. Even with centuries of bloodshed and brutal survival, Tristan's heart swelled whenever he was in his kingdom of Skeletonia—walled and safe from the bloodthirsty undead outside.

Sunlight glinted off his silver crown as he passed through the village. The purple gem in the center glimmered a soft lavender color. Buildings made from wattle and daub lined the streets in an orderly fashion. Between them sat prolific pens filled with livestock. White canvas tents were erected along the cobblestone curb, overflowing with food, tools, and miscellaneous trinkets. Townspeople bustled through the streets like water flowing down a stream. A myriad of people, skeletons, elves, and even a few demi-zombies greeted the king with reverence—a reverence that was too much for Tristan.

Unlike most rulers, Tristan didn't abide by the whole kowtowing thing. He felt it was highly unnecessary. Words like *sire* and *your highness* placed frivolous blockades between cordial relationships. These people weren't merely his subjects; they were his friends—his family.

I wish they'd understand I'm not pompous like the zombie king. I don't rule with an iron fist. I want to protect them, not subordinate them.

So, as he traversed the city streets, Tristan waved off the superfluous greetings and responded with a kind smile and said a casual, "Hi." It was the same way he greeted his closest friends, and that was the way he wanted to treat everyone, whether he knew them well or not. Everyone was welcome in Skeletonia.

Tristan left the village with light spirits as he headed for the archery fields. Today, he was hosting an archery tournament and people from neighboring kingdoms would be visiting. Since the fields were outside the walls, he passed the daunting forest off to his left— the Zombie Forest, as it was known. Tristan suppressed a shudder. The undead ruled the forest, and those who wandered in usually never returned. Torn remains were all anyone ever found, or the victims underwent full zombification themselves. It wasn't something Tristan enjoyed thinking about. But it was the reality of living during the Apocalypse.

Suddenly, the bushes rustled. The king stopped in his tracks and instinctively drew his bow, nocking an arrow. His pinpoint accuracy sent his enemies running. They learned very quickly that whatever Tristan aimed for, he hit. The rustling increased and a zombie emerged.

Tristan raised an eyebrow. *Only one? That's unusual . . . and a bit uncanny. They usually attack in hordes.*

While a shot to the head killed a single zombie, the monsters were lethal in numbers. But in the past few weeks, Tristan had only seen one or two zombies at a time. It was odd.

What are those zombies up to? They can't be using magic again, right? Tristan shook his head. *No, that's not possible. My parents talked about a high wizard they met. She'd given them a journal and it was hidden away, here in the Skeletonia library. There's no way. Besides, magic is outlawed anyway.*

The rotting, green-skinned zombie bound for Tristan upon first sight, unleashing a snarl no one would want to hear in the middle of the night. Drawing his arrow back, he fired, sending the projectile straight into the zombie's stomach. The monster lurched backward, growling in pain as warm blood cascaded down his midsection.

The sight made Tristan want to avert his eyes. He hated hurting anything—even his enemies. Tristan was still an adolescent, but in a world where the dead hunted the living, children had to mature fast. It had been that way since the Apocalypse started. Seeing the unfeigned agony on anyone's face was overwhelming. But Tristan forced himself to watch the wounded zombie as it relinquished its attack and retreated into the forest. The king sighed. Tristan was glad most people in Skeletonia obeyed the law because he wasn't sure he could handle an execution.

Tristan shook off the thought as he raced for the fields, warmth radiating through his body. There, in front of the hay bales, he found a zombie girl with flowing chocolate-brown hair.

"Hey, Zombia," Tristan said.

Zombia turned, facing the king with sparkling hazel eyes; she had a fistful of arrows and a longbow slung over her shoulder, like Tristan. She wore a light brown jerkin over an apple-red shirt and black pants.

The whole ensemble was tied together with deep tan, soft-leather boots—perfect for today's events.

She was one of the only demi-zombies Tristan knew, along with being his best childhood friend. Demi-zombies were rare. His father explained that those were a special type of hybrid created when the legendary high wizard, Ashley Blanchett, tried to cure a zombie by reversing the zombification. It didn't work entirely.

While the person regained their humanity and no longer hungered for flesh, their appearance remained—rotting green skin, scars, and pointed ears. Since then, if a demi-zombie and human had a child, their offspring had a fifty percent chance of being a demi-zombie or human entirely. Another nice aspect Tristan learned about demi-zombies was that their bites were not contagious. But, then again, demi-zombies didn't hunger for flesh anyhow.

I wish Mom and Dad discussed Blanchett's cure further. They couldn't, of course, it was for the better, though. With magic being outlawed, there's no point in risking exposure. Still, it would be nice to know more about demi-zombies. It's safer this way.

"Are you ready for the tournament today?" Zombia asked in a cheery tone, pulling Tristan out of his thoughts.

"Definitely, we just have to finish setting up targets and—"

Tristan glanced around. Ten double-stacked hay bales stood evenly apart. Each had a red target painted on it. Where he and Zombia stood was the shooting line. Small quivers stood across from each target. After Zombia placed her arrows in one of them, three of the quivers remained empty. He looked at them sadly. "We need more arrows. I'll head to the castle armory for more."

"I'll go with you; we'll need quite a few," Zombia said gently. Tristan glanced at the benches set up on the sidelines. Some spectators were already arriving.

Excitement rose in the king's chest. Tristan smiled back at Zombia; his face grew warm. That was one thing he loved about her: she always had others' best interests in mind. Together, they sprinted across the fields, back to the castle. Several people greeted Zombia her irrelevant title.

Fed up with the oppression, Tristan's friend made a daring escape from her hometown and crossed the border into Skeletonia. For her ingenuity and bravery, Tristan rewarded her with a position as Queen of

Skeletonia. Kings and queens usually married; Tristan didn't propose his offer in that manner. He just wanted someone with Zombia's skills and benevolence helping him rule Skeletonia—and someone he could confide in.

The towering spires and ramparts appeared. Walking into the vast castle halls made Tristan's hands tingle. He loved being king. Making life easier for his people and protecting them from zombie claws was all he wanted, but it came with loads of responsibility. Decisions had to be made, overwhelming decisions sometimes too tricky for Tristan to make. That was life in a high position of power. No matter, he took his job as a ruler with great alacrity.

Skeletons in iron armor marched along the ramparts, carrying spears and banners with the Skeletonia crest—a skeletal dragon flanked by two swords. Zombia and Tristan waved at the guards. They returned the gesture. After crossing the drawbridge, and running through the courtyard, the friends emerged into a vast throne room. It was simple; the only decorations were a few banners bearing the king's family heraldry.

Two nondescript thrones sat on a slab of carved stone. A purple curtain hung behind the chairs. Torches rested in their sconces, bathing the room in a warm orange glow. Pillars ringed the space with guards placed between each set.

A young zombie boy entered the room. His short, disheveled hair was a few shades darker than Zombia's. His chocolate-brown eyes met Tristan's ocean-blue ones.

"Hey Zombie," said Tristan. He extended his arms for an embrace. Zombie removed his gardening gloves and hugged his best friend, then did the same to his sibling.

"I was just, uhh, coming out to meet you," answered Zombie. "I'm ready for the archery tournament. Why are you guys back here? Is everything all right?" His dark brows creased.

"We need some more arrows and maybe a couple bows," Zombia explained to her brother. "Tristan and I are heading to the arsenal to get some more."

Zombie's cheeks dimpled. "Great, I'll meet you out there." Zombie was off, walking out of the throne room with a content gait.

"Come on. We should hurry before the guests and contestants arrive," Tristan said, gently tugging Zombia's arm. She nodded and strode after her friend.

A corridor yawned before them. Doors lined the

walls, holding historical secrets from the public eye. A large, locked iron door was ahead, flanked by two skeleton guards.

Tristan took another step before a noise caught his ear.

Rattle.

Tristan stopped in his tracks so abruptly Zombia bumped into him. "Zombia, did you hear that?"

His friend shrugged, confusion written across her oval face.

Rattle . . . thump . . . rattle . . . thump.

"I know I heard something." Tristan clutched his bow and pointed to the library door on the left wall. He approached and pressed his ear against it. There was a shuffle, followed by a bang, like something fell over. A cold sense of dread fell over Tristan. He motioned for Zombia. She leaned her pointed ear against the wood; a moment later, her hazel eyes rounded.

Thud.

"Do you hear—" Zombia cut Tristan off by pressing her fingers to her lips and nodding.

There are secret, enchanted items in there, thought Tristan. *Surely it couldn't be zombies, right? Why would they want enchanted items?*

Tristan grabbed his bow and drew an arrow. With his free hand, he slowly gripped the brass handle.

Chapter Two

Tristan pushed open the library door, gritting his teeth, trying to make as little noise as possible. Luckily, the hinges were oiled regularly, so no squeaking ensued. The scent of ink and old paper hit him in the nose. Zombia walked past him, dagger drawn. Though Tristan wished she had a sword, he was pleased that she had a weapon with her.

The castle library was a large circular room with a vaulted ceiling and a skylight. Tristan and Zombia were surrounded by a sea of towering shelves. Tomes of every size sat in all their glory. Years' worth of dust coated them, their spines worn, creating a mysterious atmosphere. The vast knowledge contained inside these books was daunting, sending goosebumps down Tristan's arms. Nonetheless, the library brought a sense of tranquility.

Tristan knew none of these books talked about magic, unless it was negative. The Cadre—a powerful faction of people who hunted magic-wielders—vowed to eradicate magic from the land. Being a small faction didn't matter; they basically ran the Haunted Lands. The faction rose quickly at the end of the Great Apocalypse War, continuing their reign of terror.

ALL MAGIC IS CHAOS.

The Cadre motto was drilled into the brains of every generation after the war. All history books were burned and rewritten by Cadre scribes. Magic was destructive and dangerous. All magic-wielders were burned at the stake. After years of purging, many presumed magic was dead. The only people who used it were elves, but in small quantities, far from all the sanctuaries. Magic history was erased and that never sat well with Tristan.

Tristan's parents had a few spell books hidden in their chambers. There were days Tristan and his sister would sneak into Mom and Dad's room when their curiosity got the better of them. For a while, the siblings were shooed out of the room, but eventually, their parents gave in. Every night, when the castle was asleep and the guards were on night shift, Tristan and Tibia received stories about wizards before bed.

Tristan's mother always relayed the stories in a

hushed voice, but he still enjoyed them. But as Tristan and his sister grew older, their bedtime stories became fewer and fewer until they ceased all together, leaving him with questions that remained unanswered.

Holding his bow and arrow firmly, Tristan blew out a breath and pressed his back against the wall. He whispered a prayer to the gods above, hoping the intruders wouldn't see him or Zombia. She peeked through the books, then turned to her friend.

"Tristan, come see this," Zombia hissed. The king followed her to the center of the library. Shattered glass littered the floor beneath the broken skylight. Sunlight spilled in through the opening, highlighting dusty footprints—many of them, too many to belong to a single person.

Tristan frowned. "Do you think they belong to zombies?"

Zombia shrugged. "I'm not sure. I don't see they would be here; aside from demi-zombies, most are illiterate."

There was a soft murmur of voices. Together, the two friends wove between the labyrinth of bookcases, tracking the sound until they saw it. Tristan spotted a flash of sickly green between the book gaps, followed by a distinct, decomposing smell. Tristan forced down the bile rising in his throat, triggered by the horrid scent.

Peering around the corner, Tristan felt his stomach clench. Four zombies stood around one of the study desks. Each wore full iron armor; every part of their bodies was covered by metal, save for their heads. Steel broadswords hung at their hips. Tristan's heart skipped a beat. He found himself wishing he was wearing armor instead of his favorite navy-blue tabard. Zombies weren't known for wearing armor or forging weapons. They were already seasoned predators, capable of devouring their prey whole. Furthermore, the indigent zombie kingdom couldn't afford skilled craftsmen or blacksmiths.

Was that what the zombies had been doing for the last few weeks? Gathering armor and weapons? Tristan narrowed his eyes. *What's Zokar up to?*

The quartet of zombies huddled close to the desk, ignoring their surroundings, having not spotted Tristan and Zombia yet. The king tried to keep his breathing steady. One of the monsters unfurled a map—the tall one with a long scar running over his cheek. "Blanchett's artifacts have to be here." The monster's voice had a frantic edge to it.

"Zokar's going to be angry when he discovers our failure. He needs this for the Shadowblood queen," another zombie, female this time, added.

Tristan scrutinized the zombies, goosebumps stippling his skin. *Shadowblood? I hope they're not talking about who I'm thinking of.*

The tall zombie moved to the wall and ran his thick fingers along the stones. "Aha," the zombie said. Tristan's breath hitched as the monster pulled one of the bricks from the wall, revealing a small compartment. And out of the compartment, the zombie withdrew a small oak box.

Coldness settled over Tristan's skin. He knew what was in that box—it was a journal, but he didn't know to whom it belonged. Finding the former king in his study one day, curiosity propelled Tristan to ask about the book. His father kindly told him he couldn't explain the journal's contents, for there were "ears all around the castle." Tristan understood this and he never asked again, but all he knew was it was something that if the Cadre got hold of it, his entire family would be burned.

"Good, Zokar will be pleased after all," the zombie with the scar said. Tristan concluded he was probably the leader, given his armor was fancier than the other three.

"So will Malice," added the third zombie.

The zombie flipped open the lid and pulled out the journal.

"Perfect! With this, we'll be rid of those wizards once and for all! Black magic will thrive again." The zombie's guttural voice bounced off the walls. He placed the journal back into the box. The leader glanced around.

"The king's not here. Is it worth going after him?" the female zombie asked.

The leader shook his head. "Once Zokar has the journal, he can give it to Malice. When he does, the king of Skeletonia is as good as dead."

Tristan felt dizzy. After jamming the artifact into his satchel, the scarred leader led his henchmen to the skylight, preparing to escape.

Tristan turned to Zombia; the time was right. The king took aim and let the arrow fly. It split the air, striking the climbing zombie in the neck. A cry of pain tore from the monster as he lost his grip on the rafters and plummeted with a sickening crack.

In a heartbeat, the wounded zombie jumped to his feet, the pain having not registered. Only a shot to the head killed a zombie; shooting one in the neck was a mere flesh wound.

Fitting another arrow, Tristan fired, sending the barbed shaft into the monster's head. His eyes rolled back and he slumped forward, the satchel fell with him, getting pinned under his motionless body. Blood pooled onto the stones, making Tristan want to vomit.

The leader was dead, but three zombies remained. The female lunged for the satchel under the leader's body, but Zombia didn't give her a chance. She delivered a swift kick to the monster's jaw. Bones cracked. The zombie flew back into one of the shelves. Heavy books toppled off, burying the zombie.

The two remaining zombies exchanged glances and foolishly charged—one went for Zombia, the other bounded for Tristan.

Zombia grabbed the satchel containing the journal, threw it over her shoulder, and fought. She swung her blade down in time to meet her attacker's. She spun in a wide arc. There was a flash of metal and the sound of a blade cutting through flesh. A green head went rolling as red splashed across Zombia's face.

The last zombie stood in front of Tristan. He kept the pile of books in his peripheral vision, preparing himself for the monster beneath them to rise at any moment.

"Give me that satchel," the zombie said. His red eyes glimmered with rage. "I'll ensure your death is painless."

He charged for him, but Tristan fired another arrow. It lodged itself in the zombie's neck. Blood poured down into the armor plates, but he didn't care. Tristan didn't have his sword, so he swiped one from the ground, dropped by the zombies, bringing the blade up just in time to stop the battle-ax coming down on his neck. Metal crashed against metal; pain reverberated through Tristan's arms down to his wrists

Gods above, this zombie is strong. Zombies were usually clumsy warriors—shuffling instead of running, swaying instead of dodging. Their infected teeth were their best weapons. A chill skittered down Tristan's spine at this uncanny observance. *Something's going on with the zombies—especially over these past few weeks. Is this connected to Mom and Dad's enchanted artifacts?*

In the corner of his vision, Tristan watched Zombia sprint to his aid. His breath caught when his friend tripped, her sword clattered to the ground. There, wrapped around Zombia's ankle, were gnarled, green fingers. The female zombie had crawled her way out from under the books and obtained a second chance to attack.

Tristan moved to aid his friend, but he was locked in his own battle. The zombie wielding the battle-ax was relentless. Pain sang in Tristan's arms.

The library doors swung open. A single crossbow bolt soared through the air, striking the female zombie in the back. She collapsed to the ground.

Someone barreled across the room, skidding to a stop in the sunlight. The zombie holding the satchel stood frozen.

The golden raven on the back of the newcomer's scarlet cloak marked her as Tibia, queen of Skeleteria, and Tristan's sister.

The zombie foolishly tried to run. Tibia swung

her leg out, tripping the zombie. Before he rose, she kicked him in the stomach then sent a swift jab to his neck, throwing the zombie into a tumbling heap. The satchel flew from his grasp and landed at Zombia's feet. She bent over and picked it up, turning to Tibia.

The Skeleteria queen removed her helmet, letting her short black hair spill free. Her midnight-black armor sparkled in the afternoon sun. A quirky smile formed on her crimson-painted lips.

"Thought you'd need help, little brother," she said, patting the king on the back before turning her gaze to the zombie.

"How'd you know we were here?" Zombia asked.

"When I went out to the archery fields, I met Zombie. Guests and contestants were arriving, and you and Tristan hadn't shown up. I asked Zombie, and he told me where you were. On my way, I heard a commotion coming from the library, so here we are."

"We're glad you came, sis," Tristan said, patting her on the back. She grinned before she turned to the zombie who was trying to crawl away. Tibia stomped on the monster's back, pinning him under her heel; her sapphire eyes were unforgiving and cold. "Move and you die."

Tristan looked at the zombie; his stomach clenched with sympathy. He sensed fear in those dead eyes. Fear of death, fear of the unknown that would follow. A will to live danced behind those stubborn features. Though the ferocity of a zombie's face made it difficult, Tristan sensed his emotions. Human emotions. While the body was dead and decaying, the spirit inside remained alive with the ability to feel terror, agony, joy, and contentment, and it would be cleaved by a single arrow. All zombies were once human. The king glanced at Zombia, who smiled warmly at him. Sighing, Tristan placed a hand on Tibia's shoulder; his voice came softly.

"Don't kill him, Tib."

Chapter Three

Tibia blinked at her brother, crossbow still poised at the prostrate monster's head. "Give me one good reason I should spare him. One less zombie in the world isn't a bad idea."

Tristan was taken aback. "First off, being a zombie doesn't justify his death. He's a living creature and deserves respect. Second, we need to question him. Find out what he's doing here and why." The king's voice echoed off the library walls.

Tristan understood his sister ran things differently in her queendom of Skeleteria. They were a warrior society and had the best soldiers Tristan had ever seen, even stronger than his own, making for perfect allies. While Skeletonia received regular zombie attacks, Skeleteria's formidable army staved off the undead monsters. Though force was an admirable trait of hers, Tristan did wish his sister was more compassionate at times.

"I'd listen to your brother," the zombie said, flashing his jagged teeth. Rage beamed in Tibia's eyes, but she listened to Tristan and lowered her bow.

Tristan frowned at his sister; she shrugged off his gaze of disapproval. He hated violence—he hated war. Tibia could fight anything—and she would fight anything. While Tibia usually never listened to Tristan on these matters, that wouldn't stop him from trying to curb her calloused feelings.

Tristan stared at the zombie, his ocean eyes holding composure. "Now, speak. What are you doing here?"

The zombie threw Tristan a mocking grin. "I thought you'd know. Zombies regularly attack Skeletonia, don't they? Why is my presence so different?"

"Don't try that," said Tristan. "You broke in for the box. What do you want with my family's heirloom?"

Zombia grabbed the zombie's satchel and pulled out the ornate box. Golden symbols caught the torchlight. Tristan squinted, realizing they were runes, though he couldn't read them. His parents had discussed runes and even taught him and Tibia the basics. Though they didn't study further. Instead, they pressed Tristan with his regal studies. Soon, the runes were forgotten.

Carefully, Tristan opened the box and pulled out the leather-bound journal. The leather was worn in many places and smelled of dust and mildew. On the cover was the Triple Goddess. Tristan held his breath.

"Why do you want this?" Zombia asked, her brow furrowed with confusion.

The zombie lifted his chin. "That journal belonged to the High Wizard, Ashley Blanchett."

Did Tristan mishear the zombie? Ashley Blanchett owning that journal meant that his parents must have met her. His parents were affiliated with the High Wizard. Tristan understood, after all these years, why his father couldn't disclose the journal's contents. Not only was owning a journal belonging to Blanchett enough to earn Tristan and his family spots on the stake, but the former king and queen *knew* the High Wizard personally.

Blanchett's name rarely appeared in books, and if it did it was never in a deferential manner. She was described as a power-hungry wizard who wanted the world to herself. Deep down, Tristan didn't really believe it. Though his parents didn't talk about her much, they'd never said anything negative. In fact, they discussed Blanchett with respect while simultaneously explaining the dangers of magic.

But the High Wizard had been inside Skeletonia's walls. How fascinating . . . and reckless at the same time. Would it be worth meeting the High Wizard, knowing if you were caught you'd be burned? Even kings and queens feared the Cadre. Thousands were burned for practicing spells. Tristan shook his head. *Not worth the risk. Stay safe and don't practice magic. It's too dangerous.*

"How does having Blanchett's journal help you?" Tibia pressed.

The zombie rolled his eyes. "There's a map inside, leading to where Blanchett has hidden the Apocalypse Grimoire, along with her other enchanted weapons."

Tristan opened the journal, pulling out a folded parchment. The paper was crinkled with age as he unfurled it. He marveled at the accurate detail. The entire Haunted Lands were drawn, with a compass in the far-left corner. Far north, past the Zombie Woods, resting in a plains biome, a red circle encapsulated a small building. *Crimson Citadel* was labeled above the drawing, written in the same ink.

"Zokar instructed us to get this map. He's going to give it to Malice," the zombie said. He squared his shoulders with pride. "Once the Shadowblood queen has the Apocalypse Grimoire, she'll be unstoppable."

Tristan's chest tightened. He had heard and read about Malice the same amount of times as he heard Blanchett's name. Malice was a Shadowblood, a highborn demon, and the most powerful in the Underworld. To make matters worse, Malice was *queen* of the Shadowbloods. That was as far as his knowledge went; it was as far as many dared to learn. A chill settled over Tristan as he thought about it.

"Was the journal all you wanted?" Zombia asked, placing her hands on her narrow hips.

The zombie chortled. "There's another item we came for." The monster's gaze fell on Tristan's silver crown. "That gemstone. That belonged to Blanchett too." A sinister smile split the zombie's green face. "And I'm going to bring it to Zokar, even if it means taking your head with it. Honestly, that wouldn't be a bad idea; he and Malice would love having the head of a wizard."

Tristan's stomach coiled, but not only because of the threat—it was because he knew the zombie was right. But rather than give into the zombie's words, Tristan decided to hit him with the usual societal statement. "You lie. You know what the Cadre says about magic, they eradicated it. I'm no wizard." The king tried keeping his voice firm, though he wavered, knowing he was the one lying.

"Oh, you doubt my words? You have the mark of the High Wizard. Look at your wrist. It'll confirm the truth."

Tristan gulped. Tristan wished he hadn't contradicted the zombie's statement; it only resulted in Tristan receiving a worse, more truthful statement about the royal family than he wanted. *I hid it. These monsters know about my marking. After I transformed a chair into a cat, merely by sitting on it, the mark appeared.* Tristan stole a glance at his wrist, running his fingers over the gold band. *Dad gave me this gold cuff to conceal it. Luckily, Tibia's marking is on her shoulder— easily concealed by her armor.* Not long after Tristan was crowned, bouts of magic began. They only became harder to control as he and Tibia got older. He'd never forget the time he passed the vase in the castle foyer and changed its colors.

Nor would he forget all the frogs that sprang from the pond when Tristan dipped his foot in. The gemstone wasn't helping, its magic supposedly fueled the magic swirling inside Tristan's veins. The zombie's accuracy made his knees weaken. Before their deaths, Tristan's parents were both wizards. He and Tibia are both wizards. He knew the days of concealing his family's secret were numbered—and today was the day it ended.

Tristan locked eyes with Tibia. She frowned, her face blanching. Their magic became harder to hide everyday. Tristan knew it would, he just hoped it would be under different circumstances. He flexed his fingers and looked at his wrist, trying to make sense of what to do next. Silence filtered between the king and the zombie.

Eventually, the monster smiled. Warm torchlight cast ominous shadows over his decomposing face. "Malice Sanguine is coming and she won't sleep until her revenge is complete."

Tristan promptly ordered the zombie to be dragged to the dungeon, and the dead ones to be buried; however, when the guards arrived, the zombie woman was nowhere to be found. A trail of blood leading to the skylight confirmed her escape. Tristan shook his head, removed his crown, and stared at it with burning curiosity. After a few moments, he placed the silver circlet back on his head.

"You know, this could be a chance to delve deeper into our enchanted heritage. I'd want to study it," Tibia said proudly as she, her brother, and Zombia exited the library. Her voice shook Tristan from his thoughts.

"Don't say that," Tristan scolded. "You know well what the punishment is. We can't risk it. Mom and Dad said not to." And that was true. The former king and queen of Skeletonia instructed their children to never use their powers, despite the little knowledge they imparted.

Tibia scoffed, rolling her sapphire eyes. "Mom and Dad didn't tell us enough. They should have told us more. This could be good for us, little brother. We can finally uncover the truth behind our lineage. We could fulfill our duty as wizards—stop Malice from rising again!" Tibia pounded her fist into her palm enthusiastically.

"What if the zombie was bluffing?" said Tristan. Deep inside, he knew the rotting zombie spoke the truth. But he might as well stall. Keeping his friends safe was his priority and he did so by keeping them away from magic.

"I doubt it," Tibia countered.

"Me too," Zombia said. "There's definitely something going on with the zombies—the zombie king to be more specific. His attacks have been fewer which means he's most likely planning something. It probably has to do with this Malice."

A tightness came over Tristan, making it hard to breathe. "You could be killed for this! No, we're not risking it. Let's just bury the artifacts in another hiding spot. In a place where the zombies won't look."

Tibia grabbed her brother by the shoulders. "Don't you want to know more? Don't you want to know more about our powers? I see it in your face, Tristan. You say you want to hide magic and leave our magic lineage alone, but deep down, you're just as curious as I am."

Tristan ground his teeth. *Gods, why does Tibia have to be right?*

The king shrugged out of Tibia's excited grasp and folded his arms.

"Okay, fine, keep lying to yourself." Tibia threw

her hands up. "If you change your mind, you know where to find me."

While Tibia paced, Zombia said, "Honestly, I have to agree with her. I look forward to learning more about magic."

Tristan pinched the bridge of his nose. "Why? Magic is nothing but dangerous."

Zombia folded her arms, her pointed ears twitching. "But what if it's not? Society paints magic as evil, but about the positives? Zokar always said the same thing. He burned books on magic and executed those who practiced it." Zombia paused, shuddering at the thought of the violence. "I smuggled a book that talks about the two types of magic: light and dark. Light magic is supposed to work in beneficial ways and heal others. What if this is what Blanchett's wizards do? I'm sure it is. This would be a great idea."

Agitation seized Tristan. He wanted to grab his friend and shake some sense into her—as bad as that sounded. *But I'm curious too. I want to study magic, but the ramifications aren't worth it. I'm a king, and that's where I have to stay—I have to set an example for my people.* The king chewed his lip, mulling over his next words carefully.

"Zombia, you've already risked your life escaping from Zombieshire." Tristan took her hands into his, a tingling spreading through his chest. "I don't want you risking it again by searching for enchanted relics."

Tristan could and would never forget the harrowing journey Zombia made to Skeletonia. To the zombie king, leaving Zombieshire is an act of treason. He kills anyone he can get to who defects. He hunted Zombia and her brother down for fleeing. If Zombia hadn't chosen to swim the river, Zokar's army would have caught them. The king shuddered; Tristan didn't think he could live with himself if she wound up dead at Malice's or the Cadre's hand.

His friend bristled, pulling from her friend's grasp. "You're missing the point. Your tutors taught you was how deadly black magic was. But they never bothered to mention the good. What was life like before the war? Perhaps the magic was good, and when Malice showed up, everything was destroyed, and people blamed magic—both kinds. Have you stopped to consider the type of magic Blanchett had? What was her true story?" Zombia paused to take a breath. "She was against Malice; she wouldn't have sided with black magic."

Zombia strode down the hall, her hands balled into fists. "Have you ever considered your mentors might have been wrong? That they didn't tell you the whole story? It seems to me like your parents tried to prepare you, but you ended up believing your mentors instead."

Zombia's footsteps faded and suddenly, Tristan felt empty.

Tibia passed her brother and grinned at him. "Magic might be fun too. Honestly, I don't care what the Cadre thinks. I'm learning more about magic, whether you like it or not." With a whisper of her dark red cloak, she was gone.

Tristan stood alone outside the library. What was supposed to be a fun day of archery turned into a mess of disclosed secrets and peril. He shook his *head. Zombia and Tibia are being illogical. How could something so destructive be good?* Glancing down at his wrist, he ran his thumb over the gold cuff. A pulse jolted through his body. He knew the price of magic. But he couldn't stop pondering other possibilities.

Zombia's words crept back into his head, fueling his own inquisitiveness. *"Have you ever considered your mentors might have been wrong?"*

The Forgotten Prophecy

Did magic have benefits that were masked under years of hate and fear? What if everything Tristan read about magic was false?

Chapter Four

Marcus, captain of King Zokar's royal guard, stood impatient on the grassy knoll cresting Skeletonia. He glowered at the ramparts. Since walls were built, zombie raids were less successful. And if the zombies were going to triumph—specifically Marcus's warriors—they needed more supplies and weapons.

The woods bristled behind the platoon of zombies. The leaves swayed in the soft breeze.

At Malice's behest, Zokar was instructed to steal Blanchett's artifacts, specifically her journal, and bring them to her. The Shadowblood had her own preparations, so she asked him to do this task. She even told Zokar that she didn't want to see his face unless he obtained the items. As usual, Zokar was too much of a coward to go invade Skeletonia himself, so he ordered Marcus to do his bidding.

Initially, Marcus argued, telling Zokar that if he wanted to reconcile with Malice, he should do what she asked. So Zokar went with Marcus to Skeletonia, but they reached this hill, and the zombie king retreated when the captain turned his back. *If I could just get Zokar out of the way, I could work in Malice's court and lead the zombies to proper victory.*

The sun had hit its apex, splashing the monsters' armor and weapons in a surreal glow. The zombies grumbled in discontent. They hated the sun. Nighttime was when they thrived. It was the easiest time to bite unsuspecting souls who wandered too deep into the forest.

Marcus frowned and raised his hand, shielding his right, scarlet eye from the blinding light. His left was covered by a black eye patch, concealing a wound Zokar had inflicted long ago.

"Where are the scouts I sent in?" asked Marcus. "It's been an entire hour. They should be back by now considering those were my best warriors." He released a breathy sigh; his fingers clenched his bow apprehensively. "If they're not back with the items Zokar needs for the Shadowblood queen, they'll both be displeased. Especially Malice."

One of the soldiers spoke up. "It won't be your fault, though."

The second-in-command shook his head. "The failure will fall on my shoulders and I'll be punished." Marcus stared longingly into the distance, running his fingers through his dark green hair.

"Zokar punishes everyone," another soldier said. "He'll execute someone for getting within three feet of his throne."

Marcus's posture stiffened. "It's not *his* retribution I'm worried about."

Zokar's threats had become empty to Marcus. The second soldier was right; the zombie king threatened everyone, especially the captain. So, he learned to take ridicule gallantly.

"Zokar can do whatever he wants, but if Malice isn't satisfied, I'm not either." Marcus's shoulders slumped. "If I fail her . . . " A sadness came over him, but he quickly brushed it off and cleared his throat, regaining his composure. He glared at the second soldier with his working eye, so hard it was as though he was staring into the zombie's soul. "She's warned me once. She's not going to warn me again."

"Captain, someone's coming!" one of the zombies shouted. Marcus's spirits lifted a little. He watched as a single zombie sprinted up the hill. Her armor was dented as sweat beaded on her forehead. She skidded to a halt at Marcus's feet and doubled over, puffing slowly. She had a crossbow bolt in her back. Her face was twisted with agony, tears rimming her eyes as she fell to her knees before Marcus.

Marcus saw her injury and a heaviness settled in his chest. Blood poured down her back; the bolt was lodged very close to her spine. Her wound was bad, but he wasn't about to show any compassion. If he was going to please Malice, he'd have to prove he had an iron grip.

"What's the news?"

The zombie shook her head, her eyes squeezed shut. "H-help me . . . please," she begged, her breaths coming short.

The second-in-command extended his hand as though he was going to help her rise.

Stay strong. Don't show emotion. Don't show you care.

Instead, he yanked her close and said in a low voice, "I'll help you. Just tell me what transpired?" Marcus released his grip, letting her crumple in the grass.

The zombie took a labored breath. "We didn't . . . get the items, sir," she said weakly. Pain creased her face as she spared a glance at her wounds.

Marcus's sage-green face darkened. "You failed?"

The zombie nodded, keeping her head down.

"Did you at least get one of them? Blanchett's journal, her enchanted gemstone?"

"No, sir."

Marcus clenched his jaw. "I see."

"W-wait," the zombie said, her voice barely a whisper. Marcus didn't hear her. He clasped his hands behind his back and began pacing. The soldiers remained silent. The wounded zombie's eyes were downcast; she knew escape and help were out of reach. No one dared to defy their commander's wishes by aiding their comrade. Kill or be killed; it was the zombie motto.

Marcus eventually turned back to her. The girl kept her head down. Punishment was inevitable.

"Wait," the zombie said, forcing her voice to almost shout.

Marcus stopped in his tracks, glaring at her with a quizzical eye. She recoiled as the captain approached.

"What is it?"

"I did gain something important."

Marcus furrowed his brows. The other zombies leaned closer with anticipation.

"Tristan Skeleton is a wizard, one of Blanchett's wizards."

Every muscle in Marcus's body numbed. "How can you be sure?"

"He had the marking, sir."

"I didn't think the wizards would return this soon," Marcus said, taking a deep breath. Malice had warned the zombies about this. *"Blanchett's wizards will rise again and destroy all of you,"* Malice had said. Magic was genetic and could be passed down for generations. Honestly, the king of Skeletonia being a wizard descendant shouldn't come as a shock. It was, but Marcus was more surprised by the amount of leverage this gave the zombies. The king of Skeletonia is hiding a drastic secret that could befall him and his entire family, weakening Skeletonia and leaving it prime for capture.

Marcus straightened his back. "Zokar will appreciate this information." *More importantly, so will Malice.*

Marcus extended his hand. The wounded zombie clutched his fingers, gratitude spreading on her face.

"You've done well." He allowed the zombie woman to lean into him. Some of her blood rubbed off onto Marcus's tattered doublet. It was wine-red, so the blood wouldn't show. Guilt settled in his chest. He jerked his head to a pair of zombies in the front row of the formation. "Tend to her wounds."

Gently, the warriors placed their arms under the zombie's arms and carried her away. Once she was out of sight, Marcus addressed his soldiers. "Back to Zombieshire. We have information to deliver."

A loud cheer rang out; some of the zombies banged their swords against their chest plates. He stared at the crowd, his eye wide, soaking up the praise. Marcus stuck his chest out in confidence.

This information would prove he was fit to be one of Malice's high-ranking officials. Higher than Zokar. *I'd be far better than Zokar. Malice should have chosen me instead of him in the first place. Zokar only cares about himself and ensures he gets all the power. Oppressing his people is not how a robust army is created. It keeps us all weak.*

Marcus ground his teeth and turned to the forest. Shadows danced between the tree trunks while unknown sounds echoed off rocky surfaces, launching into the air, building anxiety within him. Marcus grunted and dashed the fear.

"The quicker we report, the better off we are." Marcus strutted toward the trees, his army following behind, taking another step closer to an unspecified fate.

Chapter Five

Tristan, Zombia, and Tibia sprinted out of the library and down the corridor. Heaviness settled in Tristan's heart. He didn't enjoy arguing with his friends. He just wanted to keep them out of trouble. Keeping his people out of harm's way became his duty upon his coronation; he couldn't afford to snoop into his magic heritage. Why couldn't Tibia and Zombia grasp that? The practice was outlawed for a reason and the Cadre was craft. Somehow, someway, they'd always know when someone used magic.

He and his friends entered the throne room. The entire space was lit by a three-tiered chandelier. A cozy, yellow tone splashed across the room, highlighting tapestries inlaid with gold that flanked the throne, contrasting the purple curtain. A skeleton in full iron armor and a flowing, royal blue cloak greeted them.

"I have Sir Emerson searching the perimeter for more zombies," Radius, captain of the king's royal guard, said. "Are you three all right?"

Tristan shrugged. "If you mean physically, then yes, we are fine. However, we have a problem."

Reaching into the zombie's satchel, he withdrew Blanchett's journal and handed it to Radius. The captain adjusted his glasses and flipped through the worn pages. His pale green eyes rounded as he took a shaky breath. "Impossible."

Tristan nodded, feeling weak in the knees again. Radius had been serving as captain since his parents had the throne. When Tristan's and Tibia's powers began surfacing, they'd entrusted Radius to help conceal their magic. Luckily, the captain had a fascination with magic. In addition to his staunch loyalty, he couldn't have been more pleased to be serving a magic family.

"Blanchett's journal is the reason those four zombies broke in," Tristan explained. His fingers instinctively ran over the cuff cloaking his marking.

Radius looked up from the pages and stared at the king. "You mean the legendary Ashley Blanchett? The one who led the Haunted Lands to victory against the great Shadowblood army?"

Tristan swallowed hard, nodding.

"The thing is, how did Malice know to look here?" asked Zombia. "She's never been to Skeletonia."

"That we know of," Tibia added with a frown. "Spies maybe?"

Radius handed the king the journal. Reluctantly, Tristan opened the book and looked at the first page. The parchment was covered in faded writing. A few ink blots decorated the corners, along with some odd-looking symbols. They looked like warped letters, but they didn't form full words. Tristan knew they were runes—the ancient language of the wizards—but again, Tristan never learned to read them. Turning the page, he saw a page titled *Wizards of the Apocalypse Prophecy,* followed by several paragraphs written in the ancient language.

Radius scratched his head. "If you're interested in learning runes, I'd talk to Scribe. He'd know. I've only studied them a handful of times; guarding the castle and keeping you two out of trouble has kept me occupied." The captain winked at Tristan and Tibia. Redness crept up Tristan's cheeks; he couldn't help but smile. He'd always be grateful to Radius.

The captain pushed his glasses further up the bridge of his nose, which was hard since skeletons didn't technically have noses. "He has a book on runes. But don't tell him you're wizards. No one in the village save me knew who your parents really were and their connections to Blanchett."

Being covert made Tristan's stomach churn; it wasn't what a king should be. Candor was important between a ruler and their people. *But I don't want the Cadre coming after us either.*

Tristan gave a reluctant sigh. "Understood.

Thank you, Radius." The king's eyes fell back to the weathered parchment. The journal was short—shorter than a novella. The first quarter was written in runes; the rest of the pages were written, thankfully, in the modern language. Tristan concluded these were Blanchett's personal accounts of the war.

Zombia tucked a piece of brunette hair behind her ear as she peered over Tristan's shoulder. "She has beautiful handwriting." And she did. Perfect script, every loop and swirl done with delicate care.

One page read: *The war has begun—the living vs. the dead, light magic vs. black magic. Malice is out of control. Her armies are growing by the days.*

Tristan's mouth went dry; he turned the page with a soft crinkle of parchment.

It read: *I don't see why Malice hates me. She broke the rules, and I punished her. I never expected her to become this. She swore to defeat me in the war. She's relentless; she won't stop until the Haunted Lands are hers. She won't stop until she gets her hands on the Apocalypse Grimoire. Even with all the magic in the Haunted Lands, I remain vulnerable. I need other wizards.*

Tristan nearly dropped the journal; his face blanched. Zombia looked at him, her forehead scrunched with concern.

"Tristan, what is it?" She placed a soothing hand on his arm.

The king looked to his friend, his palms sweating. The leather became slippery against his skin as he tried processing what he just read. This was the prophecy Tristan remembered his parents discussing. The argument he had overheard between his mother and father made sense now.

He remembered the day clearly—Tristan and Tibia were engaged in a game of hide-and-seek. On his way to find her, Tristan had passed his father's study. Against his better judgment, the prince had pressed his ear to the door.

"You know what the Cadre will do if they discover our children are in Blanchett's prophecy," his father had said, distressed. "We can't train Tristan and Tibia in their powers."

"I know," his mother had responded. "But we can't leave our children in the dark about their lineage and powers. It's getting harder to hide. They'll notice and connect the dots soon enough. Did you see what Tibia did to the mirror in her bedroom? Don't forget Tristan transforming everything he touches into animals or different colors."

A tired sigh. "Their powers are manifesting, Archibald. We have to give them the basics. They just can't use them—at least not while the Cadre is in power."

A brief silence had passed before Tristan heard his father say, "I understand. We just can't have more innocent wizards burned. Gods, I hope magic doesn't remain banned forever. The Haunted Lands need it."

For years, Tristan pondered that conversation. Now, it became clearer that his parents were trying to prepare him and Tibia.

Tristan closed his eyes for a moment and took a cleansing breath. *Safety is better than magic. But what if standing back is the wrong thing to do this time? If we don't do something, Malice will destroy the Haunted Lands. I'm the king. I shouldn't be breaking the law, but I can't let Malice and her zombies destroy everything and everyone I love. I must protect them.*

"Malice is preparing for a second Apocalypse War," Tristan said to Zombia. Her eyes widened, brows creased. "The zombie was right." The words felt funny as they rolled off his tongue. Zombies were duplicitous creatures; they'd lie to get out of anything. Part of

Tristan wished the zombie had been lying, that he and Tibia weren't magic—that the magic in his family was a fabrication instead. Life would have been easier if he didn't have to worry about someone in the castle discovering his or Tibia's powers.

Tristan pulled the map out of the journal and held it in the chandelier's light. His jaw slackened as he took in the detailed drawings: the trees, Skeletonia, Skeleteria, Deadstone, all of it was illustrated with care. The Crimson Citadel caught his eye.

"We need to go here," said Tristan. He ran his finger over the drawing. "We need to get this Apocalypse Grimoire and stop Malice from raising her army." Tristan closed the journal and tucked it under his arm.

"I have no doubt the zombies have already reported back to Zokar by now," Zombia said, rubbing the back of her neck. "That would explain why the zombies have been acting so weird. They were planning this attack." She clenched her fists. "Zokar always sent patrols to confiscate magic items and execute those using them. Now he wants the location to Blanchett's cache of weapons. He's most likely working with Malice. What a hypocrite."

Tristan noticed Zombia's voice slowed when she

mentioned Zombieshire. Her voice always lowered and went solemn when she discussed the desolate zombie kingdom. The king nudged her shoulder and reached for her hand, letting Zombia know he was there for her. She squeezed his hand in return. Whether she wanted to talk, vent, or cry—Tristan vowed to be there.

Tristan looked to Radius, who was scratching his chin, staring off into space, thinking, like he always did.

"Radius, could you govern in my place while we head to the Citadel? We have to beat Malice there." Tristan's stomach churned at the thought of being caught and burned. The idea of fulfilling this ancient prophecy seemed bold and risky. But dying at the hands of a Shadowblood seemed far worse than being burned by the Cadre. It was also easier to circumvent the Cadre, too, rather than a highborn demon.

They'd hide their powers and Radius would cover for them. Magic was outlawed by most, save the three elf tribes—the Dragonbloods, the Icebloods, and Moonbloods.

An idea materialized in Tristan's mind.

"While we're in town, could you write a letter to Faye?" Tristan asked. Being queen of the Dragonblood clan, she already had a busy life. And just a fortnight ago, Faye began conducting research on three-headed dragons spotted flying around the Dragon Isles. After that, she would meet with the Iceblood and Moonblood tribes to discuss using them to battle the zombies obtruding in their territory.

That's why she told him she wasn't going to make it to the annual archery tournament. But this was urgent. Tristan knew it might take a while for her to respond, but at least she should be aware of Tristan's plight.

Radius clapped a fist to his chest. "Of course. She might not respond immediately."

Tristan frowned, but said, "That's okay, I don't expect her to. Just let her know what's going on."

The captain nodded and marched off to find a quill and parchment. *I hope she responds quickly, though. She's the only other magic outlet I have.*

"Let's go get that translating runes book," Tristan said, pointing toward the castle door.

"What book?" asked a small, perky voice from behind Tristan.

He spun around to find a chestnut-haired boy in resplendent crystal armor. Candlelight beamed off the flawless, sky-blue surface, giving the knight his own magical glow. Sir Emerson approached Radius and greeted his friends.

"Fortunately, there were no other zombies in the castle except those four," Emerson began. "Some of the guards on the ramparts saw a few up on the hill. They fled, though. Smart idea."

The knight's different-colored eyes—the right blue and the left emerald green—fell on the journal under the king's arm. "So, what's this book you need?" The knight's voice was a mix between formal and quirky. To Tristan, this was a nice change. Knights were stereotyped as being mature and composed—which Emerson was—but he also kept to his dare-devilish nature.

"We need a book on translating runes," answered Tristan. "Scribe has one according to Radius."

Emerson's thick, dark brows lifted. "Oh? Sounds fascinating. What for?"

Tristan hesitated, not wanting too many people knowing about their quest. But Emerson was his knight, he was built for quests and serving the king in addition to being one of Tristan's closest friends

"We're going on a quest," the king said. He took caution in lowering his voice. "To find a Citadel packed with enchanted weapons and a spell book."

The knight straightened his posture and clapped a fist to his chest. "Wherever you go, I go. Also, I've been dying for a new quest."

Tristan couldn't help but smile; he patted Emerson on the shoulder. He felt the cold crystal against his skin. His friend had the rarest set of armor in the Haunted Lands. Crystals were sacred for their alignment with the moon and earth. Tristan learned they could fuse with people's energy. Some aided in healing and strengthening properties. Many people collected them, but it was never enough to forge a full set of armor.

His friend's suit was the closest thing to magic Tristan had seen on a non-magic person. Another question materialized in Tristan's head.

Why would magic be outlawed, yet we continue to use crystals in our belief system? Maybe crystals aren't powerful enough to be considered magic. A small part of Tristan wondered if there was more to the Cadre's laws than merely fearing magic. Were they even right about magic being chaotic? Was it about control rather than genuine safety?

Tristan, Emerson, Tibia, and Zombia made for

the door. He looked over to his sister, watching her bold stride. Her face beamed with pride. Whenever she walked, Tristan would hear the clanking of metal. Though her crossbow was always visible, he knew of the cornucopia of daggers beneath her cloak.

"Tell him I say hi," said Radius. "I'll come visit him soon."

This was the day. Tristan might finally uncover the full truth behind his and Tibia's powers. His entire life had been a war between avoiding magic and learning more about his lineage. *What did Mom and Dad do with Blanchett? Was Blanchett looking for Tristan and Tibia, or was she waiting for their parents to bring them to her?*

So many questions and theories buzzed around in Tristan's head, even the fresh air and bustle of castle guards on the ramparts couldn't distract him. He and his friends crossed the drawbridge and headed for the village, the muddled chatter of people drawing closer.

Zombia walked beside Tristan, grinning at him. Tibia maintained her battle face to his right. Emerson walked in front of them, eagerness showing in his gait.

He made his decision. Tristan was done living in the dark; he was going to uncover the truth about his powers.

The Haunted Lands were relying on it.

Chapter Six

The village was a sea of color and life, accentuated by the sun's rays. Voices of all kinds whirled around Tristan, followed by the sweet smell of fresh baked bread and buttercream cakes. The crowd—demi-zombies, skeletons, and humans—milled about the roads, selling their wares beneath crisp white tents. Skeletonia was the only place that accepted demi-zombies. The Apocalypse drove the world into chaos, wiping out ninety percent of the world's population, and leaving the survivors paralyzed with fear.

So zombies, demi-zombies included, were banished from villages. When Zokar became king of the zombies, the hate toward zombies worsened. Many believed demi-zombies had a chance of reverting to their cannibalistic ways, but not Tristan. Guilt gnawed at Tristan's chest whenever he heard about a demi-zombie being ostracized. This was one of the many reasons Tristan, Zombia, and Zombie grew so close. He accepted them when no one else did.

Tristan traversed the crowded streets. He received many smiles. Some people even offered him and Zombia food. Of course, they both refused. Zombia reached into the pouch on her belt and produced a small diamond for a little girl who tried offering her queen a beautiful quilt. Zombia didn't want the quilt, but when she saw the girl's dirty feet and torn clothing, she knew the diamond would go a long way for her. Tristan grinned at her.

I'm so glad I offered Zombia the position as queen. Becoming queen through marriage was too common and sometimes shallow. I crowned her because of her bravery and intelligence. Escaping Zombieshire was no mere feat. Was it unusual to the rest of society to crown a queen without marriage, yes, but that didn't bother Tristan. The citizens of Skeletonia grew to love Zombia all the same.

Children ran by, weaving in between buyers and sellers with glee. They were engaged in a game of tag, not much younger than Tristan and his friends. Being a prince, responsibility weighed heavily on Tristan, leaving little time for leisure and fun.

A nostalgic smile formed on the king's face as he

turned to Tibia. She mirrored his expression as they both reminisced of the little time they managed to steal out of their busy days of tutoring.

At the end of the street was Scribe's library. Tristan had known Scribe for as long as he could remember. Scribe would visit the castle and speak with Radius frequently. He'd have to know more about this whole magic thing. Maybe he even knew about Tristan's and Tibia's powers. Worry nibbled at Tristan's nerves, but Scribe spent most of his days sequestered in his library reading. In a way, Tristan envied him. If he could spend his days reading for fun, he would. But his kingdom came first.

As soon as the thought formed, Tristan pushed it aside, and he looked to the craftsman's guild wedged between the library and baker's shop. The scent of baked bread faded as the smell of sawdust became more prevalent. To Tristan's surprise, the doors to the guild hall swung open as a young boy with disheveled black hair and leather apron emerged. He ran down the street, pushing past the villagers, and stopping right in front of Tristan.

"Hey, Cameron," Tristan said with surprise.

"What's going on?" Cameron responded with a

wide grin.

"We're heading to see Scribe," the king responded.

"For what?"

Tristan's smile withered, not wanting to tell his friend what they were doing. Cameron was talkative; he'd tell someone without even knowing it. Besides, the fewer people that knew about it, the better.

"We have to borrow a book from him," Tristan said. He clutched Blanchett's journal tighter, but it was too late, Cameron was already reaching for it. Tristan turned his shoulders, keeping the journal out of his friend's reach. His jaw slackened as he roved over the ornate cover.

"Woah, this is cool. What amazing artisanship."

When he reached for it, Tibia placed herself between the precious book and Cameron.

"You're not giving him that, are you?" she whispered into her brother's ear. "You know he's going to lose it or ruin it somehow. He may be an excellent craftsman, but he's hopeless when it comes to losing things or wrecking them. Remember what he did at the Winter Solstice ball?"

The memory appeared in Tristan's mind: food flying everywhere, splattering on the walls and table.

A few globs had made it on the chandelier and rained down on everyone's fancy clothing. The food fight had only ended when everyone joined together and began chasing Cameron. It wasn't the fondest memory he had of his friend.

"Can I come?" asked Cameron, his emerald eyes hopeful.

"Not today," Emerson said firmly. "Next time."

Cameron frowned.

"Cameron, we need you back," a voice called. The craftsman turned around to see another boy wearing similar garb, peeking from behind the guildhall door. "The next meeting is about to start."

Cameron's shoulders slumped as he tilted his head back and groaned. "See you later." After a brief wave, Cameron dashed back to the guildhall.

With a breathy laugh, Tristan and his friends continued down the bustling streets until they reached the library. Tristan reached out and pushed the door open and was overcome with the smell of pine and paper. He held the door open until his friends were through.

The place was small compared to the castle library, but bookcases lined every wall, so there was no skimping on knowledge. These books looked newer and weren't swathed in blankets of dust and cobwebs. The castle library was large enough and had books dating back to the beginning of the Apocalypse. The air smelled of fresh paper and ink—a scent evocative of the days Tristan and his sister escaped their regal studies and visited the village library to read about draconic mythology and the supposedly extinct phoenixes.

Barrels of scrolls sat beside the shelves. A staircase led up to the second story, to Scribe's living quarters. The entryway led into a backroom. There were more shelves against the right wall and a hearth to the left. Fire sputtered and crackled softly. A desk sat in front of a window, laden with parchment scrolls draped over stacks of books.

Scribe was older with blond hair streaked with some gray. His robes were the color of wine and trimmed with gold, worn over a plain linen shirt, gray pants, and soft boots. He looked at Tristan with his piercing amber eyes. Standing quickly, he almost knocked his chair over as he bowed. A snicker escaped Zombia and Tibia.

"Good to see you again. How can I assist you today, your majesties?"

Tristan and his sister exchanged glances before

unanimously rolling their eyes.

"I told you hundreds of times," said the king. "Please just call me Tristan. You've known me since I was a prince. I'd borrow books from you all the time, remember?"

Scribe straightened his back and smirked. "Apologies, I keep forgetting that. It's just . . . so unlike other monarchs who prefer being addressed by their titles."

Tristan shook his head. "I know. I find them unnecessary, even after my coronation." The king paused and cleared his throat.

"Could we have a book on translating runes, please?" asked Zombia, just getting over her fit of giggles.

Scribe smiled. "Of course." Standing from his chair, he moved from behind his desk and to the nearest shelf. Climbing a small ladder, he ran his fingers along book spines, muttering each of the titles to himself until he gave a satisfied "aha."

He pulled out a medium size book with a blue cover with gold lettering saying *Translating Runes*. The librarian handed it to the king.

Tristan took the book gently and opened it. His

jaw slackened as he saw the ancient language broken down, explaining every grammar rule and letter with precise detail.

"Thank you, Scribe," Tristan said with a grin.

The librarian descended the ladder. "I didn't know you wanted to learn runes. They're fascinating aren't they?"

Tristan blew out a relieved breath. Thank the gods that he and Tibia borrowed books from here all the time as kids. It was the perfect cover up to why he really wanted this book. "Yes, they are. I was looking to learn more about them, for research," the king quickly added.

"You and your sister were always the curious ones. Glad to see that hasn't changed."

"Thanks again," Zombia said with a wave. "Also, Radius says hi and that he wishes you well."

The librarian's face lit up. "That's wonderful. I'll visit him soon. Thanks for coming in. Happy reading," was all Scribe said.

After a brief farewell, Tristan made his way to the door. A pang of guilt rattled in his heart. Though it would cost him his transparency with his people and go against societal norms, it was better than allowing a demon to destroy the world he loved. If Tristan was going to stop Malice, he'd have to accept his powers, tradition or not.

Chapter Seven

Rose-gold light showered Marcus and his soldiers as they walked through murky, knee-high swamp water. Lanky, barren trees rose from the mud. Their gnarled branches sprouted from the ground, adorned with ribbons of sage-colored moss. The zombies grumbled as the dark, muddy liquid filled their boots, emitting a disgusting squelching sound, sucking their feet back down as they tried to walk.

Marcus hated this swamp between Zombieshire and Skeletonia, but it was quicker than going the long way where you had to cross a river. Through the haze sat the gatehouse into the zombie kingdom where Zokar was waiting for him. They were to contact Malice and she'd come to Zombieshire and proceed with their plans.

Marcus's pulse quickened; this was his chance to please Malice. He just had to endure Zokar's antics until she arrived. Loyalty to the zombie king was important.

Marcus knew he owed Zokar this information, but he also knew he wouldn't receive the same praise that Malice was likely to give. Zokar never showed any appreciation for Marcus's work. He was only there to serve his every beck and call.

A sigh of relief escaped Marcus when he saw the swamp finally end. He and his zombies climbed out of the swamp water, his boots squishing against the sodden ground. He growled as he waited impatiently for his soldiers. Hearing their commander's discontent, the zombies practically clambered over each other until every single one was out of the water. Zombieshire drew closer, spawning goosebumps along Marcus's skin, but he stamped them down with his determined attitude.

Reaching up, he caressed the patch covering his eye—a reminder of what happens to anyone who disobeys Zokar. The second-in-command didn't wish to imagine what would happen if he incurred Malice's wrath. The sun was setting quickly, and he'd given Zokar his word he'd be back before nightfall.

Marcus broke into a sprint, his zombies behind him. The air was filled with clanking armor plates and swords as they dashed through the forest, weaving around trees until they reached the dirt path, leading to the gatehouse. By the time they reached the stockade, the zombies were out of breath. Some removed their helmets, letting the evening air cool their heads. Some groaned in exhaustion; Marcus didn't listen.

Recognizing their captain, the guards scrambled to open the gates. A loud shriek of metal echoed through the trees as the portcullis rose, allowing Marcus and his soldiers inside. The foul stench hit him first. Thousands of decaying zombies ambled along the streets, darting in and out of merchant stalls, selling food and items of all kinds. Marcus didn't enter Skeletonia often, but when he did, for spy missions, it was enough times to see the kingdom was nothing like Zombieshire.

The buildings in Zombieshire were haphazardly laid out along the crumbling dirt path. Cracks crawled their way up the white-washed walls, and roof thatching was coming apart, leaving considerable paths for rain and snow. Not only were the craftsmen in Zombieshire inadequate, the reason for the dilapidated state of the town was that most Zombieshire residents were poor.

When Zokar took the throne, he turned Zombieshire into a commune, promising that no one would be poor or hungry if all the zombies shared the wealth and responsibilities. Years later, a majority of the people merely subsisted. It made Marcus's stomach churn. The zombies would never win anything in this state.

Yet another reason Malice should choose me as the zombie king.

Closing his remaining eye, he imagined Malice's face when he presented the news. Zokar would punish him for being late. Malice would too, but not after he gave her vital information that would lead her to success. All he needed to do was confirm to her that the king of Skeletonia is one of Blanchett's wizards. Then maybe, she'd reconsider having Zokar as king of the zombies.

Marcus and his warriors traversed the stone bridge stretching over the moat, emerging into a vast courtyard, but not after passing two monolithic statues of Zokar. In both, his arms were at his sides, balled into fists with a sword in each right hand. The stone faces held daunting stares. At the bottom of the statues, it read: ZOKAR IS ALWAYS WATCHING.

The wide space was crowded with zombie courtiers. Each wore tattered clothing, disheveled hair, and rotting green skin. While courtier garb and peasant clothing was supposed to differ, it didn't in Zombieshire. All the monsters wielded swords or maces; Marcus was the only one who carried a bow. Range combat wasn't something zombies were known for—close combat or hand-to-hand combat was where the undead's prowess lay.

Zokar's royal guards were easy to spot. Only the elites, including Marcus, were permitted to wear iron armor. The rest of the soldiers wore leather for two reasons.

One: it was all they could afford.

Two: leather was easier to make and easier to come by, which was perfect for the ever-growing number of zombies.

And regardless of how the zombies were dressed, the undead were perpetually caked in grime and blood. So, they'd never wear the vibrant, decorative armor of the elves or dragons. Zombies were simply too dim-witted to forge fancier weapons or armor, and no way in the Underworld would elves or humans stoop low enough to grace the undead with their skills.

Marcus frowned as he approached Zokar's throne. *After getting rid of Zokar, I can possibly form an alliance with other tribes and gift the zombies better provisions.*

Whispers rose up, reaching Marcus's ears—positive whispers—and he couldn't stop the smile tugging at his lips.

"There he is, captain of the royal guard," one said.

"So dedicated and dutiful, why can't he be our king?" said another. While that kind of talk would land them in the dungeon, Marcus never apprehended anyone who spoke against Zokar's regime. Deep down, he praised them.

The courtyard led into a vast throne room. Eerie orange light coming from braziers spread across the room, splashing against leather armor—only the zombies in Zokar's royal guard were permitted to wear iron or bronze. Guards stood in between each pillar, holding a sharp spear. Their helmets covered their heads so only two beady red eyes peered out.

A single throne sat on three-tiered steps. Torn black banners hung behind the chair, bearing two hand prints drawn with red paint to resemble blood. They crossed over one another in an X formation, creating the zombie emblem.

The zombie king sat on the throne in all his glory. He was a tall zombie clad in iron armor and a torn scarlet cloak. The letter Z stood out on his chest plate, and a spiked gold crown sat on his head. Unlike the zombies around the room, Zokar was well-muscled and starvation hadn't hallowed his face.

Marcus approached the throne and dropped to one knee.

"So, did you get it?" Zokar asked impatiently. Even after all these years, his harsh voice still startled Marcus.

Just tell him.

"No we didn't," Marcus responded, lifting his chin. "I sent four of my best soldiers into Skeletonia, and only one returned."

Zokar's eyes widened as he shot to his feet. The scar running over his right eye crinkled with anger, but his eyes darkened in terror. "Did you at least get the gemstone?"

Marcus shook his head. He watched as Zokar's face reddened, his lip curling. He lunged, grabbing the captain by the collar. His bright red eyes flared. "What are we supposed to do now? Malice is expecting those items by the end of the week! What are we going to give her?"

Marcus took shallow breaths. "Please listen, sire," he ground out, but Zokar was blinded by his own rage . . . and fear.

Crimson light enveloped the zombie king's fists as the floor beneath him cracked. The zombies in the room gasped and scattered, placing tons of space between themselves and the zombie king. Marcus glanced down to the floor in horror, seeing a jagged fissure torn into the stones. This happened whenever Zokar was angry—a magic flare-up. This was why overthrowing him wasn't an option. Zokar would wipe out any army Marcus conjured.

Besides, the first attempted coup cost Marcus his left eye. The only way to defeat Zokar and become the zombie king was through proving his aptitude to Malice.

I have to keep trying.

"If you'd listen to me, you'd know that Tristan Skeleton is one of Blanchett's wizards," Marcus said, nearly shouting.

Zokar stopped growling, his magic calming. His eyes remained livid, but his jaw slackened. "Are you sure?"

Marcus nodded, jaw set. "You above all people should know magic-wielders have a possibility of their powers getting passed down through generations."

Zokar scoffed and stepped back. "I know that, stupid. I just didn't think it would happen this soon. Well, I hoped it wouldn't happen to him. He'd be easier to defeat, now . . . " The zombie king paused. "I'm not sure."

When the zombie king began pacing, Marcus realized his plan might be working better than expected. Bringing Blanchett's journal and enchanted gemstone was his original plan, but the news of Skeleton being magic installed new fear into the zombie king. Him going up against another magic-wielder would force Zokar to rely more on Malice. He'd need her aid more than ever, putting the zombie king further under the demon's thumb—especially after she was so reluctant to reenlist him after his mistakes cost her the first Apocalypse War.

Zokar was still pacing, muttering to himself about what to do next. Sweat formed on his brow, plastering some of his dark brown hair to his forehead. Marcus forced away his smile and the pride rising in his chest. He stepped over the freshly made fissure in the floor and leaned closer to Zokar.

"All we have to do is tell her of Skeleton's powers," said Marcus. "She'll appreciate that, then we can alter our plans, and she might understand why we couldn't retrieve Blanchett's artifacts. She can guide us from there." *I know she'll understand me at least. I don't know about you, Zokar. Your approval doesn't matter. Nothing is ever enough for you.*

"She's already furious with me for the first war," Zokar shouted. His magic flared in his fists, his pointed ears folding back like an angry dog. "Malice dragged me back into this new war because she had no one else. She didn't wish to waste magic creating a new zombie king, nor did she want to spend diamonds on an assassin, nor would she trust one, so she chose me." Zokar paused, taking a shaky breath. "But, Malice said she wouldn't give me another chance if I messed up again."

Marcus bit back another grin. *Malice really has leverage on Zokar. Perfect. Just perfect. My plan is working.* The second-in-command set his jaw. "Then re-earn her trust by revealing Skeleton's powers."

Seconds bled into minutes as silence trickled by, sending Marcus's nerves into a frenzy. Finally, the zombie king stopped pacing. "All right, let's message her."

Marcus followed Zokar out of the throne room. Down the winding corridor, the zombie king took a sharp left where the hall led to a set of oak doors. Pushing them open, Zokar entered his study, which was too messy for Marcus's liking. Scrolls and books were strewn all over the desk and floor—there were more books on the floor than the shelves. Typical zombie. A portrait of the zombie king rested on the wall behind the desk, making Marcus cringe.

In the one clean spot on Zokar's desk sat a large crystal ball. Malice had gifted it to Zokar so she and the zombie king had a way to communicate. When the zombie king neared it, the orb pulsed a soft blue. Leaning over it, Zokar tapped the crystal surface. It burst to life, splashing the entire study with light. A white mist formed inside the ball then vanished revealing Malice's impatient, perpetually unhappy face.

She appeared just as Marcus remembered her. Long, jet-black hair was tied into a high ponytail with loose tresses that framed her four horns. Having four horns marked Malice as a Shadowblood. All the other demons merely had two.

"So, did you get the items?" Malice asked, her blood-red eyes flitting between Marcus and Zokar. Though she wasn't in the same room, her harsh voice reverberated through the orb. Zokar didn't answer. He maintained a straight posture to appear unfazed, but pale skin said otherwise. Marcus chewed his lip, pondering how to reveal the news.

"Why do you hesitate? SPEAK!" The demon flashed her sharp teeth in a snarl.

"I sent Marcus to get the items like you asked," Zokar said proudly. Marcus rolled his eye. "He didn't bring them back. It's his fault."

Malice scowled, her sharp cheekbones catching

the crystal ball's light. "You failed, didn't you?"

Marcus paused, pride flickering in his chest. This was his chance. "I sent four soldiers to the Skeletonia library to find Blanchett's journal and gemstone. Unfortunately, the scouts were discovered and stopped before they retrieved anything. Only one escaped." Marcus adjusted his eye patch, trying not to look nervous.

"I didn't come back completely empty handed," said Marcus. "The king of Skeletonia is a descendant of Blanchett's wizards. He's wearing the gemstone and he has the High Wizard's marking."

Malice drummed her fingers on something; the spherical frame of the orb didn't allow him to see what it was. "Is this wizard aware of his powers?"

Marcus cleared his throat. "It seems so, but he's never been trained. He knows of his powers, but doesn't know how to use them."

"This is perfect!" Malice flashed a genuine grin at Marcus. His heartbeat accelerated. "You may not have brought me Blanchett's gemstone or journal, but you've brought me crucial information. Not only is this wizard a fledgling, he knows little to nothing about how to work his powers. You did well, Marcus."

The second-in-command instantly felt taller and stronger. He'd pleased Malice this once, and this was no small task. This information was crucial to Malice's victory. Could he continue pleasing her enough for her to crown him zombie king?

"They were *my* soldiers," Zokar growled, shoving his face close to the ball. "And *my* orders," he snarled at the captain. Marcus folded his arms. This was nothing new.

"Don't push it, Zokar," said Malice, flaring her nostrils. "I still haven't forgotten your mistakes that cost me in the first war."

Zokar bristled, his scarlet eyes went flinty. "My mistakes? I was doing what I thought was best!"

The Shadowblood scoffed. "And it resulted in half of your army getting swallowed by a dragon and the other half drowning in enchanted lava. Traversing the northern Scale Mountains wasn't smart. You knew what would happen. Well done." Sarcasm dripped from her voice.

"It was a short cut to Blanchett's fortress." Raising a fist, Zokar summoned white lightning in his palm, ready to strike the crystal ball. Marcus grabbed his arm, pulling it down, throwing off the lightning's direction. The hot bolt crashed into a half-empty shelf, burning deep into the wood and leaving a large hole. The scent of charred parchment wafted off the mess. Zokar swore colorfully at his right-hand man.

"Cease your petty fighting!" boomed Malice. "I'll be paying you a visit later tonight to discuss further. I also have something for Zokar. Maybe with more of my help, I can lessen his chances of messing up again."

A low growl resonated in the zombie king's throat.

Marcus nodded, his pride nearly bursting out. "See you then."

Chapter Eight

Tristan was glad he and his friends made it back inside the castle before nightfall. Fingers of gold stretched over the castle, splashing on the walls, giving them a heavenly glow. But once the sun was down, the undead were free to prowl.

Guards going to the ramparts for night duty waved at Tristan. He waved back, but not without feeling like he betrayed them. There was no denying his magic, but hiding it didn't make him feel any better. He was already disobeying his parents' wishes by taking this quest.

In the great hall, Tristan found Radius, Zombie, and, to his surprise, Faye Dragonheart there, seated at the long oak table under a blazing chandelier. Her amethyst eyes fell on Tristan with kindness and a willingness to help.

A sense of calm and relief shrouded Tristan. *I didn't think she'd respond. I hope she can come with us.*

Zombie ran to his friend and wrapped his arms around him. Tristan smiled, taking in the scent of roses and fresh grass.

"Is everything all right?" Zombie asked. "I heard zombies broke into the castle. Why were they here?"

Tristan's throat closed up. "The usual. Another failed attempt at looting," he lied. Well, it was a half lie. They were trying to steal Blanchett's journal and his gemstone.

"Thank goodness," Zombie responded, smiling at Zombia. His eyes fell on Faye. "Oh, is this a diplomatic matter? A quest? Do you need me to leave?"

Tristan wanted to say no, but he couldn't risk his best friend learning about his powers. "I'm sorry, Zombie."

His friend nodded, his shoulders slumping, but his brown eyes lit up in inquiry. "I understand. I'll—"

"Actually," Tristan said, gently grabbing Zombie by the shoulder as his friend turned to leave. "Could you help Radius watch the castle while I'm gone? We're going on a quest." It was also true; they were going on a quest. He'd trusted his friend to care for things while he was gone in the past. How was this any different?

Zombie's face lit up. "What's the quest?"

Tristan chewed his lip, filing through his next words carefully. "It's complicated and dangerous. I can't risk you getting injured."

The corners of Zombie's lips turned downward, his green face becoming ashen. "I do hope you stay safe yourself, Tristan. But yes, I will watch the castle, as long as I can tend to the garden." A smile returned to Zombie's face.

The king chuckled. "Absolutely, you can do both. The roses need attention too."

"Great, well, good night."

Tristan held his breath as he watched his best friend disappear down the corridor. He managed to divert Zombie's questions—for now. Eventually, he'd have to tell his best friend. *Would he still be my friend if he knew?*

Tristan turned to Faye. She was a Dragonblood elf, complete with long flowing lavender hair, cool-gray skin and long, pointed ears. Unlike most queens, she didn't dress in gaudy attire. A simple pair of violet pants, red boots, and royal purple surcoat sufficed. A teal dragon eye dangled from a black choker around her neck, glinting with ancient draconic power.

"I'm so glad you could make it," he said.

The Dragonblood queen smiled at him, her eyes filled with concern. She wrapped him, Zombia, and Tibia into a hug.

"Hey, what about me?" said Emerson folding his arms. She laughed and wrapped him in too.

"As soon as I received Radius's letter, I decided I could pop by for a visit." Faye released her friends. "Unfortunately, I can't come on your quest since I'm meeting with the Icebloods tomorrow. I can't believe the zombies know about Blanchett."

Tristan laughed nervously. "Me neither. They obviously know of Tibia's and my powers, but that didn't stop them from trying, especially if Malice is governing them."

"Your parents at least imparted the prophecy to you, right?" Faye asked, her pointed ears twitching.

"They sort of did," Tibia said. "They did a horrible job of it. They always said *don't* use our powers." Tibia said the last part of her sentence in a mocking tone.

"It's not their fault, Tibia," said Faye in a sad voice. "With the overbearing Cadre, I don't blame them. I'm positive they'd have revealed more if they could."

"We only overheard them discussing that their children might be part of Blanchett's prophecy," Tristan explained. He pulled out Blanchett's journal and slid it across the table to Faye. She picked it up and flipped through the pages. While she did that, Tristan pushed *Translating Runes* to her. The moment he did, he realized that Faye most likely knew how to read them, leaving him feeling a little silly.

She smirked. "Thank you, but I learned to read runes from a very young age. All elves do. Luckily, the Cadre doesn't venture into elf territory often. I think the dragons deter them." Faye winked and stopped flipping through the pages. "I found her prophecy. It's here." She turned the book to Tristan. Zombia and Tibia peered over his shoulders. Like before, it was all written in ancient runes. "I'll read it for you."

Faye inhaled then began reading. "When the Apocalypse began and humanity fell, I knew I had to do something. I couldn't just stand by and watch the undead destroy what was left of the already-broken world. I knew my magic wasn't enough; I needed help.

I will gather people to train as my apprentices, then choose three of them to serve in my council as the Wizards of the Apocalypse. They will be the only three capable of controlling all four elements and the only ones who can withstand black magic—the only ones

who can end the Apocalypse and bring peace to the Haunted Lands. When those wizards die, the next generation will replace them until a cure is found."

Tristan's head throbbed, filled with information. This was the prophecy his parents had discussed. It all made sense. He and Tibia were to serve in Blanchett's court, just like their mother and father. This was their destiny. But, how were they going to fulfill it in a world that hated magic?

Faye closed the journal and handed it back to Tristan. "From the Dragonblood archives, I learned the elf tribes ceased their fire to aid Blanchett against the zombies. With dragons and wizards fighting side by side, we were able to defeat Malice's army. Even after the war, the elves helped Blanchett find a cure. She believed dragon magic was the only magic powerful enough to cure the zombie infection."

Tibia's eyes rounded. "If dragons can cure the virus, then why isn't it cured?"

Lowering her head, Faye's usually peppy voice grew somber. "Victory didn't come without losing many dragons. The ratio of dragons to zombies is extremely low, and with the undead multiplying as fast as they do, the dragons couldn't keep up. So we stopped trying that method altogether." Her hand rested on Tristan's shoulder, and it felt heavy. "That's why it's so important for you to fulfill this prophecy, Tristan."

Tristan looked at Zombia then Tibia with determined expressions. Their mission was clear: get the Apocalypse Grimoire before Malice and stop her from raising an army of the undead.

"While you're heading to the Citadel, I'll return to the Dragon Isles and see if I can convince the Icebloods and Moonbloods to fight at our side once more." Faye squeezed his shoulder reassuringly, reminding Tristan of how fortunate he was to have her as an ally. The three elf tribes agreed to a ceasefire to battle the zombies, and maintaining peace between them kept Faye busy. But, in the midst of her own kingdom's turmoil, she still found time to help her friends.

Tristan locked eyes with Faye, his heart feeling full. "Thank you."

The rest of the day was spent packing and reading Blanchett's journal.

Since Radius and Zombie were sent to watch over the castle, it would just be the king, Zombia, Emerson, and Tibia who went on this daring mission. While Tristan's sister had her own kingdom to care for, Tibia insisted that a few days away didn't seem so bad, much to Tristan's disapproval. The last thing he wanted was for his sister to get in harm's way. After a few minutes of excuses and constant pestering, he said yes.

When moonlight seeped through the windows, Tristan bid Emerson and Tibia good night.

"I can't believe you're finally getting to use your powers," Zombia said, her voice bouncing off the corridor's walls. Tristan grabbed her arm gently, shushing her.

She blushed in a way that made Tristan smile. "Oops, sorry, I'm just so excited. I've always wanted to see someone perform magic."

"We're still keeping secrets from everyone," said Tristan. "And using magic is still breaking the law. But yeah . . . I guess I've wanted to learn more about our powers."

Tristan and Zombia began ascending the winding staircase to the castle's second story. Torches crackled, filling the momentary silence. He liked these times when he and Zombia got to be alone, where they could talk and enjoy each other's company. It was one of the reasons he crowned her queen of Skeletonia.

When they reached the top of the stairs, Zombia laughed. She glanced over her shoulder to smirk at Tristan. "You're the king; you make the law, don't you?"

Tristan nearly tripped on the top step. "By the gods and goddesses, you're a queen. You should know what will happen if someone discovers Tibia's or my power. The people will turn against us; we'll be overthrown and executed. Even worse, all our friends will become the Cadre's targets too!" Tristan was so wrapped up in his concern that he didn't realize he was holding his friend by the shoulders. He briefly let go, heat rising in his cheeks, though he liked being that close to her. He wished he could have held her longer.

Zombia looked down. "My mother mentioned magic. She said it was wonderful, but she never got the chance to tell me in detail since leading the Resistance was more important."

"I'm sorry," the king said. "I just don't want to lose you, Zombia. I almost lost you when you decided to make the perilous journey to Skeletonia. I almost lost you to Zokar. I don't want to lose you to the Cadre."

Tristan and Zombia stared into each other's eyes for a long while. After the two met in the forest as kids, they continued writing to each other and even meeting for covert picnics and hunting trips. When Zombia decided to leave her desolate hometown, she wrote to Tristan, detailing her escape and how he could help her. She spent months using her hunting trips as cover-ups for scouting backroads and bypassing the many heavily guarded checkpoints.

She'd been lucky in avoiding capture. She'd survived this long, and Tristan didn't want to tempt fate into taking her away. Sighing, Tristan released his grip.

"Promise me you'll be careful on this mission, please," he said, his voice soft. "I don't know what I'd do if something happened to you."

Zombia squeezed Tristan's hand, sending warmth up his arm. "I will. If we're going to get that Grimoire, we'll have to stay alive. Goodnight, Tristan." She walked down the castle halls for her bedchamber.

That empty feeling found Tristan again. He pushed open the doors to his own room. After closing him, he went to his closet and changed into his nightshirt. He pried off the gold cuff, revealing the marking staring back at him. It was simple: a crescent moon with three water drops under it, imprinted forever onto his fair skin. With a shaky sigh, he climbed into bed, blew out the candle on his nightstand, and gazed at the ceiling for a long while until sleep took him.

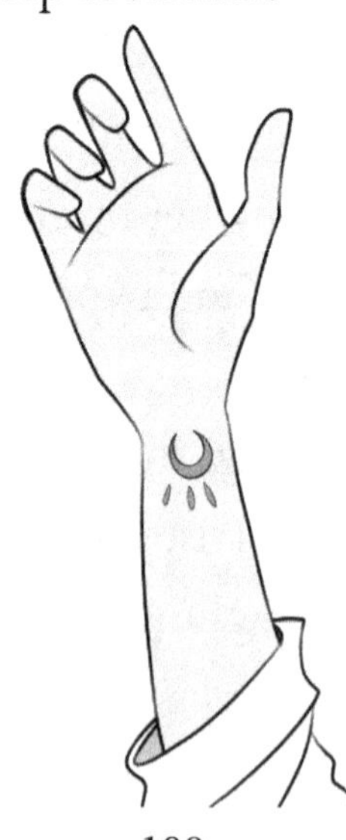

Chapter Nine

Tristan opened his eyes, finding himself on an unrecognizable cobblestone road. He blinked a few times to be sure. Trees surrounded him as a cool breeze rushed through the air, causing goosebumps to form on his skin. Out of instinct, Tristan reached for his bow. His heart skipped a beat when he felt it wasn't there. Not only did he not have his favorite weapon, but he was also still in his nightclothes. Though the metal pressing into his head told him he had his crown.

Weird. I have my symbol of authority but no weapons. Just great.

A mist settled close to the ground, but a full moon shone overhead, lighting Tristan's way. He began walking up the path, a sense of unease creeping through his body when he realized his situation. Being alone in the zombie-infested woods was never a smart idea. His heart began racing so hard Tristan swore he heard it. Through the mist, a figure appeared. Tristan bent down and grabbed a jagged rock, but his hand passed right through it.

The king saw his hand and his heart leapt into his throat. It was transparent, as was the rest of him.

Is this a . . . dream? I've never dreamt this vividly before. Could I be a dream-walker? That was something I heard my parents discuss. Some magic-wielders could be dream-walkers. Driving away the shock, the king focused on the approaching figure. They didn't shamble like a zombie, nor did they smell like one.

And there she was. A youthful woman with light blond, almost-white hair. Her locks flowed down her back, tied in a single ponytail. A crown forged from the purest gold sat on her head, adorned with bright garnets. Robes of the same color, trimmed with gold, covered her tall, broad form, complemented by epaulets made of blue crystals. Tristan blinked again, seeing the epaulets were composed of the same crystals as Emerson's armor.

In her hand, she held the most beautiful staff Tristan had ever seen. It was covered in gold leaf and curved at the top, like a shepherd's staff. Except, the curve wasn't just a curve; it formed an ornate dragon's head. Resting in its maw was a red orb. The king stared, overwhelmed by the artisanship that reminded him of Cameron.

The woman gave Tristan a heartwarming smile. Astonishment widened the king's eyes. This was *the* Ashley Blanchett. He recognized her from all the wanted posters he would see lying around the forest. Tibia even showed him one she found on their father's desk. Except, seeing her now, she didn't have that ominous, angry expression the posters depicted.

"Tristan Skeleton, I've been expecting you," Blanchett said, her voice soft but serious.

No words formed. Tristan continued staring at her with a quizzical expression. After a few moments, he realized what he was doing and blushed.

"I'm sorry, I wasn't ... um ... expecting to—"

The High Wizard simpered. "No apologies needed. Compared to how others would have reacted, you handled our meeting rather calmly."

"I have so many questions. Where have you been all these years? Were my parents your wizards? Did you know Tibia and I were going to be in your prophecy? Why—"

Blanchett held up her hands. "Slow down, Tristan. All your questions will be answered in time.

Unfortunately, as this is a dream, I only have little time. Thus, I must show you what you need to see."

Before Tristan could say anymore, the High Wizard grabbed his shoulder and waved her staff in front of her. The path and forest morphed into a hill overlooking a motte and bailey. It was still dark, but the fortress held an ethereal glow. It seemed as though the bricks themselves had a light inside them, banishing the shadows. Another rush of icy wind whisked by, sending shivers down Tristan's back.

"The Crimson Citadel," Tristan breathed.

Blanchett nodded, her electric-blue eyes growing wide. She was impressed.

The king shrugged and smiled. "It was in your journal."

"Keep that journal close, Tristan. You'll need it."

With another wave of her staff, they were no longer outside the motte and bailey. Now, they stood inside a vast courtyard. The walls and floor were constructed from the most elegant marble. Ancient runes were scrawled along the pillars, crafted with seasoned artistry and care. Along the walls, multiple doorways led to other parts of the fortress where other magic-wielders might have lived. Torches hung silently in their brackets, dimly lit. The open sky drifted overhead, calming Tristan's nerves.

Moving to the far-left wall covered with more archaic runes, Blanchett waved her hand over the smooth stone, and the wall receded, revealing a dark, foreboding hallway.

She led him through, more torches ignited out of thin air. Tristan heard a few rats squeaking in the walls; his gooseflesh rose. They emerged into a chamber with a vaulted ceiling. The pillars resembled the ones in the courtyard. Chests lined against the wall right across from them. Beside them was a vertical, rectangular mirror.

In the center of the room sat a single monolithic pedestal. The top was round, bearing Blanchett's symbol—the same one imprinted on Tristan's wrist.

ᛈᛖᛉᛞ
ᛏᚱᛟᛒ

Tristan inhaled the scent of old wood and mossy stone.

"You see, this gemstone in your crown doubles as a key. I gave it to your parents so long ago," said Blanchett. She reached up, plucked the gemstone from its place, and approached the pedestal. Lo and behold, a diamond-shaped lock was set at the pedestal's base. Carefully, Blanchett pressed the stone into the lock and twisted. Once done, Blanchett gave the gemstone back to Tristan.

The grinding of stone resounded through the chamber. The middle of the pedestal's surface shifted away, and a platform rose out of it, holding a massive, leather-bound tome. It was plain except for the turquoise dragon eye embedded in the cover. Tristan ran his hand over it; it looked so real for being a glass eye. He anticipated it to blink at him. To his relief, it didn't.

"The Apocalypse Grimoire holds every magic spell known to the Haunted Lands," Blanchett said, her posture bold. "If Malice gets her hands on this . . ." Her eyes locked with Tristan.

The king finished her sentence. "She'll conquer the world again."

The High Wizard only nodded. Tristan reached to

touch the Grimoire, nearly jumping as his hand passed through it. *Oh, right. I guess you can't pick up things in dreams. Makes sense.*

"During the war, I constantly experimented with potions and various weapons to ensure the wizards' victory. Here, I wrote down all the recipes, formulas, and spells needed for magic. It took me years to write this, but it was well worth it."

Tristan nodded as Blanchett placed the book back on its pedestal. The king watched the High Wizard, a single question forming in the back of his mind. "Four zombies broke into the Skeletonia library today to steal the items you gave my parents. They said something about you betraying Malice. What was that about?"

Blanchett sighed and closed her eyes, turning her gaze. Tristan regretted asking, wondering if that was too blunt of a question.

"She was one of my apprentices," said Blanchett with a sorrowful tone. "Malice was once a girl named Astrid. She was a curious little thing."

Tristan tilted his head. "Really?"

Blanchett nodded. "I know it's hard to believe a sweet girl turned into a heinous demon, but it's true. I have a book that contains all the secrets of black magic. I told all my students to stay away from it. If they were to study that book, they'd learn spells a good person should never know. It would open their minds to the world of dark magic." The High Wizard sighed, prompting Tristan to place his hand on her arm.

She took a deep breath. "One night, I heard a commotion down in the sparring room. I rushed down there and saw Astrid with the dark magic book. She was standing over it chanting. I raced to her and threw the book across the room, but it was too late. Black magic had already taken her soul."

Blanchett paused as she stared off into space with a longing expression. Tristan's chest tightened. *At least that's one form of magic the Cadre protects us from.*

"I was forced to banish her from the Wizard Council. Since then, she's never forgiven me. We briefly fought before she left, and that's how I got this scar."

Reaching for her sleeve, Blanchett rolled it up, revealing a nasty burn mark. It ran down from her elbow to her wrist. Tristan hissed as though he felt her pain.

"I'm . . . so sorry." He didn't want to imagine that happening to one of his friends. Gods, what would he do? Could he bring himself to banish them?

Blanchett said nothing, letting her sleeve fall back into place.

"After I banished Astrid, she changed her name to Malice Sanguine and retreated to the Dragon-Fang Mountains. Since the mountains overlook the Zombie Woods, she began amassing an army of zombies. She granted them dark magic. And that's how the Great Apocalypse War started."

Tristan looked at his feet, immersing himself in thought. "How did the zombies know about my gemstone or that the journal would be in the Skeletonia library?"

"Before she turned evil, I took her and my other apprentices to Skeletonia where they could meet and work with your ancestors. I saw no harm in it since she was one of my best and most trusted apprentices. I never thought she'd do what she did. The bad part is, now that she's evil, she can use all the knowledge I've imparted on her against me."

Tristan's pulse quickened. *Malice knew that much. I wonder what else she knows about my family.* Tristan didn't blame Blanchett. He knew the High Wizard was only teaching her young wizards and she didn't know one of them would become a demon. Still, the thought of Malice knowing about his family's magic frightened him.

The High Wizard took a long breath. "Zombies are dangerous enough on their own. But with magic, they become unstoppable. The wizards nearly lost the war. We were only victorious because of my wizards and the help from the elf tribes. But it wasn't without many casualties."

Tristan couldn't force his limbs to relax. "That's what the zombie meant by Malice's revenge."

"She now realizes the zombies weren't enough; she needs stronger forces. She read about this dimension called the Otherworld, where other demons—Shadowbloods included—reside. She is heading to the Hall of Black Mirrors to free them. It's the only portal to that realm."

Blanchett took another shuddering breath. Instinctively, Tristan reached to place his arm around her like he did when his friends were sad, but this was Ashley Blanchett. It didn't seem appropriate to be so informal with a powerful wizard. So he retracted his hand.

"She plans to release those monsters, Tristan. If she does, Malice will have an army of the undead *and* demons. That will be the end. It's up to the Wizards of the Apocalypse to stop her. Follow the map in my journal and everything will unfold."

The king scratched his head, contemplating the information. He knew Blanchett sensed Tristan's apprehension when she looked at him with crestfallen eyes.

"I know that look," said Blanchett, her voice flat.

"Oh, no, I wasn't—" Tristan began.

"No, I understand perfectly. The Cadre has painted magic as chaotic, leaving the world loathing it. But it's quite the contrary. Magic has balance like everything else in the world. Yes, magic can be chaotic, but it can also be beneficial. And it's with the beneficial magic that you'll stop Malice."

"How do we stop her, though?" asked Tristan. *If that's even possible.*

"There's a weapon that can kill her, but until you have it, the only thing you can do is capture her."

"What's the weapon?"

"It's a dagger crafted from a dragon's claw. It's one of the many dragon weapons the Dragonblood elves forged for us. Only magic from a dragon can withstand a Shadowblood's powers. When the war ended, I gave the dagger back."

Tristan's face lit up. "I'll ask Faye about it. She's a Dragonblood elf; she'd have to know." *Hopefully she solidified alliances with the other elf tribes.*

Blanchett smiled approvingly. "Her clan helped us immensely. Those elves have arcane magic of their own. You should seek her assistance."

Tristan glanced around the courtyard, pondering the best way to ask Faye. He listened to the braziers crackling. Surely she would help him. Faye was open and amicable. On the other hand, he felt bad asking for a family heirloom. He understood. He wouldn't just give his gemstone to anyone.

Before Tristan could think anymore, Blanchett guided Tristan to the mirror.

"Before you go, I have one more thing to show you. Stand before this, and let the glass recognize your gemstone."

Tristan cocked his head. "So this gemstone acts as a key?" Blanchett nodded and gestured to the mirror.

Tristan gazed at his reflection, waiting for the gemstone to work its magic. The glass flashed purple. A jolt flickered through him like lightning, leaving a tingling sensation after. Blanchett tapped the glass with her knuckles; the glass rippled and vanished.

The two stepped through the mirror into a small chamber. Dank air wafted up Tristan's nose. The room was nondescript, save for the Triple Goddess symbol resting in the center of the floor, inlaid with gold.

Blanchett reached the base of the full moon and pressed her foot down, activating a pressure plate. Gears shifted, and the Triple Goddess parted as three pedestals rose. Each held a different weapon: one had a bow, the middle held a single glaive, and the third held a crossbow. Tristan marveled, jaw going slack.

"Weapons of my wizards," Blanchett said, walking closer to the stands, her red robes whispering over the tiles. "Once you have the Apocalypse Grimoire and these items, you can fight against Malice, but until you procure the dragon-claw dagger, she'll live."

Tristan walked over to the weapons. The bow looked exactly like his: crafted from yew. However, tiny runes were carved into its limbs. Reaching out, his hand passed through it, reminding him this was only a dream.

"Tristan, the sun will be rising soon," said the High Wizard. "You must return home. I'll be sending someone your way. She'll guide you."

The king looked to Blanchett, his chest tight.

Tristan clenched his fists and bowed. "I won't let you down." He knew the risk he would be taking, but it was worth it if it meant saving his friends and the Haunted Lands. It was a mission he was willing to take.

"I know you'll do the right thing, Tristan Skeleton." Her voice began to fade as everything went dark.

Chapter Ten

Malice materialized outside the Zombie Fortress. Those all too familiar walls stood firm, defying any entry. Fingers of moonlight shrouded broken spires and cracked gargoyle statues. Everything about the fortress appeared disorganized. The demon scowled at it; the sorrowful, angry groans of zombies filtered through the air.

Zombie Keep. I hate this pitiful kingdom with its craven ruler.

The Shadowblood didn't want to be there. It was stressful enough convincing Zokar to rejoin her in taking the Haunted Lands. It was even more stressful deciding whether she *wanted* to work with Zokar again. Malice persuaded the zombie king, telling him Blanchett was their common enemy and it would be easier to fight her together than apart. After she promised high positions to all the zombies, Zokar agreed.

Her grip tightened around her staff as she surveyed

the dilapidated city of Zombieshire. How could anyone live like this? The hovels were crammed on a crooked road. Unlike most other cities built on a grid pattern with straight streets, this place had no specific plan at all. And oh gods, the smell! The revolting scent of decomposing flesh and unwashed clothes would drive any survivor away; instead, Malice shook her head in disgust.

"The foolish monsters would be nothing without the Shadowbloods," Malice muttered. Frosty air nipped at

Malice's milky skin. No one but her would be out on this cold autumn night wearing only a thin robe, riding pants, and boots. The metal epaulets and knee pads she wore did nothing to fend off the chilly atmosphere, but she didn't care. Her disdain for Zokar and his kingdom kept her warm.

I wish I didn't have to take Zokar back, but I don't want to waste time and power creating and training a new zombie king. And Kane, the assassin, is out of the question. That inane zombie king is my best option. Hopefully these weapons I'm going to make for him will help.

Like all Shadowbloods, she has the capabilities to spawn creatures from her mind and breathe them into reality. Malice decided to put her evil powers to the test years ago, right as the Great Apocalypse War began. Realizing the zombies needed a leader other than her, the Shadowblood queen poured her dark magic and powers into creating Zokar. What Malice didn't realize was that the zombie king she created would grow arrogant. He'd focus on what *he* considered best for the army and how to win the war, leading to many disastrous mistakes, and eventually costing Malice her victory.

And that was something she'd never forgive him

for. But what else could she do? Creating a new zombie king might beget the same problem. Maybe enough threats would bend the zombie king into shape. She hoped. With Blanchett's wizards growing stronger every day, Malice knew her days were numbered.

The demon's anger boiled like a potion in a cauldron. Sighing through her nose, the Shadowblood pressed forward, approaching the leather-clad guards. Startled, they aimed their spears at Malice.

She looked down her nose at the zombies and smirked. "Please, gentlemen, I come as an ally of Zokar. Don't you remember I'm his maker?"

Maybe one of my bigger mistakes. The amount of dark magic it took to spawn him wasn't worth it. But he'll have to do.

The zombies shifted, their eyes flitting to the four burgundy horns jutting from her head. They gripped their spears tighter, but lowered them.

"You may enter, but it's late," said one of the guards. "I doubt the king will be interested in visitors."

Malice's lip curled. She flicked her fingers, releasing a tiny lightning bolt. It struck the closest guard on the backside, setting his pants on fire. He zipped around the gatehouse, screaming in a way that made Malice snort with laughter. She turned to the remaining soldier.

"Bring me to the zombie king before you're nothing but a pile of ash on the ground."

The zombies nodded vigorously. Malice strutted into the courtyard. More of the rotting creatures were gathered. Braziers dotted the courtyard, filling the area with warm orange tones and making Malice's navy-blue robes pop. A set of large doors swung open, revealing a pillared corridor.

The monsters moved out of Malice's way without question. A satisfied grin formed on Malice's face.

At least ruling his kingdom using fear was the one thing Zokar did right.

Zokar and Marcus stood in front of the throne. While the second-in-command stood looking composed, the zombie king quivered whilst trying to maintain false bravery.

"Greetings, Zokar and Marcus," said Malice in a low, flat tone. "Let's skip the pleasantries and get to work. Since you don't have the items I asked for"—her eyes flicked to Zokar—"we have to work faster than before."

Marcus flashed Malice a proud grin; Zokar grumbled to himself.

"I did what you asked, Malice!" Zokar shouted. "I sent my second-in-command to get the items. Blame him!"

Malice poked Zokar's chest with her claw. "Don't argue. You're already treading on thin ice with me. From what I see, you sent Marcus to get Blanchett's artifacts because you were too much of a coward to do it yourself. And even though it cost him a few casualties, he still brought me vital information. On the other hand, I had no choice but to reenlist you. Let me say it wasn't an easy decision."

Zokar threw his hands up. "Whatever. We don't have Blanchett's stuff, so what's your *brilliant* plan? Skeleton is a wizard. How can we ensure our victory again after failing the first time?"

The demon pinched the bridge of her nose. *Why must I suffer this fool? Maybe creating a new zombie king isn't such a bad idea. He's so far hampering my revenge plans.*

"You underestimate me," said Malice. "While you were hiding, I spent years planning and preparing. Have you noticed you and the other zombies obtained the power to speak and think? You're no longer mindless, flesh-eating zombies. That's part of my plan and the power of my magic. Blanchett is weak and in hiding, and best of all: the world fears magic. They're unprepared. Once we have the Apocalypse Grimoire, the undead will be undefeatable."

The demon backed away from Zokar and raised her staff. "Now shut up, I have something to make."

Before Zokar could respond, Malice already went to work. Gathering her dark powers, she cast a rune on the ground at her feet, forcing it to split. Magma bubbled up from the castle floor. Marcus stepped back, and the zombie king shrank behind him. Next, two thin globs of molten rock rose into the sky, then began to warp. Malice moved her hands meticulously until the magma took the shape of two daggers.

When the spell ended, the ground closed up, and the newly forged weapons landed handle first in Malice's hands.

"Behold, enchanted daggers."

Zokar approached and looked them over, mouth agape. The handle was wrapped in black leather bindings, the hilt was a hoop, and the blade was delicately curved, ending in a sharp point crafted from pure obsidian. Once he finished inspecting them, he shoved the blades into his belt.

Malice clutched her staff. "We're heading to the Hall of Black Mirrors. There, I will release the rest of the Shadowbloods trapped during the last war. Along the way, we are going to invade any village we find. Loot all their supplies and bite everyone you see. The more zombies we have, the better."

Zokar nodded, his eyes lighting up. At least the zombie king was brutal, which was the main reason she reenlisted him. Marcus recoiled. Malice could tell the captain wasn't a fan of sheer brutality, but he made up for it with intelligence.

The demon tapped her staff on the ground and faced the fortress door. "You are to follow my orders if we want to defeat the wizards. Show Blanchett I'm no weakling. We failed once, and we aren't going to fail again." She glanced over her shoulder at Marcus and Zokar, black hair moving in a wave. "And I won't think twice about eliminating any obstacles."

Chapter Eleven

Tristan woke with a start. His heart pounded heavily; sweat clung to his nightclothes and forehead. Warm light streamed through the window as the sun's face greeted him, punctuated by the sound of morning birds. Sitting up, the king rubbed his eyes. Nothing in his room was disturbed; he glanced at his wrist, finding Blanchett's mark still there. He reached over his nightstand, grabbed his gold cuff, and snapped it around his wrist, concealing the mark once more.

A knock at the door made him jolt.

"Tristan, are you up? Can I come in?"

Tristan smiled, recognizing Zombia's voice. Throwing off the covers, Tristan strode to the door, wincing as the cold floor bit his toes. Outside his room, Zombia stood there wearing iron armor over simple gray leather boots, dark pants, and a scarlet shirt that complimented her green skin tone well. Her trusty sword was belted at her hip, which relieved Tristan. At least she'd be safer with all that on. He must have looked exhausted because worry danced in Zombia's hazel eyes.

"Is everything all right?" she asked.

Tristan paused, recalling his dream briefly. "Y-yeah, I'm fine."

"That's good because everyone's waiting downstairs in the courtyard. We're ready to leave."

Tristan's cheeks reddened as he presented a sheepish grin. "Sorry, I'll be ready in a moment." He shut the door and heard Zombia giggle as she listened to her friend's hurried footsteps.

Five minutes passed before the king came out dressed in a white kilt and full iron armor, his bow in hand and a quiver of arrows over his shoulder. Everything was iron except for the blue crystal epaulets—a gift from Cameron.

Together, the king and Zombia started down the castle corridors, heading for the spiral stairs. Usually, he and Zombia would chat, but today, silence seemed more appealing.

A few moments passed before Zombia placed a hand on Tristan's shoulder, sensing his angst. "Something's bothering you, isn't it?"

Tristan stepped back, blushing. "I'm fine, really."

Gods, she knows me too well.

"I know when something's bothering you, Tristan," said Zombia with a smirk. "You go quiet and look at the ground. Please, tell me what it is."

Tristan sighed as he exited his room. "Blanchett visited me in a dream. She told me what Malice's plan is. After she gets the Apocalypse Grimoire, she's heading to a place called the Hall of Black Mirrors. She plans to release an army of demons."

Zombia stopped in her tracks at the top of the stairs, her face darkening. "Oh that's horrible. We have to go now!"

"But it gets weirder," added Tristan. "Blanchett said two of my friends are also wizards. Tibia's one, but who's the other?"

Tristan locked eyes with Zombia, looking for answers, but she shrugged a little too nonchalantly.

"I'm not sure, but we'll find out," Zombia answered calmly. Heat flushed Tristan's cheeks when she squeezed his hand.

"This is getting harder to hide, isn't it?" Tristan said woefully as he descended the steps.

Zombia followed him. Her presence behind his back made him feel lighter. "We can hide it."

Reaching the bottom of the stairs, they found the courtyard. Guards from the nightshift lumbered through, their bodies racked with fatigue from a monotonous night peering into the wilderness for threats. Emerson and Tibia waited; full packs hung on their shoulders.

Cameron, Radius, and Zombie stood beside them.

"Are you sure I can't come along?" Cameron pleaded. Emerson frowned at his friend. While the knight and guild master were close friends, Emerson always made that stern face—frown, hardened gaze, and down-turned brows—to show he wasn't joking.

"Not this time, sorry. As much as I'd enjoy your company, this mission can afford no mistakes."

Cameron nodded, flashing his friend a sad smile. "Don't die out there. If you do, who will I prank?" Humor had returned to his voice. Balling his hand into a fist, he punched his friend playfully in the shoulder. Cameron retracted his fist quickly, clutching his knuckles.

Zombie extended his arms, embracing Tristan and Zombia. "Radius and I will take care of the castle." The captain gave an affirmative nod. "Stay safe," Zombie said.

"Thank you, my friend," Tristan replied. His heart felt heavy.

Parting, the king waved bye as the four friends made for the castle door. A sudden emptiness flowed through Tristan as the doors shut behind him.

Towering pines, low-hanging branches, and brush became their new surroundings. The soft detritus of pine needles carpeted the floor, crunching under Tristan's boots. The distant sounds of forest denizens bounced through the treetops. A few chipmunks scampered across the path, making Tristan smile. He inhaled, taking in the sweet scent of pine. It reminded him that beauty still thrived in the Zombie Woods.

It wasn't nighttime, but darkness bathed the scene. Only tiny rays of sunlight managed to pierce the leafy canopy. There was enough light for seeing, but it was the looming shadows Tristan didn't trust. The friends trekked through the Zombie Woods with weapons drawn, prepared to face the many volatile threats lurking behind the foliage. Zombies being green made the forest the perfect hiding place.

They continued north with nothing but looming pines and close-packed needles for miles, making the sense of direction difficult. Tristan knew that moss only grew on the north side of trees, so he used that to point the way.

"We need torches," the king said.

"I'm on it," called Emerson. The knight reached into his satchel and withdrew some linen, then wrapped it around a branch and dipped it in pitch. After taking out some flint, Emerson struck a rock with it. A couple tries later, a flame sputtered to life. Shoving the flint back into his bag, the short knight handed the torch to Tristan.

"Thank you. I wish more sunlight got in here."

Walking a little further, Tibia sniffed the air and asked, "Do you smell smoke?"

"Em just lit a torch, sis," Tristan retorted sarcastically with a grin. In return, she flashed her brother an irritated scowl and elbowed him in the shoulder.

"No, it's heavier and stronger than the torch."

"I smell it too," said Zombia.

Tibia loaded her crossbow and charged up the path. She skidded to a halt. "Look there," Tibia said frantically, pointing her finger ahead.

In the forest clearing sat a small village. Several columns of smoke floated into the air from charred houses.

"Follow me!" The king's sister took off charging toward the smoldering homes. Bursting through a line of trees, Tristan and his friends stood in front of the village. The acrid smell nearly overwhelmed them. Smoke made Tristan's eyes water as a sandpaper feeling bit the back of his throat; his heart sank.

He scanned the scene. There were no cries or screams, and the fire was out. Smoke snaked out from collapsed wooden frames. Trinkets spilled out of empty carts and smashed stands littered the land. Tristan sighed and turned to Emerson.

The group made their way through the now-dilapidated houses. The walls and foundations were burnt beyond recognition. Zombia held her breath as her face scrunched up in disgust. Tibia's face remained stoic. Tristan knew she cared; she was just reticent, but judging by her scowl, he could see she was burning with rage toward the attackers.

"Spread out; scour the area for survivors," said Tibia curtly.

"Will do." Emerson was off, Tibia on his heels.

Tristan sniffed the air, thankfully not sensing any burnt flesh or corpses.

"Whoever did this is going to pay dearly," Zombia muttered as she and Tristan marched down the linear streets.

Tristan stepped through the smoldering remains of a doorway. The frame was severely burnt and blackened. Flaky soot blanketed the floor, shattered furniture littered the foundations, but no one appeared to be present. Since the walls caved in, Tibia and Emerson were visible in the other buildings.

"No one's here," called Tristan.

"Not in here either," Emerson responded over his shoulder.

A sinking feeling settled in the king's chest. *Where are the people? There are no dead bodies around. If the zombies bit them, the time between the raid and us arriving isn't long enough for the infected to reanimate and wander off. I hope they escaped.* This was life in the Apocalypse—villages of survivors were constantly beset by the undead, leading to these horrible raids. Tristan bowed his head, whispering a prayer to the gods that the town's residents made it out alive.

When the king turned to leave, his foot hit something, followed by the crack of glass. Soot puffed off the discarded object. Looking down, he found a broken window, half-covered by a black banner bearing two crisscrossed gory handprints.

"The zombies were here," Tristan grumbled. "No doubt this is Malice's doing. She's already on the move."

"I can smell the black magic," Tibia answered. "That was one thing mom taught us." She eyed Tristan. He agreed. He could smell the magic too. Black magic smelled of sulfur, making the king wrinkle his nose.

Emerson tilted his head. "Magic has a smell?"

The Skeleteria queen nodded. "Everything has a unique smell."

"And when people use magic, it leaves a scent trail," Zombia added, arms behind her back as she inhaled again. When Emerson kept his brows furrowed, Zombia explained further. "Magic isn't just something you use; it's part of your body and soul."

Tristan's eyes widened. *Zombia seems to know a lot about magic, despite it being banned in Zombieshire. Perhaps she smuggled a book on the topic?*

Looking down again, Tristan saw footprints leading out of the house. "Whose are these?"

"Not mine," Zombia responded.

"Mine neither," Tibia said.

"Certainly not mine," Emerson said. He drew his sword and walked ahead of Tristan, ready to defend his king. "Maybe a zombie?"

Tristan followed Emerson; they led him and his friends through another broken door frame. Entering, he found more burnt furniture strewn everywhere. To his left someone dashed across the cobblestone streets.

Tristan drew his bow and nocked an arrow. He sprinted after the person, following them to the next house over. Pushing open what remained of the door, he found a young girl. She wore a burgundy cloak trimmed with gold. Her long brunette locks were tied into a neat braid dangling over her shoulder. She turned to the king, revealing her scratched face.

A survivor. She lacked the pointed ears of a zombie, demon, or elf. Tristan put away his bow and offered a hand.

"Hey, it's okay; we're not going to hurt you."

The girl paused, jamming an apple into her satchel. Her emerald eyes fell directly on Tristan, then shifted to Tibia. She looked at them with recognition as though the girl was reconnecting with old companions.

"Are you Tristan Skeleton?" the girl asked.

Tristan took a step back, lost for words. "Yes . . . why?"

The girl swept aside her braid and extended a hand. "I'm Cerys Runeblaze, a member in Ashley Blanchett's court. She sent me to find you. On my way to Skeletonia, I passed through this burned village." The girl frowned at the wreckage.

The High Wizard's words popped in the king's mind. *"I'll be sending someone your way. She'll guide you."* This *must be the someone she referred to.*

"So you're one of Blanchett's wizards too?" asked Tristan.

Cerys rolled her eyes. "No, I am a mage. There's a difference. Here's your first lesson: mages only have access to certain types of magic and don't nearly have the spell capacity wizards possess."

Tristan grasped the girl's hand. "Sorry, my parents didn't tell me as much as they would have. These are my friends: Zombia Deadfall, Sir Emerson Valor, and Tibia Skeleton, my sister."

"It's great meeting you, but we need to get to the Crimson Citadel," Cerys said. "Malice isn't waiting, and neither should we."

Tibia scrutinized Cerys. "But you're so . . . young. Aren't most mages adults?"

Emerson cocked his head. "And how'd you finish training so quickly? Knight training takes seven years. Magic training must be longer."

Tristan agreed; the girl was a year or two younger than him.

The mage lifted her chin, her eyes narrowing.

"Contrary to popular belief, a lot of magic-wielders are very young. I know enough to guide fledgling wizards. I'll explain more later. We should get out of here before dark. Malice's zombies might return to pilfer whatever's left."

Cerys sprinted out of the burnt town, leaving Tristan and his friends in the dust. The air still smelled of smoke. Swallowing his discomfort, Tristan turned to Zombia and Tibia.

"Do you think Blanchett really sent her?" Tibia asked as she moved to her brother's side. "Can we trust her? What if she's one of Malice's henchmen posing as one of Blanchett's mages so she can get close to us?'

"I doubt it. During the dream, Blanchett told me she was sending someone to help us," answered Tristan. "This must be that someone. We should give her a chance."

"I agree," said Emerson, rubbing his face. "At this point, we need all the help we can get. Those zombies aren't going to fight themselves."

"We might learn some new stuff too," Zombia added with a wide grin. Warmth spread through the king's cheeks. Zombia always saw the good in people, which has come in handy in times where humanity teetered on the brink of extinction, and the few survivors had to trust and rely on each other. *More people should replicate her optimism.*

Tibia blew her black bangs out of her face. "Be careful around her. I swear Tristan, one of these days, your softness is going to bite you in the backside. Don't say I didn't warn you." She stalked after Cerys, hand on her crossbow. Emerson walked next to the mage, probably talking her ear off.

"Tib—"

Zombia grabbed the king's shoulder. Sparks shot through Tristan's heart at her touch. "She just cares about you. Let's go."

The two friends followed, disappearing back under the foliage onto their next lethal adventure. Tristan pursed his lips in thought, knowing Tibia had a point. Malice could have anyone claim they're one of Blanchett's mages. But after his dream, the two events seemed too coincidental. Also, he needed someone to teach him and Tibia about their powers. There was no other choice but giving the mage the benefit of the doubt.

Chapter Twelve

Zokar watched Malice as she led the army. *His* army. The zombies marched all day, destroying one village after another, infecting everyone inside. Nightfall would come soon; the sun had dipped below the treetops. He walked beside the demon, then ran his hands over the knives belted at his sides and smiled.

The more magic she gives me, the easier it will be for me to overthrow her, thought Zokar. *After the first war, I considered leading the zombies against Blanchett again, using the magic Malice gave me against them, but it wouldn't have been enough. Lying low for so many years became dull. Now that Malice wants me back into her army, I'm closer to her, earning her trust. That will be her first and final mistake.*

But while he was thinking about overthrowing the demon, Zokar also couldn't help the sneaking feeling that Malice might do the same to him. *I'll kill her first.*

Malice brought the zombies to a halt on a hill overlooking another doomed village. This one was on flat plains, untouched by trees, making for an easy target. Hundreds of zombies shambled behind her, growling. Their armor and weapons glinted in the setting sun.

Zokar drew his knives. Iridescent blue light undulated over the blades like ocean waves: beautiful but deadly.

Armed guards stalked along the stockade, bows slung over their shoulders and swords at their hips, ready for any impending threats. All villages had walls around them since the Apocalypse began. This manifestation of perpetual angst restored joy in Zokar's twisted soul. He looked to Malice to see she was most likely thinking the same.

"Are you sure infecting and raiding these villages isn't slowing us down?" Zokar asked, furrowing his brow. "We could have the Grimoire by now if you didn't want to stop at every town."

Malice scowled at the zombie king, narrowing her crimson eyes. "We're growing an army, Zokar. We can't face the wizards without one. We have to prove to Blanchett who's superior. By the Triple Goddess, you zombies are so impatient." Malice pointed to the bustling town. "Now, get in there and attack the soldiers on the ramparts. Once inside, open the gates and let the zombies in and have them bite everyone, women and children included."

"Doesn't that seem a little . . . harsh?" said Marcus from behind Malice. "Can't we spare them? Just bring them under zombie rule instead?"

Zokar scoffed. "You fool, we're zombies. Our purpose is to infect and kill. The larger our army, the better."

Malice nodded in agreement. "Get in there, raid the place, take any food and weapons you find. "

"It will be done," said the zombie king.

"For your sake, Zokar, I'd hope so. I bestowed powers on you for a reason; use them wisely."

Those powers were a mistake to give me in the first place. When you created me, you should have considered I might dethrone you. Which I will. Zokar's fists clenched and unclenched, the heat of rage slithering through him like a venomous snake, ready to strike. He yearned to say these words to Malice, but he held his tongue.

Instead, the zombie king turned to face the village gates. A smile broke across his face, revealing many serrated teeth as he considered the spoils he'd gain. He wasn't going to overthrow Malice yet; he still had a ways to go before she fully trusted him again. For now, Zokar would help the Shadowblood.

Drawing his knives, Zokar addressed his warriors. "Attack! Leave none uninfected."

A handful of zombies surged from behind Zokar and Malice and ran—some limped—for the gates, weapons out. Another group of zombies carried a massive tree trunk for a battering ram. To Zokar's disappointment, the undead lacked the proper siege weapons. A catapult or ballista would have been nice; Malice taught the zombies to use them in the first war. But this time, she wanted to waste no time enacting her revenge on Blanchett.

The ground shook when they slammed the heavy trunk into the village doors.

BAM, BAM, BAM!

The doors didn't give way, only a few cracks spider-webbed across the wood. Their tactic was ineffective against the strong oak. All it did was attract the sentinels' attention.

"We're under attack!" one of the guards cried, alerting everyone else. Soon enough, dozens of soldiers in bronze armor stood on the ramparts, bows aimed in the zombies' direction.

"FIRE!" shouted the same guard.

Hundreds of barbed shafts rained on the zombies, tearing into flesh. Monsters collapsed only to be replaced with three more—proving just how deadly zombie hordes were. Pained cries echoed from below, zombies still dropped, and Zokar's rage boiled. Judging by the few cracks in the doors, the battering ram hadn't gotten them anywhere.

"Climb!" he commanded. The zombies rearranged their formation and began mounting each other's shoulders.

"They're climbing the walls!" one of the soldiers shouted. The archers pointed their bows down the walls, continuing to fire. The monsters clung close to the stone, avoiding some of the shafts; others weren't as lucky. Seeing the zombies evade the arrows, a few soldiers marched forward with a cast-iron pot filled with boiling oil. They poured it on the undead masses. Growls of anger and pain echoed, followed by the scent of charred flesh.

What made Zokar proud was that despite all these attacks, the zombies didn't relent. When one layer fell, another appeared, the green monsters snarling and scaling closer. Once at the top, they jumped the wall's lip and attacked the soldiers, biting into any exposed skin. Zokar smiled. This was perfect. When humans attacked, the ground was littered with the dead. When zombies attacked, they could infect, quickly raising an army with just their contaminated teeth.

Zokar's chest tightened when he saw some of the soldiers throwing the zombies off the wall. Green bodies plummeted to the ground. If this wasn't successful, Malice would have his hide.

Sheathing his knives, the zombie king clapped his hands together and closed his eyes. Magic formed inside from all corners of his mind. Drawing the enchanted tethers together, Zokar pulled the power into his hands. His body and eyes glowed as a ball of white energy formed between his splayed fingers. Bigger and bigger until. . . BOOM!

The explosion left zombies and villagers alike strewn in the dirt. On cue, the undead poured through the shattered barriers, falling on the guards. Several stormed the stairs leading to the top of the ramparts. Another volley of arrows rained down, but it no longer mattered. The stockade was breached.

"Magic zombies!" one of the guards cried.

"Quick, we must—" A swift slash to the throat silenced the soldier. Warm, slick blood coated Zokar's hands and knives as he seized his enemy's head and bit into his neck, then let him fall to the ground. Marcus appeared behind Zokar and dragged the body back to Malice. The second-in-command's face wasn't one of pure delight. He looked . . . apologetic.

Weakling.

Zokar stalked through the lantern-lit streets, a turquoise sheen coating his body, his fists sparkling with magic energy. With a flick of his wrists, houses combusted; whenever villagers came his way, he tossed his knives at them. The blades soared through the air, cutting into his opponents, before returning to Zokar.

Red stab wounds blossomed on their chests. Too weak to defend themselves or flee, Zokar lunged for their arms. His teeth sank into their flesh, just as Malice had instructed. They slumped to the ground, whimpering as they stared hopelessly at their arms—at the bite marks. Zokar stepped back with a satisfied grin, wiping blood from his mouth.

More zombie soldiers came to drag the bodies away. The villagers would turn soon enough, but Zokar wished the transformation was immediate. He found

Marcus at his side again, looking down at a young girl, blood seeping from her stomach from an arrow wound. The second-in-command's knuckles were white from gripping his bow so tightly.

"Hurry up and bite her!" boomed Zokar. "What are you waiting for?"

Marcus reluctantly knelt down by the body, took the girl's arm and clamped his jaws around her wrist. Releasing, Marcus stood and threw her over his shoulder, brows pulled together.

"That's better. For a second, I thought you were becoming more human than zombie."

Smoke and ash filled the air as flames engulfed the once peaceful homes. Zokar continued down the streets until he came upon a single villager. The tan leather apron wrapped around his waist told Zokar he was a blacksmith.

"I don't fear you! It's the Apocalypse. We're accustomed to your *kind*." The blacksmith's words just made Zokar smile. Fear lurked beneath them.

The blacksmith barreled for the zombie king, swinging his sword toward his opponent's chest. After evading the petty attack, Zokar brought his foot up, connecting with his adversary's gut. The young man doubled over, but managed to stay on his feet. His eyes flitted to the blades in Zokar's hands.

"Y-you're magic?" he stammered.

Zokar's grin grew. "Quite an observation, considering you've denied magic all these years." His arms slackened.

"Come, fight me, I'm right here."

When the villager didn't attack, Zokar rolled his eyes. "Look, I'm offering you the first shot."

The blacksmith didn't wait another second to take the zombie king's offer. He aimed for Zokar's shoulder and cut in. The pain made the zombie king decide it was time to reveal his true powers. A magic blade hurtled through the air. It was an effort to keep from laughing when the keen edge sliced the smithy's sword in half as he parried. The dagger returned to Zokar's grip hot to the touch.

"Still in doubt?" the zombie purred.

"Impossible," the man breathed, eyes wide as he backpedaled. Zokar approached and tossed his knife again. It twirled around the blacksmith and back to his hand. Neon-green tendrils circled his opponent's body as a pallid look fell across his face. Within seconds, the villager fell to his knees.

"What's wrong?" Zokar asked, stepping closer. With a stiff foot, the zombie king pushed the villager to the ground. A weak groan escaped his lips.

"What did you do to me?" the man asked. Zokar snorted.

"If you studied magic, you'd know every living thing has energy inside." The zombie king ran his green thumb over the flat side of the blade. "These daggers allow me to draw energy from surrounding objects."

"That'll be the day," the villager spat. He rose on shaky legs. "That'll be the day I surrender to a rotting corpse." Fists ready, the blacksmith lunged for the zombie king, but the daggers were already sailing. He gasped as they pierced both shoulders, pinning the smithy to the wall. Blood blossomed on his shirt and apron. Gritting his teeth, the man jerked and twitched; the blades didn't relent.

Zokar stepped forward and grinned balefully. "That was a valiant effort, but Malice is waiting."

"W-what are you doing?"

Zokar didn't answer. His sharp teeth sank into the man's neck. Horrified screams split the air. He kicked and pushed against Zokar's grip as blood splattered his face.

Stepping away, the zombie king yanked his knives from the smithy's shoulders, letting his form slump to the ground. A sick smile crept on Zokar's face as he eyed the fresh bite mark decorating the man's neck. He glared at the lifeless body, knowing he would reanimate soon. His face was frozen in a scream, and Zokar couldn't stop from wishing it was Malice.

The Forgotten Prophecy

An emptiness filled Marcus's chest as he bit into the forearm of an adolescent boy. Agonized screams filled his ears before the body went limp. Releasing his grip, Marcus watched his victim fall to the ground, a fresh ring of teeth marks embedded in his skin. Feeling sick, Marcus spat out the taste of flesh before slinging the motionless form over his shoulder, and making it through the smoky haze back to Malice.

This was his second kill that night, luckily, he was able to lay low and carry bodies back to Malice outside the gates. But one kill was already too much. These were real people who had jobs and families, and the zombies had deprived them of those rights.

Nighttime had fallen by the time the entire village was infected and looted. The second-in-command dragged the boy to the pile of soon-to-be zombified villagers. He approached Malice. Unlike Zokar, she didn't scowl at him. In fact she looked pleased. The tightness in Marcus's chest vanished, but his guilt remained.

"Well done, Marcus," she said. "Quick and coherent, I like it."

She said them, the words I've been waiting for. Next step, grant me the position of zombie king. Prove I'm more competent than Zokar.

A commotion came from the shattered village gates. The rest of Malice's army returned, carrying villagers over their shoulders. Others dragged carts of food and weapons—all the supplies she'd asked for. The grin on the Shadowblood's face widened, exposing her long sharp teeth, though it faded when the zombie king came into view. He strutted through the sea of monsters, dragging two limp townspeople behind him. The crowd parted to let him through.

Marcus could only guess the zombie king was enjoying himself, playing with his enemies before sealing their miserable fates with a single bite. Marcus found that unnecessary and highly inefficient. Judging by Malice's folded arms and clenched teeth, she felt the same way.

Another reason she should choose me as the zombie king, thought Marcus.

"Well, Zokar, at least you did what I asked, for once," said Malice.

The zombie king muttered under his breath and tossed his two villagers in with the rest. Malice looked at the considerable lot. People of every age lay close together, their clothing torn and covered in soot, bite marks covering their arms. Marcus knew they'd turn soon, but not for a few days, some longer than others. Very few of the people wore armor already; unfortunately, most of them would need to be provided for. When zombies came out carrying carts of blacksmith weapons and armor, the tension in Marcus's limbs eased.

The Shadowblood sighed looking at the townspeople's limp forms. "I'll have to use some magic to expedite the zombification process." She raised her staff and muttered an incantation. A complex rune hovered in front of Malice's staff and she flung it toward the motionless crowd. A sapphire-blue sheen descended on the bodies like a thick shroud. The magic embers seeped into their skin, absorbed like a sponge. None of the zombies spoke, none of them could. What would they say?

Horror rippled through Marcus. No one wanted to get on Malice's bad side, especially not him.

When the sheen faded, Marcus bent down to look at the closest villager—a youth. A few seconds skipped by until the boy's eyes popped open. They beamed a vivid red as he twitched and clambered to his feet. It was dark, but the light from Malice's staff showed off the villager's features perfectly. His skin was green, his ears were pointed, and he growled incessantly. One by one, the crowd of once motionless people staggered to their feet as bloodthirsty zombies.

Gooseflesh prickled Marcus's skin as he stood upright.

The newly turned boy's gaze flitted between the demon and Marcus. "Who are you?" he asked in a gravelly voice.

The Shadowblood flashed him a smug grin. "I'm the one leading the undead to victory." The zombie boy didn't move, probably filled with questions, but Malice didn't wait to listen.

"Now, suit them up with armor and weapons and let's move."

Chapter Thirteen

The moon's pale face told Tristan and his friends it was time to rest for the night. Cold air caressed the treetops, shaking their needles. Tristan had to make another torch to navigate through the dense woods. An icy feeling settled into his bones; silvery light seeped through the leaves, providing little light. Further away, darkness melted the pines together, creating a meshed curtain of danger.

"We should settle in soon," he said. "Nighttime is zombie time."

His friends nodded in unison.

"I'll scout the area ahead for danger," said Tibia. The king's sister sprinted forward, her black armor melted into the darkness.

Cerys walked next to Tristan. She was a skinny thing. Her crimson cloak brushed the ground; the gold embroidery glimmered in the moonlight, accentuating the mage's enchanted aura. Bottles dangled from her belt, softly clanking against each other like delicate wind chimes. The colorful liquid sloshing around inside caught Tristan's curiosity, making him wonder what those potions were for.

Were they beneficial or poisonous? What did it take to brew them; what was it like to brew them?

He almost tapped Cerys on the shoulder to ask, but decided not to. He'd just met her. Would that be too personal of a question? On the other hand, Tristan and Tibia would most likely need to learn brewing potions.

After Tristan's parents died mysteriously, his tutors took over, constantly spouting negativity about magic. Looking back on it, Tristan wondered if Malice had something to do with their untimely deaths. It was a cold winter night when Mom and Dad said they were embarking on a mission. Weeks passed and they didn't return. That was the end of Tibia's and Tristan's magic learning. The Cadre killing them seemed plausible, save for they liked to make a public spectacle of their magic-wielder discoveries.

"Your mentors only taught you the negative side of magic. What about the positive?"

Zombia's words bounced inside Tristan's head like an echo off a cave wall. But all his life, it had been his obligation to follow the laws. As the king of Skeletonia, he had to set an example. He wasn't like Zokar—a hypocrite. Looking at Cerys again, he realized there was no other option but to delve deeper into the complex world of magic-wielders. In a way, he was excited to learn what his parents didn't get the chance to pass on.

Hurried footsteps jolted the king out of his thoughts; Tibia made her way back to the group.

"There's a clearing up ahead," she said. "Follow me."

The group followed her and found they stood in a lush, grassy clearing. The bejeweled sky stretched above them combined with crisp, sweet air. The moon revealed itself, bringing Tristan a sense of tranquility. Some of the land had bare patches due to grazing deer herds.

Tristan lifted his satchel off his shoulder with a relieved sigh and let it plop on the ground. Carrying both Blanchett's journal and *Translating Runes* ignited a nagging soreness.

I wish Faye could've come with us, thought Tristan. However, he was thankful she was solidifying her alliance with the other elf tribes in preparation for Malice's return.

"Tibia and I will gather some firewood," Emerson said as he dropped his bag to the ground in a puff of dust.

"Sounds good; we can set it here." Tristan gestured to a shallow recession in the dirt.

Tibia and Emerson nodded then disappeared into the trees.

Zombia gathered small rocks. Cerys took them from her and placed them in the recession until they formed a neat circle. Tristan loaded his bow and scanned the tree-line for threats. Forest animals scampered around at play while the owls hooted, filling the sky with their nocturnal songs. The king's nerves relaxed. The sounds reminded him that even in the Apocalypse, beauty still existed.

Tibia and Emerson returned with armfuls of branches and placed them in the makeshift fire pit.

Tristan took the torch he'd been carrying and tossed it in. Flames burst to life with a *whoosh* and dimmed to a soft crackle.

Tibia rolled a log next to the fire. Emerson sat on a rock next to her. He put his hands out in front, warming himself. Then the knight took a piece of bread from his satchel and took giant bites out of it. After finishing that, he pulled out some dried, salted beef.

Zombia sat on another log Tibia had rolled over, and gestured to Tristan. "Come sit."

The king glanced over his shoulder one more time, scanning for threats. Pleased, he sat next to his friend and set his bow at his feet. Tristan began removing his armor; the plates clanked together. He stretched, his muscles complaining in response. Reaching into his satchel, he took out an apple, and handed it to Zombia. Their hands touched briefly, sending a spark through Tristan's hand and conjuring a warm fuzzy feeling inside. Accepting it, she thanked him.

"So, your name's Cerys, right?" Tibia asked, gesturing to the girl. The mage nodded before plopping down across from Tristan and Zombia. She scooted away from Tibia, her emerald eyes focused on the crossbow at the Skeleteria queen's feet. The king took out another apple and handed it to Cerys.

"Thanks," she said curtly before taking a bite.

There was a short silence before Emerson asked, "You're one of Blanchett's mages?"

The mage nodded again.

"What's it like being a mage?"

"From our youth, we're taught the use of magic and enchanted weapons," Cerys began. "After a mage finishes their apprenticeship, they're assigned to groups of wizards and witches to impart their knowledge to them. When the war ended, Blanchett had some of her mages protect and guard her enchanted weapons, keeping them from falling into the wrong hands. But to this day, mages continue training wizards in secret, in Blanchett's hideout."

"Where's that?" Emerson asked through a mouthful of dried beef.

"I'll explain when you're ready." Cerys took another bite of apple. "She sent me to find you, like I said."

"She visited me in a dream last night," said Tristan, shifting his sitting position. He took a piece of bread and goat cheese from his bag and nibbled at them, though the overwhelming questions filled his stomach better than the food.

Cerys rolled her shoulders back. "Yes, Blanchett does that with her apprentices. It was how she maintained contact with them when she sent them on missions."

There was a long silence. "You're the next three Wizards of the Apocalypse if that's what you're wondering."

Tristan exchanged a confused glance with Tibia. "Three? Who's the third?"

Cerys's eyes fell on Zombia. "She's the third."

Tristan's muscles went numb. His limbs trembled. It felt as though time stopped and the world went completely still. The fire continued to crackle, owls hooted in the distance, but it did nothing to calm Tristan after what he'd just heard. It felt like a dagger in the chest. Zombia was magic and she never told him. She trusted him enough to allow Tristan to aid in her escape from Zombieshire. She trusted him not to alert Zokar of her and Zombie's escape. Why was her magic any different? If Tristan didn't tell the zombie king about Zombia leaving Zombieshire, why would he expose her to the Cadre? On the other hand, a fluttering of surprise erupted in his belly.

What was it like for Zombia having to hide her magic in Zombieshire? She smuggled a few books on magic, but did she have magic flare-ups like he and Tibia? She must have used her ingenuity to divert suspicions, like she did with planning her escape. Tristan couldn't decide whether he was more curious or hurt.

That explains how she knew what black magic smelled like. And why she read contraband books on magic in her hometown. I'll ask her later.

Cerys sat up and tossed her apple core into the grass, which made a dull thud. "Yes, you three are descendants of the greatest wizards in history." She turned back to Zombia, who was now doubled over, hugging her knees. "Yes, your family was magic too. Blanchett told me your mother was a witch. She invented incendiary armor for the dragons and people so that any projectiles that hit them would burn up upon contact. Her job was very important. She passed her powers onto you."

Zombia's eyes fell on the king and she drew her shoulders up as her body tensed. She blew out a breath. "I didn't know I was magic at first. My mother was like your parents; she knew the practice was outlawed, especially in Zombieshire with Zokar being as paranoid as he is. I was outside playing in the yard with Zombie and I tripped and cut my knee. However, it healed immediately, leaving no scratch or bruise." Zombia paused.

She had bouts of magic too. Just like the time Tibia lost her favorite wooden sword and she got so upset, she shattered a mirror and set a pile of books ablaze with her emotions. Same with Tristan accidentally conjuring frogs or changing the colors of the family tapestry when he walked by it; he, Zombia, and Tibia all had magic.

Zombia didn't meet Tristan's gaze, adding to the hurt. "That's when my mother knew my powers were coming in. And my mark formed."

Cerys took in Tristan's quizzical look. "When wizards' powers surface, Blanchett's marking appears." She took one last bite of her apple then tossed it over her shoulder.

Zombia nodded, her brows creased. "I've never shown you it, Tristan, and I was going to, I promise. I just was looking for the right time." She rolled up her sleeve to expose her shoulder and sure enough, Tristan saw a crescent moon with three water drops below it. "Since you wanted nothing to do with magic, I withheld telling you."

Tristan frowned. She was right, but not entirely. He *did* want to learn more about magic, his family's magic. Staying safe and obeying the law was more important, though.

Emerson finished his bread and asked, "Oh, am I magic too?" his heterochromatic eyes twinkled with hope. Tristan breathed a sigh, half-glad his knight was diverting the conversation from Zombia's magic. He still needed time to process what he discovered about his closest friend and why she didn't confide in him.

Cerys giggled. "No, sorry."

The knight looked down at his armor, the blue crystals glimmering in the firelight. "Oh? I went on a whole quest for this meteorite composed of these crystals. My sword is made of the same material too. So are Tristan's epaulets. Aren't crystals magic?"

The mage shook her head. "Not exactly. Crystals are used for protection and boosting your inner energy. While they can also provide healing properties, only a magic-wielder can harness their full power or enchant them. Non-magic people can use them for healing in place of medicine, but that's about it."

Emerson's shoulders slumped. "Well, that's still good, I suppose. I just thought how intriguing and thrilling it would be to have magic."

"Don't worry, crystals are still beneficial, Emerson." Cerys patted the knight on the back.

"You're still the finest knight in the realm," said Tristan with a grin. Emerson's frown fizzled, replaced with a proud grin.

"What kind of magic did our parents do?" Zombia asked Cerys. "It wasn't black magic, was it?"

Cerys looked offended. "Of course not; there are two types of magic: dark and light. Light magic is drawn from nature and four elements. Dark magic is attained from demons and evil forces. Blanchett's wizards only practiced light magic. One creates, the other destroys. Anyone caught using black magic was banished from her Citadel due to the chaos it brings."

Tristan's heart dropped as he thought about what Blanchett said about Malice. In a way, he felt bad for her.

Zombia paused, immediately regretting her rash assumption. "Sorry, Cerys."

"Yes, your mother served the council well. She sacrificed a lot for the Haunted Lands." The mage turned to Tristan. "So did your parents. Archibald and Ulna Skeleton were some of Blanchett's best wizards."

The king stared into the fire, listening to every sputter and crackle. He felt he knew the answer given the events of today, but he decided to ask anyway.

"How'd they die?" he asked.

"Malice ambushed a group of our wizards." Her sad eyes locked with Tristan's. "I'm sorry, but they were killed in the process. After I began my apprenticeship, Blanchett showed me an obelisk that listed all the fallen wizards' names. Your parents' names were two of many. She keeps it in her courtyard. That ambush caused so many casualties that the High Wizard formed an alliance with the elf tribes. Every year after, that day became one of memorial."

It felt like the wind had been knocked from Tristan's chest. Initially, Tristan believed the Cadre was responsible. He believed Kieran, leader of the faction, had discovered their magic, hunted them down, and ordered their executions.

Tears blurred Tristan's vision. He couldn't shake the tightness that wrapped around him as rage built against Malice and her zombies. Who else would Malice take from him? He and his friends sat in silence. Zombia wrapped her arms around Tristan, supporting him in his mourning. Tibia sat next to her brother at his left. Her arm wrapped around him, her muscled form acting as a buttress to a crumbling building. Aside from sibling rivalry, Tibia was always there to support Tristan, both emotionally and physically in war.

When Tristan wiped his eyes, he inhaled deeply. Cerys maintained a sorrowful expression. Emerson whispered words of comfort, which Tristan appreciated. Brave in battle and chivalrous on the inside was everything a true knight should be. Tibia on the other hand looked like she was ready to hit something. Her face was red, her posture tense.

"When I find Malice, I will fill her body with bolts until she's barely alive. Then I'll leave her dying form for the birds."

Tristan grimaced at her words, but deep down, he didn't blame her.

Cerys leaned in, her face filled with compassion. "I'm here to help you and your friends with your magic," the mage said, staring intently at the three wizards. "We're ending Malice's reign of terror here. Our first task: retrieving the Apocalypse Grimoire and stopping Malice from opening a portal to the Otherworld in the Hall of Black Mirrors."

Emerson leaned forward so far he nearly fell into

the fire. "What's the Otherworld? Would it be a place fit for adventure?"

Cerys snorted and doubled over. This made Emerson frown and narrow his eyes, offended.

"Far from it; the Otherworld is the lowest level of the Underworld. It's where the high-born demons live. There's a spell in the Apocalypse Grimoire to access the dimension and that's why Malice wants the book."

The knight's eyes grew wide as he sat back against the rock. "Doesn't sound great. I think I'll remain in the surface world, thank you."

"I didn't think so," Cerys said as she snickered again. She turned to Tristan. "Is your friend always like this?" she whispered.

Tristan rolled his eyes. "Emerson's my best knight, filled with gallantry, but it worries me sometimes. He's always sticking his nose into things he shouldn't be, aside from quests. Yes, he's always out for a new adventure."

"I can see that. Anyway, I'm going to train you three in your abilities." The mage held up her wand.

Tristan tensed. "Are you sure we have time? We need to beat Malice to the Citadel."

"I'm going to train you on the way. You need to learn your magic if you're going to fight her," said Cerys in a matter-of-fact tone. "You're going to lose if you battle her without proper knowledge and training." Cerys stood over the fire, wand pointed at the dancing flames. "I know, it's tedious. When I was beginning, Blanchett had me reading the Apocalypse Grimoire for hours every day. I was bored, and fell asleep sometimes, but it paid off because now I can do this."

Cerys murmured an incantation under her breath. The flames followed her movements, bending at her will like a slithering snake. The fire shot out of the pit and formed every phase of the moon.

Tristan's eyes widened as he watched the flames dance. "Wow."

"Very fascinating," the knight said, blinking rapidly. "Imagine what you could do with that. Cam would love this. No doubt."

Cerys pointed back to the pit, sending the fire crawling back into its place. "When your training is done, you three will be able to bend the elements and form weapons from pure magic. Spellcasting and mind magic will be a great start."

"Incredible," Zombia said excitedly. "When do we start?"

Cerys yawned. "We'll start in the morning. A

brief lesson on runes, levitation, and teaching you how to use that gemstone of yours."

"I want to start now!" Tibia said, shooting to her feet. She reached for her crossbow.

"No, we need to rest. Magic doesn't function as well without rest." The mage removed and folded her cloak after locating a soft spot in the grass, and sat down. Tibia opened her mouth to speak further, but the mage rested her head on her makeshift pillow that was her cloak and rolled over, indicating she was done speaking for the night.

"I'll take the first watch," said Emerson. The brave knight drew his sword, marched to the perimeter of the encampment and stared off into the ominous tree-line.

Tibia stepped away from her crossbow reluctantly, also making a pillow out of her folded mantle. Tristan, too, wanted to begin learning immediately, considering their time crunch, but he agreed. They'd get nowhere without proper sleep.

Questions raced around the king's head as he removed his own cloak and rolled it into a pillow. Soon all his thoughts coalesced into one: how were they going to stop Malice and learn magic without alerting the Cadre?

Tristan's thoughts were interrupted by a warm hand on his back. He turned to see Zombia, the firelight giving her chocolate-brown hair a subtle halo. That stabbing feeling in his gut returned, but even that couldn't divert him from her beauty. She sat beside him and leaned against her friend's shoulder. Though he was still upset with her, Tristan couldn't say no to her closeness.

"Why didn't you tell me you were magic, Zombia?" asked Tristan in a steady voice.

"I was waiting for the right time to tell you," she responded.

"Right time? Did I do something that caused you not to trust me?" the king asked.

Zombia shook her head immediately. "No, not in the slightest. It was a lot to process, you know with the Cadre lurking around every corner. When you crowned me queen, I never forgot about my powers. I knew I needed to keep a diplomatic, serious appearance. Ruling Skeletonia with you came first, but every day, I yearned to tell you about my powers. You didn't approve of your own powers when you told me about yours and Tibia's magic bouts, so I remained silent, thinking you wanted nothing to do with magic. I wasn't going to discuss something if it made you uncomfortable."

Tristan's lips parted as lightness took over his chest. While he still felt the sting of his closest friend not confiding in him, he grew to understand, realizing it might have been partially his fault for being so pejorative about magic. His response to his own powers must have made Zombia think he wanted nothing to do with the banned practice. But deep down, curiosity found its way into his mind every time.

Zombia took Tristan's hand. Her palm was warm and comforting. "I didn't do this to hurt you, Tristan. I hoped for a day when you'd accept your own powers, and then I'd tell you about mine. Remember how I told you Zokar had my mother and father executed for leading the Resistance against his regime?"

Tristan nodded.

"I learned later that he targeted my mother after discovering she was a witch. Zokar claimed no one was allowed to have magic since it threatened the safety of Zombieshire. Though, I think that brute was just intimidated and wanted no one more powerful than himself. So, that was the final straw. I decided to leave Zombieshire."

A sickness swept over Tristan. *How could Zokar be so cruel? I bet he's harboring some magic of his own.* Zombia released her friend's hand but kept her gaze on him. Tristan knew Zombia fled Zombieshire to escape Zokar's tyrannical rule, but she didn't once mention her mother was magic. Was that a shock? Yes, it always would be. Was Tristan feeling hurt? Yes, but he replaced it with understanding. Five years prior, back when Zombia started her plan for escape, Tristan swore to protect her, to aid her in her escape. That wasn't going to change. He'd still protect her, still care for her, still . . . love her.

"I guess I'm sorry too," the king said calmly. He

closed his eyes apologetically and opened them. "I made you believe I hated magic, but the truth is, I wanted to learn more about it. But with all my regal training, I never got to read the books you did. Tibia and I would read books on magic occasionally, books we borrowed from Scribe's library, but as we grew older, those times became less frequent. Eventually, they vanished altogether." Tristan wrapped his arm around Zombia. She leaned into him, her head under Tristan's chin. "But I understand you now. Thank you for thinking of me." He smiled full-on.

Zombia blushed. "Of course. Now, get some sleep."

"Oh, one more thing," Tristan asked. "Does Zombie have magic?"

Zombia nestled under her cloak. "None that I can see."

Tristan smirked. "Does growing a beautiful garden count as magic?"

"Well, he does have a green thumb," said Zombia with a giggle. "However, that's not considered actual magic. Good night, Tristan."

"Night," Tristan responded before turning over to face the looming curtain of forest pines, listening to the animals, listening to the fire—still trying to accept his new life.

Tristan sighed and closed his eyes. "Gods help us."

Chapter Fourteen

"Do not read this book; anyone who opens it will destroy themselves."

"I told you not to open the box. I'm sorry, Astrid, but I must banish you from my court forever."

Malice growled and shook her head, the memory of her arguing with Blanchett fading with the soft nighttime breeze. "You can't run forever, Blanchett. This time, I will prevail."

"What?" Zokar asked, throwing her a quizzical glance.

The demon waved him off. "Never mind." These thoughts often circled in Malice's mind, perpetuating her desire for revenge. Blanchett turned her back on her, the one apprentice who did everything in her power to prove her knowledge and please her mentor. Malice clenched her fists.

As soon as night fell and the moon trekked its way into the sky, Malice led the zombie army to their next destination. Looming shadows masked their presence.

"Are we almost there? My feet are killing me," a displeased zombie grumbled. Malice rolled her eyes, refusing to pay the monster any attention, choking back her anger.

As soon as I defeat Blanchett and her wizards, I'm going to give the zombies all attitude adjustments. How can a creature with the deadliest virus gripe so much? Marcus so far hasn't complained, which is great. Other than him, from what I remember, Karneleth never complained. Malice stared into the distance at her destination peeking through the leaves. *He'll help me.*

"Patience, we're almost there. I would expect fewer complains from so-called *'fearless creatures.'*" Malice made air quotes with the hand that didn't carry her staff.

The zombie turned his head to look at the walls of trees around them.

Malice groaned and turned to Zokar, who walked beside her. Marcus walked to her left.

"Zokar, you must do a better job of keeping your soldiers in line. So far, all they've done is gripe about food, marching, and everything else."

The zombie king scowled. Malice didn't meet

his gaze. She straightened her back and kept moving as though he wasn't there at all. Malice knew she couldn't mess up her one chance for revenge due to the dim-witted zombies. She couldn't afford any miscalculations.

Zokar strode up, syncing with Malice's steps. "Painful feet may be one thing, but being brave is another. Our bravery is not dependent on exhaustion. Also, we've been walking for hours!"

A sneer stretched over Malice's face as she stopped in her tracks. She spun around, moonlight glinting off her four horns. "Since you're so tired, why don't you stay here *alone*? I'm not afraid to stalk the wizards myself."

The zombie king flinched, then shook his head. She saw it on his face—that feigned gallantry she always hated. Though Zokar talked tough, she knew he was anything but. The slightest noise would send him bolting for cover. The thought nearly caused a smile to sprout on her face.

The zombie king eventually shook his head.

Malice leaned in to Zokar's face, their noses inches apart. "Then keep up and quit sniveling." She flicked a tiny bolt of lightning at his rear for good measure. His pained yelp drew a laugh out of the demon.

They walked in blissful silence the rest of the way. After slicing through a thin layer of low-hanging branches with the sharp end of her staff, Malice saw her destination—a graveyard. A spiked iron fence surrounded a sea of tombstones, dwarfed by a giant mausoleum.

Cemeteries produced the first generation of zombies, thus starting the Apocalypse and leaving the world broken. With burials becoming pointless, graveyards became zombie hideouts and rendezvous spots.

Withered trees sprouted from the ground up. Their gnarled branches jutted from the eroded trunks like broken, bony fingers ready for unlucky souls. A dirty white mist lingered at their feet, hiding them. Crows landed on lifeless tree limbs, emitting shrill screeches and causing some monsters, Zokar included, to jump. The Shadowblood stopped at the front gate. Looking up, she saw faint orange dots in the thick, gloomy fog lining the mausoleum walls.

"You're sure Karneleth will help us?" Zokar asked, shivering.

The demon sighed through her nose. *More irksome questions.* "When Karneleth sees I've returned, he'll be on his knees, *begging* for me to help him and his zombies vanquish the Haunted Lands."

When the war ended, some zombies became warlords, ruling their own portions of land in the forest. Malice went into hiding to plan her revenge, leaving the zombies with Zokar as their leader; however, many rejected his rule and formed their own separate clans and territories. Though Zokar had bragged about keeping excellent control over the undead, Malice knew he was too afraid to fight the warlords. This graveyard belonged to Karneleth and to him alone.

The Shadowblood marched down the path and ascended the stairs to the large squeaky doors of the mausoleum. She turned to the army.

"Wait here for us," commanded Malice. She snapped her fingers at Zokar and Marcus. "You two, with me."

She pushed the doors open forcefully, revealing a modest marble hallway covered in a decade's worth of dust. Sconces lined the walls, illuminating the murals depicting the Great War. Zombies versus humans in a battle for the Haunted Lands. The paint was faded and chipped in most areas; years of abandonment rendered the faces indistinguishable. As Malice continued down the halls, she heard voices ahead.

Clenching her fists, Malice sped up, her heels clicking on the white marble as she swerved around the corner. She cursed when she found the door to the crypt locked.

Zokar sashayed forward and drew his daggers. "I can slice the lock."

"I don't think that's possible," Marcus said behind them.

Before Zokar could object, Malice chanted another spell. A soft red glow encased the top of her staff. Stepping back, she tapped the lock and instantly, the metal glowed a hot scarlet then melted, leaving a pool of liquefied copper on the stones. The demon turned back to Zokar. He had wide eyes filled with awe, but his brows creased with fear. Malice gave a haughty smile as she held up her staff and blew away the smoke wafting off the top.

Behind the door, stairs led down to the crypt. Zombies loved crypts and that's where they'd stay unless it was feeding time and they'd emerge to scavenge for food or they wanted to pillage the nearby towns. More torches lined the walls, but the dim light made the stairway appear as though Malice was walking down a dragon's throat. With each step, they plunged deeper and deeper beneath the mausoleum. The voices grew louder. When her feet clicked on the bottom step, Malice found another door where the overlapping voices were prominent. A low agitated growl escaped her as she eyed another lock.

"What are we waiting for?" Zokar asked, his obsidian knives already gripped in his hands. "Let's barge in and show them who's superior, force them to capitulate."

Malice's gaze flicked upward in annoyance. *Why does Zokar have to act before he thinks? I'm really starting to rethink reenlisting him. I'll talk to Marcus. He's proved competent.*

Marcus turned to Malice. "What do you think?"

"Shh!" Malice lifted a finger to her lips. She pressed her ear against the wood, the voices becoming clear.

"We're tired of hiding down here," one voice said.

"When can we take back the Haunted Lands? With

Zokar around, usurping and controlling everything, it's nearly impossible," said another. "We aren't strong enough on our own."

Zokar bristled at the zombie's treasonous words. Malice somewhat understood the zombie. How could anyone take the Haunted Lands if the zombie king's greed was impeding their need for unity?

There was a loud bang; someone pounded their fist on a wooden surface. "Stop prattling; we'll have the world soon enough. We just need magic. Without it, we don't stand a chance against the zombie king." Malice recognized Karneleth's voice immediately. "When Malice returns, we'll be unstoppable."

At least Karneleth trusted her plan, unlike Zokar. *Maybe Karneleth won't question me every five seconds.*

The Shadowblood drew in her magic and used her staff to melt the lock. Pulling her foot back, she swung into the door, kicking it open. A dimly lit room full of piercing red eyes zoned in on Malice. The crypt was filled with at least three dozen zombies, each wearing various kinds of armor: leather and bronze mostly, only a few wore iron. They all sat around tables covered with assorted animal parts; bones littered the floor.

Malice stepped in, shoulders back, chin up as she

observed the crypt. Alcoves lined the walls. However, instead of containing remains, Malice saw various weapons lying in them: swords, spears, maces, weapons of all kinds.

The demon's eyes flickered with anticipation. "Karneleth, get out here!"

The crowd of monsters parted and a single zombie marched forward. He was taller than the rest. His black leather armor was ornate, designed to resemble dragon scales. The small plates overlapped each other, shiny and decorative. Scars covered his face, hands, and arms. They were tokens of the battles he'd survived during the Great War, serving at Malice's side as one of her best generals. To zombies, scars were medals of honor; the more disfigured their flesh, the greater their prowess in combat.

Karneleth stared down at Malice. The warlord's right eye was milky white; the left was scarlet red.

"You've finally returned," said the warlord. "I was beginning to lose hope."

It's official, all zombies are impatient. Malice accosted him until she stood toe-to-toe with Karneleth. "Planning revenge takes time, if you want it done right."

The warlord's lips pressed together. "I thought

you'd ditched the zombies. You were gone so long. Not very fair."

Malice splayed her arms. "I'm here now, aren't I? Let's get to work, we have lots to do and you have a new task."

"Should I trust you again?" The warlord's eyes flitted to Zokar. "Why is he here? I'm certainly not participating in anything with *him*."

Malice sighed. "He's going to help you using the magic I gave him and the same magic I'm going to give you."

"What can that coward of a zombie king do? He's too afraid to fight Skeletonia soldiers alone," Karneleth scoffed. "There's no way he could battle the elf tribes or Blanchett."

The zombie king growled and darted forward, jumping over the table knives in hand. The warlord jumped out of the way, but not quick enough. Zokar's blade sliced his cheek. A snarl erupted from the warlord as he wiped the blood away. Drawing a broad ax, Karneleth charged, summoning five of his best soldiers with a loud whistle.

Zokar seemed unfazed. He stepped back, angled one of his knives and threw it at the coming monsters.

Karneleth ducked, narrowly evading the blade a second time. The obsidian blade spun through the air, guided by the zombie king's magic, and slashed the five zombies' throats. It cut so deep their heads flopped to the side as their bodies collapsed. Blood pooled in the uneven stones. The rest of the monsters stood, terror rounding their dead eyes.

Zokar stood straight and brushed off his cloak. The knife returned to him, handle first. Malice pinched her lips together. Zokar had acted out of rage rather than with logic.

Karneleth paused in his tracks. "What's this? No zombie has controlled magic since the war."

For a split second, the Shadowblood wondered if his actions would cost her Karneleth's alliance. But those were *Zokar's* rash actions, not hers. The zombies went rigid with fear. Zokar's brutal attack at least proved Malice's magic was effective and put Karneleth and his monsters in their place.

The demon stepped casually over the fallen bodies. "And that's why I'm here. To help you with your dilemma. You want to conquer Skeletonia and the rest of the Haunted Lands, don't you?"

"Every zombie wants that," the warlord said in a flat tone.

"Listen, the king of Skeletonia is magic. Blanchett is already training her next generation of wizards. We have to stop them. He's on his way to the Crimson Citadel to retrieve the Apocalypse Grimoire, Blanchett's book of spells. The king and his friends will pass through this graveyard and you're going to stop them with this."

She began weaving magic between her hands and tapped her staff to the ground. The earth before the demon split open. A neon-green light rose and enveloped Malice's hands. The light soon began to take shape, forming a new enchanted tool. The earth closed, and above Malice, a staff that closely resembled her own hovered. It wasn't an orb; it was a single crystal wrapped in tendrils of ebony wood, and it wasn't blue. It was a shimmery lime green, so bright it bathed the room in that daunting hue. Malice handed the staff to the warlord.

Karneleth took and inspected it. "What's this?"

"It's a magic staff that allows you to conjure zombies from far and wide," Malice explained, gesturing to the staff. "Plus, you can control any zombies that cross your path. Say you kill some of the wizards' friends; once they reanimate, they're yours to govern."

The warlord stared at the staff. Light emanated from the crystal, highlighting his face. Tiny fern-green embers danced along its length, standing out against the black wood.

Malice leaned closer to the warlord. "Think about the power, think about conquering Skeletonia. Imagine the revenge and wealth; the zombies will rule the world again."

The monsters whooped and shouted, some

drawing their weapons and smacking them against their armor, making the metallic plates ring like a hundred gongs.

"It's set then. I'll stop the wizards when they arrive," said Karneleth in a gravelly voice.

The demon nodded. "You know your task. Don't fail me." Pivoting on her heels, Malice muttered under her breath. "You may have won the first war, Blanchett, but I guarantee you won't survive the second."

Marcus left the crypt with a heavy heart. What Zokar did, killing some of Karneleth's soldiers, was extremely brazen of the zombie king. To Marcus, angering a possible ally was a huge mistake. Use of force was an excellent tool, but all Zokar succeeded in doing was incurring the warlord's wrath. If the undead were going to win this war, they needed to make friends, not enemies. Marcus could see what Karneleth meant when he said, *"With Zokar around, usurping and controlling everything, it's nearly impossible."* Marcus had to agree. Zokar made everything more difficult.

Once out of the mausoleum, Malice headed out of the graveyard, continuing north to the Crimson Citadel.

The army had grown significantly since invading all those villages. Though, it was hard for Marcus to look at the zombie children.

Once under the dense canopy of the forest, Malice turned to the second-in-command.

"Marcus, can I have a word with you?"

Marcus's lips parted and nodded. *I wonder what she wants to discuss with me. A promotion maybe?* The Shadowblood walked faster, putting a few feet between her and the rest of her army. Marcus followed her until they walked in lockstep.

"You want the zombies to rule the world, right, Marcus?" asked Malice.

The second-in-command nodded vigorously. "More than anything, your Highness."

Malice looked off into the distance. "I can see you're proficient. You do everything with efficiency, and that's something I admire about you. There should be more zombies like you."

Marcus lifted his chin, eye widening, a much-welcomed lightness spread through his chest. She finally praised him! He'd been waiting years for this kind of recognition; someone who appreciated his skills, unlike Zokar who always took Marcus for granted. Too often he forgot why he gave Marcus the position of being his captain in the first place. Malice slowed her walk, almost stopping as she focused her narrowed eyes on Marcus.

The next words that came from Malice were the ones that the second-in-command had been yearning to hear.

"Once we have the Apocalypse Grimoire and Blanchett is dead, I want you to lead the zombies."

Chapter Fifteen

Dawn broke less than a half hour ago, and Tristan was already up. He stared at the sunrise, watching the colors merge in various reds, yellows, and brilliant blue. A single shaft of sunlight beamed, piercing the foliage and bouncing off the king's silver crown and the gold leaf on Blanchett's journal.

Tristan had already donned his armor and had been staring at the journal, contemplating what had taken place: he, Tibia, and Zombia being wizards, his parents' deaths, and obtaining the dragon-claw dagger. Sighing, he picked up the book, and began flipping through.

Though this isn't the Apocalypse Grimoire, Blanchett's journal might tell me something, Tristan thought.

Opening the journal, the king found crude sketches covering the pages, detailing experiments, runes, and a few spells. The entire thing was a mix of the modern language and runes. Some of the writing was scratched out, suggesting they were Blanchett's discarded ideas.

Magic, without knowing its mechanics, was dangerous; Tristan knew that much. He found himself searching for the answer to defeat Malice. Did Blanchett write anything in her journal about the dragon-claw dagger? Then he remembered this was a journal, notes from the High Wizard's perspective. Not an encyclopedia of magic. Tristan frowned; he and his friends had to reach the Crimson Citadel before the Shadowblood did.

Reading further, he found more history about the war, written in the modern language, not runes thankfully. From what he'd seen so far, only the prophecy itself and the few spell formulas were written in the language of the magic-wielders. Tristan found himself enthralled.

Blanchett's notes on the war detailed how the three elf nations ceased their bickering and banded together to fight the undead. Wizards, witches, elves, and even dragons died in combat. Faye was right; so many dragons died that their numbers were depleted significantly. Even if their magic did cure the zombie virus, the zombies multiplied too quickly. For every zombie cured, ten more would rise.

What Tristan read on the next page was what made him see eye to eye with the High Wizard. She wrote how the gruesome battle had *changed* people, sending them into a depressed, anxious state. Due to how chaotic magic could be, the Cadre banned the practice. Remaining magic-wielders were driven away or executed. Though Tristan knew that, it was interesting reading the events from Blanchett's perspective.

When Tristan flipped to the next page, he caught a glimpse of Cerys approaching. She was gnawing on a piece of dried chicken for breakfast.

"Morning," she said softly. Her eyes drifted to the journal. She gobbled down the rest of the meat and smiled. "The High Wizard is a phenomenal writer, isn't she?"

Tristan paused at a loss for words. "Uh, yes, she is." Though this was just the High Wizard's journal, the king was impressed at how much history and a few spells he learned in the past two days. Would his parents have shown him and Tibia the journal if they got the chance? Most likely, just in secret like they did everything else regarding magic.

Cerys sat in the grass next to Tristan. "Blanchett was always invested in reading and writing, prompting her to write this journal with entries about the Great War and new discoveries."

Tristan nodded as he glanced back to the journal with a determined face. Soon enough, the rest of Tristan's friends rose. After greeting the king and mage, they sat and ate some of the left-over goat cheese and dried meat from last night. When the sun shone on the mage's face, Tristan noticed the dark rings under her eyes.

"Didn't you sleep well?" asked Tristan.

The girl shook her head. "That constant groaning of zombies doesn't allow for a peaceful sleep. I'm not accustomed to having them so close by."

Tristan raised an eyebrow.

"You're not used to zombie noises?" Emerson asked with surprise as he donned his crystalline armor.

Cerys shook her head. "In Aramore, Blanchett's new hiding place, there are no zombies around. Only demi-zombies. It's a boon to a good night's sleep not hearing them growl all the time."

"Interesting," said Zombia, scratching her chin.

Emerson swallowed his bite of meat and

continued, "When I was training for knighthood as a squire, I'd have to go on quests through the forest all the time. That got me used to zombie noises pretty fast."

After a brief silence, the group began packing their things. The fire had sputtered out overnight leaving charred wood and tiny orange embers speckled against the dark remains.

Tristan opened the journal to the map. Moving the silver ribbon bookmark out of the way, he saw a small clearing surrounded by little round bumps. A spiked fence was illustrated around the clearing. At the center a large building was drawn, dwarfing all the tombstones. Tristan recognized the place immediately as a graveyard. A chill settled over him. His friends exchanged glances with each other, their faces creased with dread.

Cerys took a sudden deathly pallor. Tristan noticed, his smile fading. He looked at her calmly.

"Cerys, what is it?"

The mage gulped. "Karneleth lives there. He was one of Malice's best generals in the Great War. When Blanchett won, the zombies were sent back to Zombieshire, but some of them broke off into their own clans, each clan ruled by a warlord. Karneleth claimed that graveyard as his. He lives there to this very day."

Tibia and Emerson exchanged enthusiastic glances.

Emerson stuck his chest out. "That should be easy enough. I've fought many warlords to save villages from being raided."

"Same," Tibia said with a huge grin. "It's a good thing children are taught combat skills from a young age in Skeleteria. And since we get a lot of warlords around my kingdom, I've sent plenty running—or killed them."

Birds chirping wildly filled the few moments of silence. No one said anything. Tristan felt weak in the knees. It wasn't that he hadn't fought warlords in the past to protect Skeletonia, but Karneleth being one of Malice's generals couldn't be a good sign.

Tristan turned to his sister with a frown. "You know how dangerous they are."

Tibia rolled her eyes. "Baron Xerin and I battled one by *ourselves*. There are five of us. We'll be fine." The Skeleteria queen picked up her crossbow.

"Do we have to pass through there?" Zombia asked looking to Cerys.

The mage nodded. "The other trails are too long and they're in denser forests than this. It will waste more time than we have. That's our best bet."

Tristan looked at the map and realized Cerys was right. Trees were drawn all around the graveyard, obscuring other paths. One of them looked like it led into a swamp. Sighing, Tristan nodded as he closed Blanchett's journal.

The five companions were back under the leafy forest canopy and had been walking for a while.

Cerys said, "As I said last night, you three need to begin your training."

Tristan's throat closed up. "We need to get to the graveyard, don't we?"

Cerys nodded. "But you also can't go charging into battle without being prepared. Luckily, these lessons will be quick and easy enough to do as we make our way to the graveyard."

Cerys took her wand and drew a shape in the air and the rune burst to life. It looked like a very geometric letter P. The mage scanned the wizards.

"This is called Thurisaz. It stands for defense and protection," explained Cerys. The rune hovered in her open palm. "When you write this rune in the sky, on paper, or anything really, you will summon protection magic." The rune dissipated as quickly as it appeared. "Try it."

Tristan thanked the gods that Scribe had given him and his friends *Translating Runes*. Cerys wanted to prove the protection spell's effectiveness, so she asked Tristan to throw a rock at her. At first, he hesitated, but when she insisted, he did. The rock didn't even make it to Cerys, the stone bounced off her shield, landing in the bushes behind her. The next few minutes were spent with him, Tibia, and Zombia writing various runes in the sky. The air shimmered with different each one a different color. After the basics, Cerys showed them elemental runes: earth, fire, air, and water.

Of course, Zombia had taken to the gentler runes. Tibia, on the other hand, enjoyed destructive ones such as fire and earth. At one point, Tibia spoke the rune's name and the spell didn't function. Cerys had to explain that a wizard couldn't get the pronunciation wrong; spells don't function if even one letter is off. Tristan, Zombia, and Emerson laughed. Tibia ignored them in a huff, righted herself, and successfully performed the same spell.

"A magic-wielder can't afford imprecision in their craft," the mage had said.

The king remembered to keep that in mind as he practiced. Tristan had never felt magic like this. With each rune he wrote, he felt the magic thrum through his limbs. It felt like a warm heat moving through him like a wave, but at the end of each spell, it left Tristan feeling a little light-headed as though a piece of his physical and mental energy was whittled away. He assumed the sudden tiredness afterward was the cost of using magic; it weakened the wielder.

The dirt path began to widen as the trees became more dispersed, allowing the sun to shine down fully. Tristan smiled; it felt good to see the sun again.

Taking a quick respite from his magic, Tristan pulled out the map. According to it, the cemetery would be just through the few bushes obscuring the path.

On their walk, Cerys decided to teach the wizards levitation. Pulling an apple out of her satchel, the mage tossed it in the air, but it never made it to the ground. The fruit hovered in front of her face.

The fruit floated before their eyes. Cerys moved her hand, the apple moved with it. She eventually put her hand down and flicked her head left and right. The apple moved in sync. Tristan and his friends watched, charmed by her skills.

"All right, now, your turn." Cerys kept the apple afloat.

Tristan closed his eyes and reached deep within himself, drawing out his magic. This time, he noticed it was easier. The warm, tingling sensation spread through his body and out his fingertips. Suddenly, the king felt a snap within. It was like he was pulling on a rope, then feeling it break as his magic was unleashed. When he opened his eyes, he saw the apple was no longer in Cerys's hand. It was in his.

As the friends traversed through the bushes at the base of the graveyard's hill, they each practiced levitation. They levitated whatever they could find.

Tibia and Tristan levitated branches, pebbles, and leaves. Zombia had more trouble balancing the apple alone. Seeing her disappointment, Cerys explained that magic doesn't come easy for everyone, and certain types of magic were more difficult for some magic-wielders.

"Good job, now push yourselves," said Cerys with an encouraging voice. "Try lifting your friends."

And they did. Tristan even managed to lift Tibia upside down, incurring her wrath of angry curses and hilarious threats. Zombia couldn't lift a person yet. When Tristan saw her discouraged face, he wrapped an arm around her, speaking encouraging words to her.

They had reached the graveyard gates by the time that was over. Approaching the gate, Tristan found it was already opened. Instinct made him draw his bow and nock an arrow. Rows and rows of tombstones sprouted from the ground, a mausoleum dwarfing them. A spiked fence surrounded and protected them. The entire land was covered in a soft mist; silhouettes of dead trees peeked through. Their gnarled branches arched over the headstones with crumpled, discolored leaves beneath them.

"Looks exciting," Emerson said sarcastically.

There was a series of light wing beats and cawing in the branches above. Tristan looked up to see crows perched on the branches. Their pitch-black eyes stared down at the king as though he were a piece of carrion.

"Stay vigilant," Cerys warned. She held up her wand. Small embers of magic danced on the top. "Remember, zombies hide out here."

Tristan proceeded, then felt something crunch beneath his boot. Looking down, he found the earth was charred. It wasn't only the grass, but the soil looked as though it were licked by a flame. Crouching, Tristan examined the ground. He found burnt flowers, the petals disintegrating at his touch. To his left, there were footprints. Standing, he looked to Cerys.

"What happened here?" he asked. He looked at Zombia, who shrugged in response.

Cerys bent down and rubbed her fingers in the charred remains. Her hand came back covered in ash. Her eyes narrowed as she looked toward the mausoleum.

"Malice's been here," Cerys said.

Emerson sniffed the air and made a face. "You smell black magic again?"

Cerys nodded with a frown. "That, and the fact that it destroys anything it touches," the mage explained, pointing to the bushes on the side of the path. The edges of the bushes' leaves were entirely singed; some were completely gone, leaving behind a bare, crooked limb. Blades of grass curled in on themselves, burnt, no life present. Tristan's skin crawled, feeling like a million tiny spiders skittered down his back.

"Malice has probably spoken with Karneleth already, recruiting him like she did in the war," Cerys said solemnly as she continued down the path. Her crimson cloak brushed against lifeless leaves, shaking them loose.

Tristan didn't respond and just followed. He watched the headstones as he walked. It was hard knowing graveyards had lost their purpose, that everyone who died turned and became a zombie. Death existed without existing at the same time. Tristan's head spun whenever he thought about it. Even worse, Malice was gifting the undead with dark magic. Zombia moved to Tristan's side. Her hand brushed against his.

"Guess I have to work on my magic," she said, trying to lighten the situation.

Tristan grinned, his nerves easing when he looked at her. "We're all going to have to work on our magic."

"Agreed, especially now that the entire Haunted

Lands is relying on us."

Through the gray haze, the spiked exit gate was visible. Tristan's fears abated now that the mission was at hand. However, a new smell assaulted his senses. The smell reminded Tristan of fetid carrion left out in the sweltering summer sun. It wasn't the burnt scent of black magic.

Cerys's voice cut through the air. "ZOMBIES!"

Chapter Sixteen

Tristan heard the hungry growls before zombies emerged from the mist. His heart thudded in his chest. There were at least a dozen of them, each wearing armor and wielding weapons, blocking the group's escape. There was no choice except to stay and fight. Tristan didn't hesitate. Remembering what Cerys just taught him, the king gathered his powers. Three zombies charged his way.

Tristan imagined a huge hand picking up the monsters. At his very thought, the tingling sensation rippled through and out him, lifting the zombies off the ground. Their faces showed a mix of confusion and fear. Concentrating, Tristan threw his adversaries toward the spiked fence. The monsters flew through the air, their angry growls turning into cries. Their screams were cut short when they smashed headfirst into the serrated gate.

Tristan stared nonplussed at the three impaled

zombies. His magic had done that—he had done that. His stomach churned; his heart filled with regret. Zombia sprinted past him, her sword already slick with red. Her keen blade whistled through the air as she parried her enemies' attacks and thrust her blade through their skulls. Tristan fired arrows at approaching monsters, magic thrumming through his veins. Zombies littered the ground with arrows jutting out of their bodies—a few with crossbow bolts thanks to Tibia. He found his sister through the haze; one zombie made the mistake of getting too close. She flicked her wrist and the zombie went crashing into the spiked fence, impaled like his comrades.

Emerson didn't leave Tristan's side the whole time. He fought beside his king, like any loyal knight would, cutting through the zombies with his crystallized sword. Two zombies approached Cerys, but she waved her wand, summoning several shards of what appeared to be glass. The edges glided through the air, slicing the monsters' throats. The grass became sticky with blood as they crumpled into it.

I wonder if I'll have that power. Seems sort of brutal. But efficient. Tristan's eyes locked on the graveyard's exit and he charged for it. Something grabbed his foot, sending Tristan falling face first into the dirt. His bow flew from his hand, landing by one of the headstones. Blinking dust from his eyes, he found green fingers wrapped around his ankle. A zombie burst from the loose soil, teeth snapping, sword in the monster's other hand.

"Tristan!" cried Emerson. The knight dashed to his king's side to help when an undead creature barreled into him. Tristan bit back a scream. He shook his foot, but the monster's grip was strong. Not only was the zombie trying to bite him, he swung the sword with the prowess of a warrior. Tristan made the connection. The zombies were gaining intelligence, learning to wield weapons, just like the ones in the library.

Grunting and kicking at the zombie, Tristan reached for his bow, his fingers barely grazing it. Dirt scraped against his armor as the zombie relinquished his sword and pulled the king in for a lethal bite. There was a flash of metal, and the monster's head went rolling; the body crumpled to the ground. Zombia stood over Tristan, her face wrought with worry. She extended her hand and helped her friend to his feet.

"Thank you," said Tristan. He bent over and retrieved his bow. He searched for Emerson, breathing a sigh of relief when he found the zombie that attacked the knight lying at his feet.

Breathing deeply, Tristan surveyed the graveyard. There were only a dozen zombies, but their corpses were scattered everywhere, weapons held in loose fingers. A single growl erupted from behind Tristan, but was silenced with a crossbow bolt. Tibia approached her brother, bowing her head in relief.

"Was that all of them?" asked Emerson.

"I think so," Zombia answered, frowning at the blood splattered on her clothes and sword.

Cerys turned to the king, grinning from ear to ear. "Great job using your powers."

Tristan grinned back. "Thanks. Now let's get out of here before—" The king's voice was cut off by more footsteps. Figures materialized in the mist, drawing closer as another wave of zombies approached Tristan's group. The king counted the zombies, wondering how many he could levitate and throw. There were more than the last time, at least three times the last wave.

The monsters closed the space between Tristan's friends and the exit. One zombie, more robust than the rest, pushed through the crowd and stood directly in front of Tristan. His armor was decorative; the black leather overlapped like dragon scales. His left eye was milky white; the right was red like most zombies, except a few shades darker.

Tristan's muscles stiffened. Cerys talked about Karneleth owning this graveyard, and now they were facing the ancient warlord. What made Tristan's stomach clench was the staff the warlord wielded. Crafted from ebony wood, the staff twisted and spiraled up, cradling a bright green crystal. Waves of magic pulsed across the gem's surface, radiating formidable power that made Tristan weak in the knees.

"So you're the pesky wizards Malice told me to exterminate?"

"Listen Karneleth," Tristan began, holding a hand up. "We don't mean any harm."

The warlord barked a laugh. "Seems a bit late for that. You wizards botched the zombies' victory, but not again. The Haunted Lands belong to the undead. Malice promised we'd get our land back and we'll start by ridding the world of Blanchett's goons."

Tristan shivered, though he stood as still as possible. Karneleth's eyes fell on Tristan's crown—on the gem. The king scowled at the warlord.

"You're not taking the Haunted Lands," Zombia

said, her voice was firm and serious. "We're the Wizards of the Apocalypse."

Zombia's words made Tristan proud. He loved the brave, determined girl she was. It was her valor that helped Skeletonia function smoothly.

Karneleth looked down his nose at Tristan. "You did this to yourselves. You could have surrendered, could have walked away.

The warlord raised his staff, the crystal beaming bright, slicing through the fog. All at once, the zombies' eyes shifted from scarlet to a blinding green—apparently controlled by the warlord's staff.

"ZOMBIES, ATTACK!"

Dozens of zombies charged like ravaged beasts. Tristan's friends circled to face the monsters from all directions. The thick mist obscured their vision; green hands and blades of all kinds sprouted through the white wall. Emerson barreled headfirst into three zombies. While he was outnumbered, his skills from knight training paid off. He quickly silenced the monsters with a few swift strokes of his sword.

Cerys waved her wand and made more magical blades appear before her. With a flick, the keen edges slashed through her attackers, sending their heads rolling across the grass.

Instinct made Tristan nock another arrow. He fired one after the other with lethal accuracy. Wherever he aimed, a zombie fell. Remorse swirled in his mind. He loathed war, he hated killing, but there was no choice. Tristan knew the Apocalypse was no trivial matter. If you let your guard down, the next thing you knew, zombies would be there, chewing your arm off.

"Make for the exit! Follow me!" called Tristan. He fired at another zombie and bolted down the path.

"Got it," Tibia responded. She fired another bolt then followed her brother. As she did, several zombies charged after her. Two of them grabbed her legs, tripping her. Grunting, she kicked, pushing them off. Tristan spun around to help her, but his sister put her novice magic skills to work. Picking up all the zombies, Tibia tossed them toward the fences. Their limp bodies now decorated the spikes.

"Are you okay?" Tristan asked, extending a hand to his sister. Tibia stood and picked up her crossbow.

"Thanks," was all she said before darting for the gates.

Tristan followed her. Luckily, Zombia, Emerson, and Cerys were close behind, fending off zombies from all around. Karneleth stepped forward in hot pursuit of Tristan's friends.

"You're not getting away that fast!" shouted the warlord.

When he raised his staff, the green crystal pulsed with a power that lit up all the surfaces around Karneleth. The ground shook. Decaying hands sprouted out of the ground, pulling themselves up. In a matter of seconds, a new wave of armored zombies appeared.

Tristan's jaw dropped. *That staff conjures more zombies too?* When Karneleth pointed his staff at the zombies, more of the creatures swarmed the group. A hand popped up from the ground; the zombie drew an iron broadsword and swung at Tristan's legs. Tristan glanced down wearily at the fresh gash in his metal boots. A heartbeat later, metal flashed and the zombie's head went rolling. Zombia darted and grabbed her friend's wrist, her hazel eyes flicking left and right at the rising wall of decaying zombies.

"There's too many of them," she said.

Tristan looked at Karneleth. The warlord conjured more monsters and herded them Tristan's way. "Until we get that staff, we're not getting anywhere. Karneleth is going to continue conjuring more zombies. We need to get it from him."

Tristan formed a makeshift plan in his head. He wasn't pleased with it, but it was all he had.

"You three," Tristan addressed Tibia, Emerson, and Cerys, "fend off the zombies while Zombia and I get that staff from Karneleth." The words tasted bitter in Tristan's mouth, but he knew this was the only way out. Putting his friends in danger wasn't something he enjoyed, but if he didn't have help fending off the zombies, they'd all die and Malice would win.

"Understood," Emerson said, clapping his fist to his chest in a salute. When the three broke off, Tristan and Zombia sprinted to Karneleth. They found the warlord standing on one of the tombstones. When his red eye fell on Zombia and Tristan, he aimed his staff at them, sending five zombies in their trajectory.

Tristan fired more arrows at the furthest zombies. He set the two that got closest on fire using the new fire-starting rune Cerys taught them. The golden-orange letter flung through the air, splitting and striking the two monsters in the chest ablaze. The scent of burnt flesh clogged Tristan's nose, making his eyes water and bile rise in his throat.

Tristan took aim for Karneleth's head and loosed an arrow. The warlord spun at lightning speed and deflected the arrow with the head of his staff, sending it harmlessly into the grass.

"Malice is going to be so pleased when I bring her your head," shouted Karneleth, his neck cording. The warlord pointed his staff at Tristan; when nothing happened, Tristan realized too late who the real target was.

"And your friend here"—Karneleth aimed his staff at Zombia— "is going help me kill you."

A lurid, green glow enveloped her body; she dropped her sword, crumbling to her knees. The king ran to her side, but when he tried helping her, Zombia violently pushed him away with supernatural strength. For a moment, it felt like he forgot how to breathe and not just because he slammed into a headstone.

"Stop!" Tristan shouted. A part of him wondered if this spell could even work. The zombies Karneleth controlled weren't demi-zombies, but Tristan didn't want to wait and find out.

Gathering his powers, he gripped the warlord with an invisible hand. The warlord laughed at the king's petty attempt to levitate him. Each time Tristan's magic grasped Karneleth, it passed through him like a phantom, not having moved him even an inch.

Did he block my magic? Tristan thought, his brow furrowed. *I didn't know you could block magic.*

"That was a little trick I learned from the demon queen herself. Too bad you're still a fledgling wizard. Otherwise, you could save your friend here."

Tristan watched in horror as Zombia's eyes shifted from hazel to a pitch-black. A toothy smile painted across her face. Zombia's movements followed Karneleth's staff.

Resentment roiled through Tristan. *She's under Karneleth's control!*

Karneleth laughed. "She'll make a great member of my army."

Zombia lunged for Tristan. Before she got close, the king lifted her off the ground using levitation. Guilt surged through him. The king was using his magic on his closest friend. While in the air, Zombia's pitch-black eyes flitted back to hazel. Pitch-black. Hazel again. Karneleth kept his staff aimed at her, cursing as he saw her eyes flickering back and forth. Relief spread in Tristan's chest. *Karneleth's control isn't working on her.*

Tristan noticed Karneleth was so focused on Zombia's transformation that he became careless about his surroundings. Zombies were unable to multitask, especially in combat, and Tristan was thankful for it.

Pulling back an arrow, the king fired. The arrow

struck Karneleth in the hand. He yelped, letting his staff fall to the ground with a dull thud. Though the fog hung low to the ground, obscuring the crystal, it dimmed, and the green hue around Zombia evaporated. Her body went limp, still hovering in the air, suspended by Tristan's magic. Her sword dropped from her grasp, smacking against a gravestone and onto a patch of dirt.

Bow still clutched in his left hand, Tristan lowered his friend to the ground and severed the spell. Ending a spell felt like cutting strings, letting whatever he was holding release. It was then a wave of nausea washed over the king. His vision spotted for a second when he snipped his magic tethers, followed by a sudden internal heat.

Why did that happen? Is using magic supposed to have these side effects?

Leaning over Zombia, Tristan lifted her head, pleading to the gods that she'd wake up. His prayers were answered when her eyes fluttered open, revealing those hazel eyes he too often got lost in. A huge breath escaped him; Tristan didn't want to imagine a world without Zombia in it.

Zombia smiled wearily as she blinked a few times. "I feel like all the blood in my body has been drained."

Tristan tenderly brushed one of her brunette tresses from her face. "You'll be all right. Karneleth tried controlling you using that staff but it wasn't working."

In his peripheral vision, Tristan watched as Karneleth cradled his hand, looking at the arrow sticking through it. He listened to the awful yell that tore out of him as he yanked the projectile out.

Tristan stood, helping Zombia to her feet.

Zombia looked at herself as she retrieved her sword. "My powers seem to have negated Karneleth's. Or maybe the staff doesn't work on demi-zombies. I'm not sure, but I'm glad he didn't get hold of my soul."

Just as Tristan bent down, collecting the staff, a booted foot swung into his vision, connecting with his nose. A coppery tang filled his mouth as he flew backward onto the hard ground. The sounds of battle were deafening. Tristan's vision blurred for a moment. A moment later, something sharp slashed down Tristan's forearm. More pain blinded him as he dropped back to his knees, clutching his wound. Looking up, Tristan saw Zombia in a headlock. Blood oozed from the wound in the warlord's right hand; the arrow was gone, leaving a jagged hole. In his other hand, he held the staff. Crimson was smeared over the shiny edges. Tristan looked from his arm to the staff, putting two and two together. It made sense. Not buffed, crystals were as keen as a sword.

He pressed the sharp crystal to Zombia's neck. The warlord, having discovered the staff's magic didn't work on Zombia, opted to use the non-magic aspects of the staff. Push too hard and it would cut cleanly across Zombia's neck like a dagger.

Tristan scrambled to his feet and aimed an arrow at Karneleth. "Don't you harm her," he seethed. "It's me that Malice wants you to kill, isn't it? Do it, but promise me you'll spare her."

"Well, she instructed me to kill all three of Blanchett's wizards, but you'd do just nicely."

Zombia writhed in the warlord's grip. Tristan growled, taking aim, but there was no way he could shoot Karneleth without him slicing his friend's throat in the process.

I can't cast a rune. Karneleth would see it and kill Zombia. And levitating him is useless. I can't wait until Cerys teaches us new spells.

Suddenly, Karneleth's eyes went wide, his grip on Zombia loosened. She pried herself from the warlord's grasp in time to see a jagged point protrude through his chest. Red splattered over a recognizable shiny blue blade.

Emerson.

Tristan knew stabbing a zombie in the chest didn't kill them, but at least it stunned Karneleth. A bolt zipped by the king's vision, and embedded itself in Karneleth's forehead, right between his eyes. Red trickled down the bridge of the warlord's nose. His eyes rolled back as he plummeted face first onto the ground. The staff rolled out of his motionless hand.

Tristan turned and saw Tibia standing behind him, crossbow held high. Tristan retrieved the staff. Right now, the crystal was dim. The remaining zombies had stopped their assault, but they still formed a rotting wall in front of the graveyard's exit.

Tristan stole a moment to examine the wound Karneleth inflicted on his forearm. The cut wasn't severe, but it was deep enough to require attention sooner rather than later. He tore off the hem of his kilt and wrapped the cloth around his wound.

Wincing from the pain again, Tristan looked from Karneleth's prone form to the zombie-controlling staff.

"Let's end this battle."

Chapter Seventeen

To gain higher ground, Tristan climbed into one of the contorted, lifeless trees. Gathering his powers, he poured them into Karneleth's staff. It felt like pouring water into a glass, pouring and pouring until the vessel was full. Another wave of nausea swept over him, but he gritted his teeth, pushing through his swaying vision. He held the staff high and pointed it at the remaining zombies. The crystal beamed bright, piercing the fog, grabbing the zombies' attention one by one.

The monsters stopped in their tracks. The ones chasing Cerys halted; the ones pursuing Tibia ceased their assault. All their cold, dead eyes turned to Tristan. Magic thrummed through his veins. He felt their emotionless gazes swivel to the staff like a moth to a flame. Wherever the staff moved, the monsters followed. A thickness balled in Tristan's throat. He was *controlling* them.

It was an effort not to let his shoulders fall. This

was one thing he always hated about magic; the one thing he remembered his father telling him.

"Never use magic to control someone unless absolutely necessary," the former king of Skeletonia had said.

Controlling the monsters made Tristan feel like Zokar. Skeletonia wasn't a dictatorship. His people didn't have to worship him like a god while he dithered, allowing them to starve. The feeling was sickening.

But this was Tristan's destiny. He, Tibia, and Zombia were humanity's last hope. Pushing aside his feelings, he loaded more energy into the staff. Brighter and brighter the crystal grew as though it were a delicate green sun, keeping the zombies focused while Tristan sorted through his options.

Of course, he didn't want to kill the zombies. And Karneleth was dead. He could no longer control them, nor could he report back to Malice. Without Karneleth, perhaps these zombies will scatter. Tristan swallowed as he kept the monsters tethered with his magic. More nausea washed over him, but he blinked it away.

"What are you going to do with them?" asked Cerys. She approached the bottom of the tree Tristan sat in. Her face was bruised, but luckily, there appeared to be no bite marks. None of his friends had any bites.

"Place them somewhere else," suggested Zombia. She wiped blood off her sword in the grass. "No killing, no wounding necessary. Just send them back into the forest."

Tibia's sapphire eyes flared. "Are you crazy? Releasing them back into the woods is the worst idea, Zombia. They'll continue being threats, even without Karneleth."

"I highly doubt it," said Emerson. "They're lost without Karneleth, and since the warlord has already rallied them against Zokar, they won't go back to Zombieshire. On their own in the forest, they'll be pretty harmless. But in the end, it's up to you, Tristan."

Tristan swallowed again. The zombies' eyes were still locked on the king. Their growls were low, but they stood entirely still, weapons in hand, waiting for their next command. In the back of Tristan's mind, he wondered if Malice would return and regroup them, but the more he thought about it, the more unlikely it sounded. She'll have assumed Karneleth was successful and continue on her journey for the Apocalypse Grimoire.

Tristan looked from his friends to the snarling ocean of green. Inhaling deeply, Tristan formed a message in his head, forcing it through the staff and into the monsters' minds. The zombies sheathed their weapons, then vanished into the mist. The monsters didn't run or drop their weapons. They just casually walked away as though nothing happened.

A sharp pain erupted in Tristan's head, his temples throbbing. He barely managed to keep hold of Karneleth's staff. Why was his head hurting? Why did it feel like his magic was sputtering, like a flame ready to extinguish? Was there a limit to his magic?

Tristan ignored the questions and continued feeding his message to the zombies' minds until they disappeared, their green armored bodies merging with the white curtain until the graveyard was empty save for Tristan and his companions.

With all the zombies gone, Tristan allowed himself to relax. Sweat coated his forehead; soreness sang through his muscles and mind. The crystal on Karneleth's staff dimmed. He had saved his friends. Seeing that many zombies so close to his friends was a horrifying sight. Skeletonia was one of the safest havens in the Apocalypse. Tristan's kingdom had never been overrun; they had come close, but thanks to Emerson and Radius's battle strategy skills, they kept the undead at bay.

Tristan's thoughts were broken by wild screams. The king relaxed when he realized those screams were ones of joy.

"We stopped the zombies!" Emerson shouted.

The knight leapt into the air. Tibia punched the air with her fist, a wide grin on her face. Cerys shot Tristan a smile of approval and glee. The tense feeling in Tristan's body abated and he allowed pure gratitude and happiness to consume him.

He turned to Zombia and embraced her, resting his head on hers. Part of him didn't want to let go; the king wanted to keep his arms around her. After a battle like this, Tristan wanted to be closer to his friends more than ever. With the Apocalypse besetting them every day, Tristan learned life as he knew it could end at any moment.

When they parted, Tristan also noticed the sharp, searing pain in his forearm was reduced to a dull nagging one. The amount of blood on his makeshift bandage wasn't nearly as large as before. And this all happened as soon as he touched Zombia.

Did she heal me? Tristan knew about healing magic from his mother. Though, of course, the Cadre never touched on it. Every book written after they became a powerful, influential faction only revealed the chaos magic brought. *Maybe if the world knew about healing magic, they'd stop being so afraid of it. Maybe even the Cadre would think twice.*

"You controlled the zombies! I can't believe magic can do that," Emerson said in wonder. "Very interesting. Still wish I could do magic. Then I could protect you instead of you protecting us."

Tristan smiled at the knight. "It's a king's job to protect his people. Now let's get out of here."

Tristan's chest felt lighter as the graveyard disappeared behind them. It was late afternoon, judging by the angle at which the sun pierced the treetops. Evening would set in soon. As he held Karneleth's staff, magic hummed low. Though the crystal was dimmed and inactivated, it was still very warm in his hands as though it just came out of the forge. In fact, Tristan felt extremely warm himself.

Cerys was farther up the dirt path than he was, so Tristan caught up to her. The mage turned to him, her eyes already anticipating his question.

"Feel this," said Tristan, proffering the staff to Cerys. "Does it feel—"

"Hot?" the mage finished for him. Tristan's brows rose.

"Yes . . . why does it feel like this?"

"Magic items heat up when they're used," Cerys explained, slowing her gait. "When a weapon is scalding hot, that's a good sign you might want to reserve your energy."

Tristan's jaw slackened. "Wizards don't have

infinite magic?"

The girl nodded, her emerald eyes filling with seriousness. "Magic-wielders aren't eternal pools of magic, Tristan. Our energy can be just as easily spent as anyone else's. Magic is like a fire: it will burn for a while, then eventually die down, needing to be rekindled."

Tristan glanced at Karneleth's staff, pondering. If that was so, then the amount of zombies one could control with it would be limited, unable to surpass a certain number before the wielder's magic expired.

"What happens if you use too much of your magic?" Zombia asked, popping in between Tristan and Cerys.

The trees' shadows fell over the mage's face in an ominous way as she said, "You burn up. If you keep at it, you'll literally explode."

Tristan's stomach did a flip. That explains why he felt feverish and nauseous. With each zombie he controlled, a piece of his energy was sacrificed. He could've died just by using too much magic.

Tristan's face must have looked worried because Cerys followed up with, "Don't worry too much; you just have to know your limits. All wizards do. Whenever you feel your magic reaching its end, stop immediately and allow yourself to rest. Allow your magic and energy to regenerate then resume. Knowing your limits is foremost to being a fully-fledged wizard."

Reaching up, Tristan felt his gemstone. It, too, had cooled but still radiated warmth. His heart beat fast. What about his friends? What were their magic limits? Swallowing his questions, Tristan strapped Karneleth's staff to his back.

The group continued walking until they found another clearing; this one was smaller than the last, but it'd work. Tristan thanked the gods when they found a spot to rest. His limbs felt leaden, his brain sore, like he'd been hit over the head multiple times. Tibia and Emerson retrieved firewood, and Cerys ignited the fire with a flick of her wand. Tristan watched the mage use her powers, inspired by how helpful magic could be if in the right hands.

After another meal of dried meat, goat cheese, apples, and bread, Cerys showed her apprentices a few new runes, keeping the magic lesson easy since all of them, Tristan especially, were fatigued.

"I can't wait to tell Cameron," Emerson said as he watched Cerys conjure water from her canteen and shower her new friends in a sprinkle. "He'll be so impressed."

Tristan nearly jumped. "No, Em, remember? We can't tell anyone we're magic. You know what will happen to us." The sentence tasted foul on his tongue. This power was costing Tristan his candor. He lowered his head, gazing into the fire. This would be the first secret he kept from his people, and he hoped it would be the only one.

Though he got a strange feeling this was only the beginning. Many more secrets would surface that he'd have to hide, and it made Tristan's chest ache. He removed his crown and stared at the gemstone. His eyes flicked up to Cerys.

"Is there something specific this gemstone does other than act as a conduit for magic?"

Cerys chewed on the dried meat in her hand and nodded. "Yes, it actually allows the user to shapeshift into a skeleton. Or human if you're already a skeleton to begin with. Your father used it a lot."

Tristan's brows rose, and his mouth gaped as he looked at Tibia. With their mom being a skeleton and their dad being human, Tristan wondered why he and his sister were both human. He had to admit, battle was easier for skeletons. He'd watched Radius and the other skeletons in his army fight for years. They never had to worry about blood loss or getting stabbed to death. A shattered skull was the only way to kill one.

Tristan turned the crown in his hands. "How do I shape shift? Is there a special rune?"

Cerys nodded. Finishing off her food, she took her wand and etched the symbol in the dirt.

"The word is *Cweorth*."

Tristan was about to start the spell but stopped. "I probably shouldn't do the transformation tonight," he said, remembering his close brush with death a few hours prior.

The mage smiled. "You're learning. Well done. While we continue to the Citadel, you can try it."

When Tristan placed his crown on his head, Cerys's face paled. "You're wounded," she said with alarm.

Tristan glanced at his wound. The blood had dried to where the bandage chaffed and itched. "Karneleth got me with the tip of his staff." Tristan held up the weapon; firelight feathered against the crystal's sharp edge. Then he turned to Zombia. "I think you healed me. When I hugged you, the pain and bleeding stopped."

Cerys's eyes gleamed. "She is indeed a healer.

Though, the number of healers is small. While healers have weaker combat magic, their ability to cure and heal wounds and ailments is a nice counterbalance." She faced Zombia, whose face lit up. "Yes, your power is truly singular."

"Were our parents healers?" Tibia asked.

"No, neither of them were," said Cerys. "Both had powerful combat magic that could destroy enemies. They were the most powerful apprentices Blanchett had."

Pride warred with regret inside Tristan's head. *I didn't know our parents were so powerful. They must have saved many lives before their death. But is that my destiny? To destroy?*

I don't want to be a wizard if that's true.

Zombia tossed her apple core into the woods. "Can I heal myself, or just others? Either is fine with me as long as I can heal others."

The mage nodded. "Healing applies to the wielder, other people, and animals."

"This is great!" Zombia nearly squealed. She wrapped her arms around Tristan and Tibia. "Whenever you get hurt, I can fix you up."

"And me?" Emerson said playfully.

"Of course, Emerson! Anyone and everyone."

Emerson snorted. "I was kidding. I'd sacrifice my life for you and Tristan any day." Zombia grinned and wrapped the knight into a warm hug.

Cerys laughed before her voice grew severe. "But, like I said, wizards aren't limitless fountains of magic. You have to know your capacity. For example, don't try raising people from the dead. Every wizard who tried that combusted."

Zombia's face grew a few lighter shades of green, and her shoulders slumped.

Cerys stretched and yawned. "We should get some sleep. We'll reach the Crimson Citadel by mid-morning. After that, we must head to the Barren Lands to reach the Fortress of Portals."

"What's the Fortress of Portals?" asked Tristan.

Cerys laid down and folded her cloak, making a pillow. She looked agitated as sleep tugged at her eyes. Tristan immediately felt a pang of regret; he didn't want to keep Cerys awake.

"It's the only portal to the Underworld. The rest were destroyed and most magic-wielders can't summon portals. At least not ones to other dimensions. Now goodnight."

The mage turned over and snored softly. Tristan couldn't tell if she was seriously snoring or faking it. It brought a smile to his face.

"Sounds good," Tibia said. She looked out into the woods. "I'll take the first shift this time." On cue, her crossbow reloaded itself. Patting her brother's shoulder, Tibia stood and made her way to the encampment's perimeter.

Tristan nodded but didn't say anything. As he settled on the soft grass, he expected another restless night.

The same silvery mist that told Tristan this was a dream had returned. Rubbing his eyes, Tristan found himself back in Skeletonia. He stood in the vast space of his throne room. His and Zombia's oak thrones sat on the dais, untouched. Guards milled about, spears in hand. But something didn't feel right. None of his friends were there.

There was a loud crash followed by the ground shaking violently.

Tristan sprinted outside in time to see a fireball smash into one of the towers. Up in the daytime sky, he saw dragons. Tons of them flew for the castle. Dragons of different colors, shapes, and sizes. He recognized them from the lessons his parents gave him and Tibia. He learned dragons were usually peaceful creatures that coexisted with the elves. Each elf tribe had their own species of dragons. Icebloods had ice breathers; the Dragonbloods had fire breathers. Tristan had even read about moon dragons who breathed silver fire and supposedly could only hatch under a full moon and whose powers were heavily affected by its phases. However, the dragons approaching looked anything but friendly. They breathed fire down on Skeletonia. Tristan drew his bow and shot at the winged beasts. After a few loose arrows, which skimmed harmlessly along their tough scales, he saw a dragon he recognized. His stomach clenched.

This one was larger than the rest with scales as black as night; the underside of his wings was a cool gray and shimmered as though they were speckled with white gemstones. Iron plates wrapped around his underbelly and his head, fitting perfectly around two curved horns.

It was Shadowstalker, the largest dragon known to the Haunted Lands and Faye's personal steed.

Shadowstalker swooped down and breathed fire on the village. Orange flames licked the houses; villagers screamed. More scaly beasts roared, adding to the tumult. The horrid smell of burning flesh reached Tristan's nose, making bile rise in his throat.

Tristan furrowed his brow. *Why is Faye having her dragons attack Skeletonia? Why are any dragons attacking? Where are my friends?*

Tristan didn't dwell on the thought as another fireball smashed into the castle, felling another tower. As more dragons neared, Tristan saw the riders were zombies. Zokar was atop a dragon, like Shadowstalker, but smaller. An emerald-green dragon carried another familiar zombie—Marcus, captain of Zokar's royal guard. He'd seen him fight alongside the zombie king many times before this whole magic fiasco. Marcus was dangerously intelligent for a zombie, which often worried Tristan.

But now the zombies had dragons!

"Ah, I see my old friend," screamed a feminine voice.

Tristan looked skyward to see Shadowstalker hovering above him. The dragon's eyes burned with a hatred that weakened the king's knees. It was the rider that made his heart stop: Malice. A cruel grin was plastered across her face; her crimson eyes sparkled with malevolence.

"What have you done? Where's Faye?" Tristan asked, rage laced in every word. "Why do you have her dragons?"

"Don't worry," said Malice, her voice like oil. "Faye cordially helped me raise this army. Well, with a little persuasion of course."

"She'd never do that!" cried Tristan. It had to be a spell the demon cast, or she killed the Dragonblood queen to take the throne and her dragons.

He aimed an arrow at the Shadowblood, red in his vision. He didn't want to kill Shadowstalker. The dragon opened his mouth, and that's when Tristan heard his name.

It was another feminine voice, not Malice's.

"Tristan!"

The king's eyes snapped open, only to realize the ground was no longer beneath him. "Tristan, you're floating!" Tibia shouted.

The moment she said that, Tristan yelped as the ground rushed to meet him. Groaning, he sat up to see Tibia and Emerson staring at him. His sister had her hand cupped over her mouth, trying not to laugh.

"Are you okay?" Emerson asked, moving to the king's side.

Tristan rubbed the back of his neck. "Yes, I'm okay . . . I think . . . I was dreaming."

The stars were still out, and the waning crescent moon was high.

"Go back to sleep. We need rest," was all Tristan said before lying back down. His eyes wouldn't close and all fatigue became elusive. One, because Tibia would tease him incessantly in the morning, and two, he was too shaken by his dream. Was this just an absurd nightmare or a premonition?

Chapter Eighteen

The sun caressed the top of the trees too soon. Birds chirped in the distance, welcoming the day with their uplifting music. Tristan felt like he had rocks for eyes. Through the rest of the night, Tristan didn't really go back to sleep—not after that nightmare.

Was it possible for Malice to obtain the power of Faye and her dragons? Was this dream what would occur if he didn't defeat her and her army? Tristan blinked a few times before sitting up and stretching, feeling grateful Faye was in the process of forming a possible alliance with the other elf tribes. He found Zombia sitting up as well, rubbing her eyes and smiling.

The king smiled back, but the nightmare was replaying in his mind. He needed to tell his comrades. Although the idea of Malice controlling dragons was wild, Tristan decided it was something they should know.

Once everyone gathered their belongings, the

group was back on the road for the Crimson Citadel. A perilous journey didn't allow much room for jokes or small talk. Booted footfalls crunching against the dirt filled the silence.

Zombia approached Tristan, her hand brushing against his. *Was that deliberate or a wonderful accident?* Gooseflesh studded his skin. He hoped Zombia would stop beside him so he could divulge what he saw in his nightmare, but she continued to the front of the group with Tibia, both girls going over the journal's map. Tristan's shoulders slumped.

Cerys appeared by his side, her eyes focused on the king as they walked. Her brows furrowed when she sensed the king's discontentment. The usual cheerful Tristan had dwindled on this journey, much like a candle's flame slowly burning out.

"I understand how you're feeling," she said.

"You do?" the king replied, slowing his gait, putting distance between Emerson, Tibia, and Zombia. At first, he wondered if she knew of his dream already.

The mage nodded. "After the war, mages and wizards became the Cadre's targets due to their closeness to the High Wizard. We were forced into hiding ourselves. We tried blending into normal society just like you and your family. It worked relatively well."

Not the response Tristan was expecting, but it was still relatable. Tristan could count all the magic bouts he had that his parents had cleaned up after. Levitating items with mere excitement, changing the colors of tapestries and furniture with a mere touch, and his sister's rage that shattered mirrors and broke doors off their hinges; he and his family had to hide it all.

"How did your parents feel when they found out you'd be training the next Wizards of the Apocalypse?" asked Tristan.

A flock of birds rustled in the trees, but no answer from Cerys, not immediately.

She slowed to a shuffle. Tristan frowned, seeing her sudden sorrow. He began to regret asking. "They never got to see me as a mage. Zombies attacked my village, killing them." Cerys paused again. Her hands clenched into fists, her entire body rigid with undulating agitation. "If we were allowed to use our magic, we could have stopped them, but we couldn't. The only survivors of the attack were me and my sister, Ingrid."

Tristan's eyes darkened; his heart wrenched. Death by a zombie was unavoidable in most of the surrounding areas. No one could ever fully be prepared.

"I'm so sorry, Cerys," said Zombia. Tristan looked from Cerys to the rest of his friends. Having noticed he and Cerys fell behind, they waited.

"Malice will pay for what she's done," said Emerson. His thick brows tilted inward with rage.

Tristan couldn't agree more. Tibia didn't have to say anything for Tristan to note her resentment. Her fists tightened around her crossbow's barrel, and her scowl hardened.

Cerys wiped a single tear from her eye and picked up her gait, eager to get to the Citadel, as they all were.

"Blanchett found and took us in, nursing my sister and I back to health. Ingrid was in worse condition than I. When the zombies invaded, they set the village ablaze. We were trapped inside our burning house. I managed to get us out, but not without Ingrid suffering severe burns; thank the Moon she recovered. However, it wasn't without lasting scars. Afterwards, Blanchett began training us. When I wasn't sparring, I studied in the Citadel library or potions room, working with the High Wizard herself. My entire childhood consisted of preparation for the new war."

Tristan focused on the girl; his brows creased with empathy. Cerys reached into her cloak withdrawing her wand. "Blanchett gave this to me as a graduation gift from the apprenticeship."

"That's wonderful! You deserve it too. You must've worked so hard," Tristan said, his voice returning to a more cheery tone.

"I love my job imparting magical knowledge to others. Especially now that magic has been outlawed." Cerys put her wand away and stroked her braid. "It saddens me that so many have forgotten the positive side to magic. That magic can be good; it can benefit people. Like everything in nature, magic has a beneficial and destructive side. There's good and bad in the world; in times of turmoil, many choose to seek out the good. Why should magic be any different?"

Tristan nodded in agreement, chewing his lip in thought. *Will people ever accept magic again? If my friends and I save the Haunted Lands from Malice, would that prove to society that light magic still exists?*

Tristan nearly noticed the trees were farther apart and the rolling hills grew nearer. Soon enough, the pines were behind them as Tristan and his companions emerged into the countryside that stretched for miles.

There was green everywhere. Lush hills of green grass and tree clusters surrounded a single motte and bailey where the Crimson Citadel was perched.

"Welcome to the Crimson Citadel, city of magic!" said Cerys, splaying her arms. "Well, former city of magic."

A palisade enclosed the entire motte and bailey. Lots of kingdoms chose the motte and bailey since it provided an uphill advantage against the zombies. However, this one was smaller than most—exclusive to magic-wielders.

Magic hummed in Tristan's veins as he led his friends down the path and to the gates of the bailey. Crossing the drawbridge, Tristan saw the gates were left ajar and unguarded. Claw marks coated the wood, implying this place endured constant zombie siege.

A lump formed in Tristan's throat. He pushed open the gates, expecting there to be signs of struggle: overturned stalls, charred buildings, runaway arrows. But there was no such thing. In fact, the entire place looked abandoned. Immediately, Emerson drew his crystal sword and stepped ahead of Tristan, eyes peeled for threats. Tristan couldn't stop the smile growing on his face at Emerson's staunch loyalty.

There were no smells of fresh baked bread or the smoky scent of a blacksmith's forge that the king was expecting. No sounds of people chattering or horses' hooves clicking on the stone streets. There wasn't even the scent of livestock; the village was entirely empty and completely quiet. Tristan broke from the group to peer inside one of the workshop's windows. Vacant save for the still-intact furniture. Everything was still in place.

It looked as though the wizards who lived there dissipated into thin air, leaving their belongings behind.

Zombia's lips pressed into a thin line as she glanced at the ghost town for a city. "Where is everyone? I expected more . . . life."

Cerys gave a rueful sigh, her eyes glued to the Crimson Citadel. "News quickly spread of the Cadre storming every village and purging it of magic-wielders. The wizard-hunting faction discovered this was Blanchett's location. One of the High Wizard's scouts returned, having sighted the Cadre in the forest, marching for the Citadel, bent on exterminating every magic-wielder in sight. So, the same night, Blanchett and the wizards packed any belongings they could and fled."

The mage's posture deflated, her eyes cast

downward. Tristan placed an arm around her, Zombia did too.

A sharp pain sliced into Tristan's chest. He couldn't fathom uprooting his entire life as he and his loved ones were pursued by an overbearing faction. He'd never met the former Cadre leader, but he had no doubt they were as severe as Kieran. Maybe worse. Tibia surveyed the village, her sapphire eyes dull. Skeleteria was a queendom built for combat. A society built for war, that Tibia governed with justice and prowess in combat. But even she looked unsure if she could handle an abrupt escape.

"But when Blanchett first built this place, it was perfect," Cerys said with a proud smile. "Our magic kept the zombies at bay, minimizing attacks. This was where she trained her wizards, molding them into soldiers to fight against the zombies and demons— where an apprentice became a guardian of the Haunted Lands." The mage stared wistfully at the tall fortress. "Yes, the wizards thrived for many decades."

When the friends continued walking, a sharp tingling sensation formed in the back of Tristan's mind like a goose feather tickling his brain. His gaze drifted to the Crimson Citadel that stood proud on the motte.

The Forgotten Prophecy

The moment Tristan took another step, the tingling sensation increased.

His eyes widened in realization. *I can actually feel the magic pouring out of the Citadel. Interesting.*

The sensation increased when the king and his friends reached the flying bridge of wooden stairs leading to the Citadel. He turned to Zombia and asked, "Do you feel that?"

Zombia nodded. Tibia appeared at Tristan's left, nodding too.

"I assume it's happening because we're wizards," Zombia said, adjusting her armor. "Perhaps they can feel other magic things."

Tristan remembered his mother had discussed certain enchantments that could be placed on buildings to protect them from the elements' cruel hands. This type of preservation magic hindered the decay of any object, allowing it to survive for years to come.

Tristan inhaled, mentally preparing himself for the secrets that lurked behind those red-brick walls.

"Here we go."

Chapter Nineteen

A bridge brought Tristan and his friends to another smaller palisade. When Tristan passed the Citadel's stockade, it became more evident of the struggle this place endured. Several trebuchets were left behind the open portcullis. Tristan eyed the weapons sadly. Those would have come in handy for Blanchett and her wizards, wherever they went.

Siege weapons were powerful against the zombies. They're the reason so many kingdoms, including Skeletonia, survived this long. Hurtling a few large stones over the walls at the zombies kept them away. Another thought hit Tristan like a punch to the gut. How long would it be before Malice taught the zombies how to use siege weapons themselves? They were learning how to use magic; it was a matter of time before the undead would utilize catapults and trebuchets.

After the ramparts, Cerys led her apprentices to a set of doors flanked by two braziers. Pushing them open with a loud creak, the group spilled into a vast square-shaped atrium. The upper balconies wrapped around the open black marble floor, supported by arched pillars. More braziers sat between the columns, igniting upon the wizards' entrance. Firelight and sunlight mixed, bathing the whole atrium in a warm glow.

Runes appeared on every smooth stone surface. It took Tristan a moment to realize Blanchett's sigil, the Triple Goddess, was in the center of the floor. Tristan marveled at the place. Though it smelled musty, the place appeared untouched by age. Multiple doors lined the walls; Tristan eyed them, wondering what cryptic secrets lie beyond them. Goosebumps stippled Tristan's skin, suddenly making him feel small. He didn't even feel like a king for a moment. A king or queen was the most powerful position in any realm, but being within a place of pure magic made Tristan feel no higher than a surf.

He tried imagining the Crimson Citadel before the arrival of the Cadre. Before the war. He imagined wizards, witches, and mages ambling around the place, going about their business, brewing potions and casting protective spells. The ancient magic was palpable, sending the king's inner energy into a frenzy like a swarm of incensed bees.

Zombia gasped. "This place is beautiful." She gazed all around, taking in the complex architecture. Tibia and Emerson were behind her, their eyes rounded with awe.

"Fascinating," said Emerson. "I only saw runes like these once on one of my quests. I've been yearning to see them again. Learn more about how they work."

More runes scaled up the pillars. Reading up on deciphering runes had been a great benefit. Though he was still new, Tristan read enough to conclude some of these texts weren't just spells; they were actual accounts of the war, how the Apocalypse began, and the adventures of past magic-wielders. One of the walls pictured an entire scene with elves on dragonback, breathing fire on their enemies below. This mural, too, was surrounded with runes detailing what transpired. The ancient language had been lost, buried in decades of loathing and fear, but reading runes had become enjoyable for Tristan.

Continuing down the walls, he found an odd—and familiar—depiction. These weren't runes, but it was a small mural depicting three individuals dressed in red cloaks. Each person wielded a different weapon: a glaive, a crossbow, and a longbow. Startlingly enough, the person in the middle wore the purple gemstone and was in skeleton form. Above the trio was another figure carrying an elaborate dragon-headed staff. Tristan recognized Blanchett immediately. A coolness settled over Tristan's skin. He knew these people. He knew what this meant.

He turned to Cerys. "That's us, isn't it?"

The mage nodded. "Blanchett knew her former wizards would pass down their abilities to their children. After a generation of wizards died, they were to be replaced by their heirs. Though, as genetics goes, the magic wasn't passed down through every single generation. Sometimes the trait skipped a generation but was passed to the next. No matter how many generations, magic would always resurface. Magic-wielders will always walk the earth."

Tristan blinked rapidly, his shoulders suddenly feeling heavy—heavy with responsibility. He never realized how much work his parents did. Ruling Skeletonia and serving as Blanchett's Wizards of the Apocalypse! That explained all the conversations he walked in on: the ones where he heard Blanchett's name and they discussed quests they'd embark on so frequently. They'd argue over teaching Tristan and Tibia about their magic heritage while also concealing their powers.

Now Tristan knew what his father meant when he said Tristan would have difficulty accepting his destiny. And it took him this long to learn his father wasn't referring to his position as Skeletonia's monarch.

Tristan felt a presence behind him. Spinning around, he found Zombia, Tibia, and Emerson—all their eyes focused on the mural. Zombia's eyes sparkled with excitement, but her hands gripped together in apprehension, mirroring Tristan's own war of emotions.

Cerys turned from the mural, facing her apprentices with a set jaw. "You three must carry the torch your predecessors left. You are humankind's last hope to purge the Apocalypse."

Tristan didn't know whether to smile or frown. He finally learned more about his heritage, he'd learn more about magic, but it was in a world that hated it.

"So, where do we start looking for the Apocalypse Grimoire?" asked Emerson. He ran his fingers through his short chestnut-brown hair and sighed. "Do we have to check every single room?" The knight faced Cerys. "Do you have a key for all of them?"

"It's not that easy," Cerys said, casting Emerson a hard glance. "A lock wouldn't protect anything from someone with magic. Magic-wielders would have ways of opening them, and by opening them, I mean blasting them apart with enchanted lightning. Also, those doors lead to classrooms and sleeping quarters."

Tristan thought back to his dream and his face lit up. The king's lips parted. "If I remember correctly, the corridor leading to the Apocalypse Grimoire would be through here."

The far-left wall caught his attention. Like in his dream, he pressed his hand to it. Magic jolted through Tristan like an electric shock. The section of the wall gave way and opened, revealing a dark hallway. Cold air rushed by, making Tristan shiver. The unlit sconces burst to life as he set food in the corridor. A warm, orange glow shrouded the walls, accentuating the red bricks.

"That's incredible," Zombia said with wide eyes and a grin. "Good thing Blanchett can contact her apprentices in dreams."

Tristan blushed, grinning at his friend. "I just hope it helps us in later battles."

The passage was damp. The walls were wide enough, but the ceiling was very low to where Tristan had to duck a little. The air was clotted with a dank musty smell, making Tristan's nose twitch. Everyone breathed sighs of relief when the passage ended and yawned into a massive chamber.

The floor was covered in black tile. Runes were written on every surface: the walls, the floor, and pillars. They shimmered a bright gold when they caught light as more torches ignited on their own. The chamber was round, wrapping around a stone pedestal standing tall in the center of the room.

Everything appeared the same as it did in Tristan's dream.

"So, where's the Apocalypse Grimoire?" Tibia asked impatiently. She walked around the room's perimeter. She even tapped the mirror before looking back to her brother.

"It's probably hidden," Emerson explained. The knight glanced at the floor, shuffling his foot over the tiles, looking for some sort of pressure plate.

Tristan looked at the rounded top of the pedestal. "It's not on the ground, Em," said Tristan. He removed his crown and plucked the gemstone from its perch.

Finding the diamond-shaped lock at the pedestal's base, Tristan inserted his gemstone and twisted it.

A sudden grinding of gears echoed through the vaulted chamber. By the time Tristan replaced the gemstone back in his crown, the middle of the pedestal shifted away revealing a giant leather-bound tome. A turquoise dragon's eye rested in the middle of the cover.

There it was: the Apocalypse Grimoire.

All eyes shifted to the book. Tristan placed his crown back on his head and reached to pick up, but quickly retracted his hand. The book must be under a protective spell. What would happen if he touched the book? Would the spell be as simple as freezing him in place or would it poison him on contact or summon enchanted wires that could easily slice him to ribbons? Tristan backpedaled.

"Wise move," said Cerys. She brandished her wand. "While some magic items simply won't function in the hands of a non-magic person, the Apocalypse Grimoire is secured with a specific spell that will dissolve any trespasser's skin upon contact like acid."

Emerson backpedaled. "Oh gods."

Tristan exchanged weary glances with Zombia and Tibia, who also took a few steps back.

"You could have warned us before trying to melt off our flesh," Tibia said in a low tone.

Cerys tapped her wand to the tome. A golden rune Tristan hadn't seen before swept over the Grimoire, swift as a shadow. The gold light faded, and Cerys picked up the book, her flesh remaining intact. She handed it to Tristan. The weight surprised him. Heavy and something he didn't look forward to lugging around.

"I was going to warn you. Fortunately, Tristan made an intelligent decision," Cerys explained.

"Why didn't Blanchett take the book with her?" Zombia asked, her eyes still glued to the Grimoire.

Cerys put her wand away. "Because she knew her next generations of wizards would need it. And since she's in hiding, she's unable to train them directly. With the Cadre around, Blanchett knew she could never return to the Crimson Citadel, nor could she give away her new location, so she cast a dangerous protective spell on the Apocalypse Grimoire and left it here for her next wizards. And she sent me to train and disarm the Grimoire."

Tristan ran his fingers over the glass dragon's eye. Another jolt of magic pulsed through him. This really was his destiny. If his parents were around longer, would they have eventually taken him and Tibia on a quest for the Crimson Citadel? Would their parents have given the Apocalypse Grimoire and taught them how to fulfill the prophecy without getting caught? Tristan closed his eyes, a sharp pain in his chest, knowing those questions would remain unanswered.

Tristan opened the Grimoire and gaped. The pages were covered in spells, drawing of potions, and paragraphs discussing dragons and the elf wars. Tristan's eyes lingered on the recipes—each detailed down to every herb, even how long to allow potions to simmer or how to stir them. His breath slowed, not only because of the magnificent information the Apocalypse Grimoire held, but he was also thinking about the book falling into Malice's hands. The terror she'd unleash on the Haunted Lands made Tristan shudder.

"This is so fascinating," said Zombia, rubbing her eyes. "Blanchett was really prepared."

Cerys nodded, her shoulders rolling back. "Indeed she was."

Tristan yearned to read more, but he knew time wasn't on their side. Closing the book, Tristan placed it in his satchel and turned to the mirror—the same mirror leading to where the enchanted weapons were stored.

With his knuckle, Tristan tapped the glass. It did nothing. He didn't know if this would work, but he had to try something. Tristan stood before the reflective surface, gem facing forward. The glass rippled and shimmered before fading, revealing another chamber.

Tristan peered into the chamber. This one was smaller; however the floor had no tiles and was less ornate than the rest of the Crimson Citadel. Luckily, Tibia had grabbed one of the torches from the corridor. A musty tang filtered through the air, but that's what Tristan expected when entering a place wrapped in years of history.

"Welcome to the Enchanted Weapons' Vault," Cerys said, gesturing outwards.

Tristan marveled at the artisanship. The walls curved up to make a dome. When he held the torch up, he saw carvings along the cusp of the ceiling, laced with gold. It was a moment before he noticed they were the constellations surrounding the phases of the moon.

Rows and rows of bookshelves lined every wall, each tome kept cozy with a blanket of dust. The center of the floor had the Triple Goddess: a full moon flanked by waxing and waning crescents, all inlaid with silver. There was a section of the room that formed an alcove. Metal coffers sat in the space, stacked on top of each other. Curtains of cobwebs coated the boxes, conveying their age. Tristan wondered if the coffers were enchanted along with being locked.

Moving to one of the coffers, Tristan eyed the oxidized copper lock and prodded it. The green patina scraped off easily, but it was still locked. Maybe even protected by that acidic skin-melting enchantment. The king cringed and turned to Cerys.

"You have a key?" he asked.

The mage shook her head. Holding out her wand, Cerys closed her eyes as an incantation slipped through her lips. Her emerald eyes lit up when a loud click resonated through the chamber. The oxidized lock clanked to the marble floor. When the spell ended, Cerys glanced over her shoulder and smirked at her new companions. "Unlocking spell," she said, then winked.

"There seems to be a spell for everything," Emerson said with a shrug.

Tristan looked at the floor, thinking about all the spells his parents never got to teach him and Tibia.

"Yes, there is. Some spells are harder to master

than others." Smiling, the mage popped the lid open. There were bottles—hundreds of them. Reaching in, Tristan withdrew one of the vials. A clear liquid sloshed inside—clear enough, he mistook it for water.

Tibia knelt beside her brother, took one of the bottles and shook it.

Reaching into the chest, the mage withdrew a bottle herself, the liquid splashing against the glass surface. "This water was blessed in a special moon ritual. It can protect against black magic and ward off evil spirits." One after another, Cerys stuffed them into her satchel until it bulged and rattled.

"Take them. They'll be useful against Malice."

So, they did. Tristan and his friends filled each of their bags with these bottles of blessed water. Luckily, the bottles were small and between the five of them, the chests were quickly cleared.

Tristan shuffled his feet over the onyx-colored marble until he stood directly in front of the full moon. The moment he did, the stone sank down. More gears squealed beneath the floor. When the floor began parting, Tristan yelped as he jumped back, not wanting to fall into the crevasse. Three pedestals protruded from their resting places. The first held a longbow, the second held a crossbow, and the third held a glaive.

Tristan's posture stiffened. Tentatively, he approached the pedestal. His hands hovered over the bow. It was constructed from the finest yew and tiny runes were carved into the bow's limbs. Tristan assumed they were spells. It looked just like his current bow. His lips parted in wonder. He had two bows: one for his wizard missions and one for tournaments. He was thankful he didn't have to relinquish his old bow. It was the one he received when his parents first taught him archery.

"Do these have skin-melting acid powers?" asked Tibia, pointing to the shimmering crossbow.

Cerys giggled. "No. These are protected by not functioning in the hands of someone other than their assigned wielder."

The king blew out a sigh of relief. What he found odd was the enchanted bow didn't come with any arrows. A question regarding the absence of arrows formed on Tristan's lips, but his sister asked for him.

"Where are the bolts?" she asked. The moment she picked it up, the string drew back, and a bolt materialized in the string. The Skeleteria queen's eyes went glassy and wide. Tristan found this highly unusual for his aloof sister, but weapons were her forte. They had been since she was born.

"This is the most amazing crossbow I've ever seen!" Snatching up the weapon, she held it close as though she were reuniting with an old companion. Like the longbow, Tristan saw small runes carved into the crossbow's surface and crafted with expert care.

Tristan picked up the long bow and pulled the string taut. Gold wreaths of light swirled up from the weapon, took the shape of an arrow, and fitted itself perfectly into the string. He marveled.

Our parents used these. They saved the world with them. I only hope we do these weapons justice.

After Tristan slowly let the bowstring slacken, the shiny arrow vanished in a puff of sparks.

Incredible.

Zombia ran to the pedestal holding the glaive. The blade was curved and sharp. More runes were etched into the iron edge. Picking the weapon up, Zombia twirled it around and jabbed the air, magic trailed behind them.

"It's really nice that Blanchett provides unique weapons for her wizards," Emerson said. He ran his hand along the pedestal where the glaive laid a moment ago.

"Blanchett designed these weapons to suit her wizards individually," Cerys said, gesturing to Tristan's new longbow. "These weapons are capable of bending all four elements, though each of you has different strengths and limits to how much of said element you have and can control at a time. Therefore, the weapons only correspond to a single wizard. This means Zombia can't use your longbow. Vice versa."

Tristan smirked at Tibia. "That means you can't use my bow, even if you wanted to."

Tibia stuck her tongue out at her brother. "I don't want your crummy longbow anyway. Crossbows fire harder." This debate had been one of many when Tristan and Tibia were kids. Her comment prompted an eye roll. Emerson and Cerys laughed.

Tristan slung his new weapon over his shoulder. Another magic jolt raced through him when it clanked against his armor. "Now that we have Blanchett's weapons, I guess next is the Hall of Black Mirrors." The mage nodded. Zombia, Tibia, and Emerson's faces all blanched and cringed—well, except for Tibia who wasn't going to act afraid. Tristan's shoulders stiffened.

"That's Malice's next destination. The Hall of Black Mirrors is in the Underworld—that's where she's going to release her army of demons."

Weakness tugged on Tristan's limbs. He had read about the Underworld. It was a world of fire and brimstone where both highborn and lowborn demons lived. It was the world the Cadre had claimed was where black magic originated from. There were rumors about a lost race of elves living there, but they were mostly written off as mythical. Tristan couldn't remember Faye ever discussing a race of Underworld elves. No, he didn't want to go there, but honestly, a fiery land looked better than demons and zombies marching across the Haunted Lands.

With another series of grinding gears, the walls opened in front of them. Tristan and his friends stared into the lush, green foliage of the forest. Sunlight spilled into the dark room, glinting off the wizards' new weapons. Fresh, clean air surrounded them. Now properly armed, the Wizards of the Apocalypse would go fulfill their destiny.

Chapter Twenty

Cool forest shade settled onto Tristan's skin. The soft trickle of a stream rushing by was gentle on the ears. His satchel was heavier than ever with the Apocalypse Grimoire inside, so heavy that if he hadn't been wearing armor, the strap would have dug into Tristan's shoulder. Tristan was loaded with weapons: both his enchanted bow and regular bow were strapped to his back, a sword at his left hip, and Karneleth's staff in his right hand.

The king walked with a bit more confidence, shoulders back and chest out.

Tibia and Zombia held their weapons too, though his sister opted to carry her enchanted crossbow in hand rather than on her back. Zombia, eyes bright with curiosity, held her glaive, running her fingers along the flat side of the blade as she walked. The sun hovered above the western horizon, ready to bid the world good night when Tristan saw what appeared to be another clearing. Upon drawing closer, he saw dead trees and a barren landscape that stretched for miles.

Cerys stopped in her tracks, looked at the few trees standing between the group and the desiccated land, then to her apprentices. "We'll head to the Underworld's portal tomorrow. For now, you three ought to practice using those new weapons of yours. We'll do it here."

Tristan and his friends nodded in unison. They held out their weapons, ready to practice when Cerys addressed Tristan. Her eyes narrowed on his gemstone.

"First, try shape shifting," Cerys said. "Here's the rune." She drew it in the dirt. "It helps to visualize yourself transforming into a skeleton."

Nodding in understanding, Tristan removed his satchel and bows, setting them and Karneleth's staff on the ground. He breathed deeply and imagined his skin melting away, leaving nothing but bones. He drew in his magic. A tingling sensation began, followed by a sudden rush of heat like liquid fire sweeping through his body, burning away his human form.

When Tristan opened his eyes, a scream of surprise nearly escaped him. His vision rang true when he stared at bony hands, breath hitching as the king flexed his fingers. All eyes were on Tristan. Of course their eyes weren't filled with terror; they saw skeletons every day. Their eyes gaped at the magic that whisked his skin away leaving Tristan's bones exposed.

"How do you feel?" Zombia asked. She grabbed his hand, inspecting his phalanges. A moment later, she let go, leaving Tristan with that fleeting feeling of emptiness.

"Lighter. Weird, but lighter," the king responded with a half smile. Tristan sprinted to the stream he and his friends passed before the tree-line and looked at his reflection. He expected his clothes to hang on his lanky frame, but they didn't. The magic somehow made them fit his skeletal form perfectly. His eyeballs remained; no hallowed sockets, and his cropped white hair still framed his face.

When he sprinted back to the forest's edge to his friends, Tristan noted how light he felt. No wind resistance or flesh weighing him down. *So this is what Radius feels like. He doesn't have to worry about bleeding to death from stab wounds or cuts. Had I been in skeleton form, Karneleth's staff wouldn't have cut me. In this form, I have a better chance of surviving battle—a better chance of protecting my friends.*

Tristan turned to Cerys, who was smiling at his new form. "Well done. Now I will warn you, you'll deplete your magic faster by being in skeleton form since you're also using magic to maintain your shift. So

I suggest practicing in human form. Save your skeleton form for real battles."

Tristan frowned. He did want to try wielding weapons in skeleton form to test his agility and flexibility, but depleting his magic wouldn't benefit his practice, so he agreed to shift back.

"Wait, how do I return to human form?" the king asked, brow bone rising.

"Use the same rune, the magic will reverse on itself," the mage explained. "Eventually, you'll be able to shift with the snap of your fingers, but it will take practice. Your parents mastered that fairly quickly." She gave Tristan an encouraging nod. "I'm sure you will too."

Writing the rune again, Tristan felt his magic being reversed. The sudden influx of power jarred Tristan's body, like tons of water rushing in at once, rejuvenating and rehydrating. He watched as a lilac light encapsulated his body, accompanied by the sensation of something shrouding his bones like a warm blanket. When the light receded, Tristan stood, back in his human form. Smiling, Tristan flexed his fingers and looked to Cerys who held the king's gaze with pride.

"Now that that's done, want to try using your

weapons?"

"Where do we start?" Zombia asked, her hands tightening around her glaive with enthusiasm.

"Use the weapons as you would normally," said the mage. "These may be magic weapons, but they're still weapons and you three are warriors. Use the Grimoire too, it will teach you how to channel the four elements with each one."

Cerys took her wand and drew the rune for fire. Instead of aiming the rune at something, she let it coat her wand and hand. Swirling her hand, flames followed in its wake, wreathing around her head. Drawing the rune for air, she pointed her wand skyward, and a gust of wind swept under Cerys, lifting her into the air momentarily. The moment her feet hit the ground, the rune for water burst from her wand's tip. Water from the nearby stream flew to her like an obedient falcon. With her free hand, she opened her canteen and directed the water inside. And last, the rune for earth sprang forward, landing at the mage's feet. The ground cracked before her and rose up in chunks.

"Do that; summon each element with your weapons." Cerys severed her magic, letting the chunks of rock drop.

"This is going to be neat to watch," said Emerson as he rubbed his palms together and plopped down on a flat rock.

Zombia gripped her new glaive with two hands and began twirling like a dancer. She leapt and jumped through the trees, swirling her weapon as she would a sword. She severed a few large branches when she landed. Pointing the blade to the ground, she lifted a few rocks. Afterwards, Zombia spun and smacked the ground, splitting a wide crack in the earth. Next, she twirled and summoned fire. The blade glowed a hot white, and she swung it forward. A ball of flame soared through the air and hit its target. Only after Cerys screamed did Zombia realize where her flame went.

"Good goddess, Cerys! I'm so sorry," Zombia shouted. She sprinted to the mage to see the hem of her cloak was on fire. Tristan drew back his bow, gathering water from the stream, and molded the droplets into an arrow. He fired at Cerys. The water splashed over her, extinguishing the blaze. Zombia grabbed her by the shoulders, scouring her body for burns. She let out a breath of relief, seeing there were none.

Cerys looked at her cloak; she ran her fingers over the blackened, frayed edge, then looked back to the king. "Thanks." She sighed and turned to Zombia.

"Good thing you're a healer. Looks like you're going to be using it a lot."

Zombia blushed. "I got wrapped up in the feeling and power. I didn't realize I had aimed at you. I'm sorry, I'll keep practicing."

Tristan snickered, drawing Zombia's attention and earning himself an elbow to the ribs.

"Run at me as fast as you can," she said.

Tristan cocked his head. "Okay." He bolted for Zombia. She ran toward him as well. When they were within inches of each other, she stabbed her glaive into the ground and leapt over her friend in a graceful arc, landing behind Tristan, glaive still in hand. The king smiled, eyes sparkling with astonishment. Emerson, Cerys, and Tibia clapped.

"Extremely impressive, my friend," said Tibia.

"That was incredible, Zombia," Emerson shouted.

Zombia bowed. "Thank you."

Tristan couldn't find words. He just stared, nonplussed, his heart racing. Zombia was learning magic as quickly as the rest of them despite her powers taking a bit longer to manifest. Nonetheless, her tenacity to learn new skills was inspiring.

After her fire fiasco, Zombia practiced the rest of the elements with Tristan practicing at her side. Summoning air was easy enough, only shaking a few branches and leaves loose. Water turned out to be the most exciting. It ended with both Tristan and Zombia summoning water from the stream and splashing each other with it until the two of them were a little less than drenched. This water battle drew laughter from Emerson and Tibia. Even Cerys laughed a little.

"How was that?" Zombia asked Cerys.

"Well done, you two," Cerys said proudly. Tristan's heartbeat drummed excitedly. He couldn't believe it. This was the magic his parents could have taught him. Deep down, Tristan felt a little shame for not sharpening his skills on magic back home. Of course, the Cadre wrecked those chances.

The mage turned to Tibia, who was already holding her crossbow ready for combat. "The crossbow works a bit differently. The user can still channel the elements, but the bolts pick up the elements, carry them, and manifest when they strike their target." Cerys brandished four apples from her satchel. "Shoot these using each element."

"Got it," the Skeleteria queen said, eyes narrowed.

One after the other, Cerys tossed up the apples. Tibia's crossbow loaded itself; the string pulled back, a bolt fitting into it, just like it did for Tristan's bow. Runes for fire, earth, air, and water struck, one at a time, at the apples. One apple burned, the second was blown high into the treetops by an enchanted whirlwind, the third cracked and exploded from the inside out, and the fourth, well, was just splashed with harmless droplets. Tristan noticed that the water element was fairly harmless and more helpful. Though, what would occur if they were near an ocean? Perhaps they could summon a water-spout or a tsunami.

Tibia spun on her heels and bowed, letting her crimson cloak fan around her. Tristan, Tibia, Cerys, and Emerson applauded.

"Thanks, I'll be here all week," said Tibia in a jocular tone.

"That's so impressive," said Emerson. His eyes took a wistful appearance. "Wish I could try. Magic would improve my prowess in battle, allowing me to better protect everyone in the village."

"But you're already a seasoned knight, Em," Tristan said, leaning down to Emerson. "Magic wouldn't necessarily make you better. You're dedication to protecting Skeletonia is already exemplary."

"No one is touching my crossbow either," Tibia said, tightening her grip on the weapon, her knuckles turned white. "One, it could fall into the wrong hands. Two, anyone else would be more likely to hurt themselves instead of the enemy."

Her gaze swiveled to Emerson. "You better not let Cameron near it. If I discover he went near it, you'll find his bruised body at your doorstep."

Tristan's face blanched. He knew Tibia didn't mean it, and he knew Tibia held a grudge against Cameron for all the pranks he'd pulled on her, but this was a churlish comment.

"Oh, that's gross, Tibia," Zombia said, her face wrinkled.

The knight put his hands up. "Okay, I'll warn him. By the gods, you're protective of that thing."

"We're supposed to *save* people. Not hurt them," Zombia added.

Tibia shrugged. "I'm saving people from the trouble he'd cause with my crossbow!"

She whirled on Tristan, pointing a finger at his chest. "Same goes for you. Keep your paws off my stuff."

Tristan rolled his eyes and put his hands up, but deep down, he saw this practice as his chance to get her back.

With the sun lowering in the sky, Cerys continued the wizards' practice. Tristan had chosen to use his levitation powers to mess with his sister by throwing one of her bolts out of its trajectory. This merited him another elbow in the ribs from Cerys.

"Let me remind you that the Wizards of the Apocalypse are supposed to be helping each other, not messing with each other," the mage said.

Tibia scowled at her brother; a red tint crept up her cheeks from both embarrassment and anger.

"Just a little sibling rivalry," Tristan said sheepishly.

"With everything we have to accomplish, we have to work together. Especially siblings. We need all the power we can get. Black magic is deadly, and the only way to defeat it is by you three working in unison."

When the sun finally sank below the horizon, plunging the world into darkness, Tibia lit the fire this time, using her new crossbow bolts. The group talked and laughed over a meal of more dried pork and goat cheese. Tristan noticed that the entire day, Emerson frowned at their magic, but his eyes were alight with awe. He could see how badly the knight wanted to learn and do magic.

But if Emerson had no magic in his lineage, it would be impossible for the knight to do magic. No matter how many spells he learned.

Once the meal ended, Tristan and his friends figured they'd begin reading the Apocalypse Grimoire, and start brushing up on all the new spells. Reaching into his satchel, Tristan retrieved the Grimoire and sat on the ground with the book in his lap. Zombia and Tibia looked it over.

"There's one more thing you forgot," Cerys said, laying out her cloak in the grass. At least another hour had passed with the trio immersed in the ancient writings nestled in the Grimoire. Tristan, Tibia, and Zombia's eyes turned from the Grimoire to her.

Cerys sat closer to her apprentices. "Tristan, generate enough magic, and it'll become a living source for your fellow wizards to use. This will be the key to defeating Malice. Other than Blanchett, only a handful of wizards have accomplished this."

Tristan nodded, stomach clenching. His magic was already low, making his head spin. He knew from reading the Grimoire that this was dangerous and difficult magic to conjure and understood why so few magic-wielders could perform this type of magic. If his magic ran out, he'd combust, causing his friends to lose their magic too.

Raising his hands, Tristan poured more magic into his palms until they glowed. He held them out. "Zombia, Tibia, try drawing power from my hands."

Zombia reached toward her friend's hand. Some of the glowing embers flowed to her. She twirled them between her fingers. Tibia did the same. Tristan's palm became a fountain of magic. Power poured over his fingers, fueling his friends; some of his energy seeped into the ground. Though his magic was low, Tristan read that magic worked best when surrounded by nature. Trees, water, everything held energy and acted as sources for magic-wielders.

Soon, the embers vanished. Fatigue swept over Tristan, his eyes growing heavy.

"You can do that whenever your friends are low on magic," Cerys said calmly. "Your energy will help prolong theirs, replenishing them as well. However, don't overuse it. The more magic you diffuse to your friends, the weaker you get." The mage turned to the ominous woods. "I'll take the first watch. And Blanchett would be so proud to see how you three are progressing. Truly. She'll be pleased to meet you." Cerys gave the king and his friends a genuine smile before sitting in the grass, eyes wide and glued to the forest.

One by one, everyone in the group went to sleep with Tristan being the last. The ground was harder than the last clearing and the grass wasn't as soft, most likely due to being close to the edge of a barren wasteland. A few more trees and Tristan and his friends would cross into a dry land lifeless as a desert.

Tristan huddled under his cloak, thinking about their mission. He truly didn't want to go to the Underworld. A land of fire and basalt wasn't a place Tristan ever dreamt of visiting. But Malice would be marching there. If they didn't go, she'd release every demon from the Hall of Black Mirrors. She may not have the Grimoire, thank the gods, but once she released her demonic army, the Grimoire would be her next target. This book was a gateway to every spell known to man, and if Malice obtained it, the ramifications would be dire. Humanity would wink out of existence.

The king stole a glance at his friends. Their chests rose and fell peacefully, bringing Tristan a sense of calm. Finally, heaviness took over and Tristan closed his eyes.

He didn't know how much time had passed when the crunch of twigs under boots awoke him. Tristan sat up and rubbed his eyes. It was still dark with nothing but greenery one way and dried out landscape the other. He was about to close his eyes again when a hand jostled his shoulder. Turning, Tristan found Zombia's horrified face.

"People are coming," she hissed. Tristan shot to his feet, tying his cloak around him. He collected both bows—putting his old one over his shoulder—and Karneleth's staff. Keeping his enchanted bow in hand, he moved in the noise's direction.

Warm yellow light flickered between the tree gaps as a fetid smell reached his nose. There was no mistaking that scent. It's the one Tristan had grown accustomed to for years.

"Not again," muttered Tibia, rolling her eyes. Her crossbow fit another bolt. Tristan inched closer.

"Who's there?" His voice was firm.

There was no answer. The king's body stiffened as he drew back the string, a translucent arrow forming in the notch. The rustling continued until clawed hands parted the shrubs. Torch light glinted off armor and swords. A gasp escaped Tristan's mouth. Ahead of them, was an army of zombies.

Chapter Twenty-One

Tristan recognized Zokar and Marcus immediately as they emerged from the shroud of pines; his eyes fell on the knives the zombie king held. He narrowed his eyes in question.

Where did he get those magic knives? I've never seen them before.

His eyes flitted to Marcus, Zokar's second-in-command. Part of Tristan pitied the zombie captain. He couldn't imagine what it's like serving such a belligerent ruler. In every battle Zokar waged against Skeletonia, Tristan noticed Marcus never seemed interested in fighting. He fought with great skill, but he seemed withdrawn from both combat and his commander like he wanted to harm as little as possible.

I wonder how he feels serving Malice instead. She can't be any better.

Tristan's breath hitched. The green masses parted as Malice stepped forward and Tristan concluded where

Zokar obtained the knives. The zombie king who'd been plaguing Skeletonia for years had been working with Malice this whole time.

Malice was a tall demon, pale with piercing crimson eyes. Four horns sat atop her head, glinting in the rising, morning sun. They were wrapped in strands of black hair pulled back into a tight ponytail. She pointed her staff at Tristan; the royal blue orb on top beamed brightly.

"Malice," the king breathed. Every muscle in his body tensed.

The Shadowblood scrutinized him; her eyes roved around Tibia and Zombia. They responded with icy stares. Malice's eyes were half-closed, paired with a mocking smile.

"You're Blanchett's new wizards? Wow, I expected someone a little less . . . pathetic." Her gaze fell on the bow in Tristan's hands. They didn't linger on the bow for long, however. Malice's jaw dropped and eyes widened when she saw Karneleth's staff strapped on Tristan's back.

"How'd you get that?" Malice hissed through gritted teeth, though her face paled like she had already made the conclusion and was just asking for confirmation.

Tibia stepped closer. "We received the little surprise you left in the graveyard. Karneleth's dead, like you will be in a minute."

A pang of guilt rattled Tristan's heart. He wished hadn't had to kill the warlord.

Malice flared her nostrils, her eyes flashing with rage as she reared her head back and screamed at the brightening sky. Her scream was earsplitting and unearthly, sending a chill slithering down Tristan's spine.

After releasing her rage, her eyes refocused on the king and his friends. Malice was beautiful for a demon. Despite her alluring looks, there was something about her, something so dark and malevolent. Trying to understand Malice would drive anyone to utter madness. Blood roared in Tristan's ears, his grip tightening on his bow. Emerson stepped defensively in front of his king.

The Shadowblood waved her hand over her shoulder. "KILL THEM ALL, BUT LEAVE TRISTAN SKELETON FOR ME!"

The battle was a blur of swords, claws, and teeth.

Tibia charged headlong with valor. She didn't pause to contemplate the ramifications or worry about death. With her new crossbow able to fire automatically, Tibia dropped zombies to the ground by the dozens. The battle had only begun, and the ground was already littered with zombies. When the monsters got too close, the Skeleteria queen levitated them and threw them into the trees.

Zombia darted into the fray. Left and right, she swung her new glaive into the accosting undead, slashing through flesh and armor. The blade's curved edge made for deadly strokes. More of Malice's army fell, adding to the green bodies sprawled everywhere. Though she couldn't levitate anyone, Zombia's quick skill with the glaive made up for it, still causing major damage. Only in battle did Tristan see Zombia push aside her kindness. Like him, she was willing to protect those she loved.

Gathering his magic, Tristan swiftly wrote the rune and shifted into skeleton form. Blades and arrows whistled past his ribs, unable to pierce any flesh. He ran faster and with more agility that made the zombies' mouths gape one last time before their demise.

Tristan fired into the crowd. Putting his powers to the test, he even drew fire out of the still-burning pit and imbued it into his arrows. Several zombies caught fire after Tristan unleashed the projectiles.

Soon, Tristan felt his magic beginning to waver like a river running dry. Summoning magic and drawing runes grew harder with each one. He was still a new wizard, so he didn't blame himself for not lasting as long as Cerys. She threw a dozen zombies into the woods and decapitated ten more with a single swipe of her wand.

But the battle against hundreds of zombies wasn't going well. For every zombie fallen, three more took its place. Putting away his bow, he removed Karneleth's staff from his back.

I have to control them again, Tristan thought with a great heaviness. It was like a boulder was tied to his heart, dragging it into the depths of the sea.

As he raised the staff, a knife zipped by, narrowly missing his ear by inches. The weapon did a delicate twirl as it returned to its sender. Spinning around, Tristan locked eyes with Zokar. The zombie king retorted with a scowl Tristan had grown accustomed to. He took in Tristan's bony form.

"Malice said not to attack me, you know," said Tristan with a slightly playful tone.

Zokar chortled. "She meant not to *kill* you. I'm not going to kill you." He looked Tristan up and down again; a crooked smile tugged at the corners of the zombie king's mouth. "I can still harm you, even without your flesh. When you're weak and every bone in your body is broken, then I'll give you to Malice for the final blow."

For years, Zokar and his zombies assailed Skeletonia. At one point, they nearly overran the kingdom. If it wasn't for Emerson's idea to lure the zombies to the wall and pour boiling oil on them, Skeletonia wouldn't be standing today. He never thought mindless zombies would attain magic.

Zokar stepped aside as four zombies in leather armor sprinted for Tristan. The king gathered his powers, allowing them to charge Karneleth's staff. Holding it high above his head, he pointed the green crystal at the approaching monsters. All four of them glowed a sickly green, their eyes turning a pearly white. They ceased their attack. Zokar watched incredulously.

"No one controls my zombies except for me!" Zokar shouted. When he bolted for his enemy, Tristan directed Zokar's own soldiers at him. Still under his spell, the monsters attacked Zokar, biting and swinging their swords at him.

"What are you fools doing?" shouted Zokar, his eyes filled with bewilderment. "Attack him! Not me!" The monsters didn't relent as they grabbed at the zombie king's clothing, pulling him further away from Tristan. More zombies closed in around Tristan, but he used Karneleth's staff to send them away. Their eyes glowed bright white as they sheathed their weapons and ambled back to the woods.

While the zombies crowded their own king, Marcus appeared behind Tristan.

"Kill them all, but leave Tristan Skeleton for me!" Malice's words repeated themselves in an endless loop in Marcus's head. Not only was he pleased to follow Malice's orders, he was slightly glad he wouldn't have to be the one to kill the king of Skeletonia.

One, because Tristan was a wizard. Marcus saw how he used that staff to turn the zombies against their own leader.

And two, because Marcus somewhat admired Tristan's leadership. It mirrored his own: duty-bound and aimed to unite the people.

Unlike Zokar who was merely focused on power over his subjects, Tristan worked to keep his friends together and fight side by side. If only Marcus was the zombie king, Zombieshire would be stronger than ever. Momentarily, Marcus looked over to see Zokar being carried away by his own soldiers, their eyes glowing bright white from Tristan's spell.

Good, that should keep him busy so I can be the one to deliver Tristan to Malice. No killing needed.

Seeing as Tristan was a skeleton, shooting him with arrows would be pointless—harder to hit.

And I don't want to do more harm than necessary. Killing would set me on the same level as Zokar, thought Marcus.

Putting away his bow, Marcus drew his sword. His hand wavered. His skill with a sword wasn't nearly as sharpened as his skill with a bow. But he had to try. Malice counted on him.

Marcus darted for Tristan, sword poised for his legs. Instead of using Karneleth's staff, Tristan waved his hand out; an invisible force wrapped around Marcus. He lifted off the ground, sword still in hand. His surroundings flew by in a blur as the second-in-command careened through the air. Pain registered through Marcus's back as he slammed into a tall pine, so hard the impact shook some of the needles from their branches.

The world spun as white spots appeared in Marcus's vision. When he rose to his feet, nausea swept over him. Collecting his sword, Marcus made it back to the edge of the battlefield, limping slightly. He winced, not wanting to imagine the angry bruise forming on his back.

Zokar was hot on Tristan's tail again. For a split second, Marcus wondered where those spellbound zombies were. Marcus got his answer when he stumbled over their prone forms. Stab wounds sat on their foreheads between open, frozen eyes. Zokar must have killed them so he could pursue Tristan.

That was no surprise to Marcus. Zokar didn't think twice about cutting down those who stood in his way.

More of Malice's army fell under the spell of Karneleth's staff and were sent after Zokar and Malice. When Zokar killed off those zombies and got too close to Tristan, the Skeletonia king lifted the zombie king into the air and tossed him away, sending him landing in a stream. Zokar cursed colorfully as he trudged out of the water.

Marcus stopped the smirk growing on his face. His grin quickly dissipated as he trekked through the carnage, back to Malice. He found her approaching the king of Skeletonia, casually sidestepping the fallen bodies. The air smelled of copper and corpses; nausea swept over Marcus.

Without magic, there was no way the captain could defeat Blanchett's wizards. That was the first order of Malice's he couldn't obey, and not because he wanted to. Marcus wasn't born with magic. His chest clenched. All he could do was *not* kill Tristan (not that he wanted to anyway) and leave him in the hands of his enemy. Marcus hoped that was enough. He'd seen what Malice did to those who disobeyed her, and he didn't want to be on the receiving end of her wrath.

A sinking feeling settled in Tristan's nonexistent stomach. Controlling these zombies and tossing poor Marcus into the woods felt so wrong. His shoulders felt heavy, and not from the Apocalypse Grimoire. He hoped Marcus was all right. His wish came true when he saw Zokar's second-in-command limp back to the battlefield, returning to the demon's side.

The number of zombies had been significantly reduced, having been sent away by Tristan using Karneleth's staff and filled with enchanted crossbow bolts by Tibia.

A bolt of hot blue lightning struck Tristan in the back. With his magic already wavering, a blinding purple light flickered over him as he was thrown to the ground. Karneleth's staff flew from his grasp as dirt and rocks scraped Tristan's flesh.

Flesh?! Great, my magic gave out and returned me to human form. Just terrific. He considered shifting back to bones, but his low energy forced him to think otherwise.

"Tristan!" someone shouted. It was Zombia. She dashed to her friend's side, hoping to help him to his feet.

Malice sauntered over to Tristan, looking him up and down. "Shapeshifting won't save you. Nothing can save you from my magic." Bending down, the demon retrieved Karneleth's staff and gave Zombia a swift kick to the solar plexus. She rolled back a few feet with a pained grunt. Emerson knelt down to help her. Tibia grabbed her glaive before Malice or the zombies did.

Rage boiled in Tristan. He looked from Zombia to the Shadowblood. Malice was the type to torture one's loved ones in order to break her adversary and get what she wanted.

Malice nonchalantly handed Karneleth's staff to Marcus.

"Now, why don't you give me the Apocalypse

Grimoire?" The Shadowblood's red eyes narrowed on Tristan's satchel. The king clutched his bag so hard, his knuckles whitened.

"You're not getting it. Your days of plaguing the Haunted Lands are over."

"No!" yelled Malice. Her face reddened with rage as she closed the space between her and Tristan. The rising sun splashed on her horns, casting eerie shadows over her alabaster face. "Blanchett must pay for what she's done to me."

Sympathy slithered in, making Tristan want to take pity on her, but he shook it away. This demon had killed his parents and tormented his people. Millions of lives were destroyed by her hand; their land usurped. There was no haggling or trying to reason with Malice. She was merciless.

Tristan steeled and shook his head. "More like what you've done to yourself."

Tristan tried levitating Malice, but she didn't budge. He tried again. When his magic flowed out his fingers, it darted for the demon, but never lifted her. His magic slammed into a solid wall.

Malice laughed. "You see, blocking certain types of magic is very helpful."

Instinctively, Tristan pulled back his bow string and fired. Two gold, incandescent arrows soared for Malice. Before they reached her, she waved her staff in a circle. A field of pulsing, lavender magic encapsulated her. The arrows pinged off harmlessly.

The king's insides quivered as he realized arrows weren't successful. Fatigue tore at Tristan's mind and body. Pain trumped thought. But he remembered his gemstone, allowing it to fuel his power a little longer.

Waving her weapon, Malice summoned fire and launched it at her foe. When he reached for his sword, Tristan's bow warped and took the form of a sword itself. Bringing up the blade, he deflected the flaming ball, sending it careening into a group of unfortunate zombies. The disgusting scent of charred flesh paired with terrified wails shattered the morning sky.

Tristan's gaze swiveled to his newly transformed weapon. It was a shimmering blue blade, mirroring the crystal sword Emerson wielded.

What in the world? This bow doubles as a sword? How convenient!

Malice glared down her nose at the king. "Shifting weapons won't save you either."

Tristan ground his teeth, too angry to respond.

He swung his new blade at the demon's head, but she stepped out of the way—not quick enough for his blade to graze her cheek, drawing a thin line of black. Inky blood trailed down her sharp cheekbones.

She slammed her staff into Tristan's sword. The force knocked him back a few feet. If he could defeat her here, he wouldn't have to enter the Underworld. But he didn't have the dragon-claw dagger.

Cold hard ground bit into Tristan's back as Malice kicked his feet out from under him. A powerful ache resonated through his ribs. His sword flew into the grass, far out of reach.

When Cerys moved to help him, Malice grabbed the mage by her braid and threw her back. A yelp escaped her as she hit the ground, but she didn't stay down for long.

Malice addressed the rest of Tristan's friends. "Come closer and he dies."

His friends stopped in their tracks, but they kept their gazes glued on the demon.

"If you won't give me the Grimoire, I'll take it by force," Malice said to Tristan. She drew a rune Tristan hadn't seen before and placed it at the king's feet. An orange light encapsulated his immobile form. It felt as though every nerve was set on fire. His pained screams shook the trees as he writhed in agony, feeling molten lava flow through his veins.

He tried to stand, but fell back as another searing wave of pain flowed over him. He flexed his fingers, but they didn't move. His legs felt leaden. His entire body was inert, held down by Malice's spell. A paralysis spell.

Tristan heard his friends shouting his name as they tried pushing through the zombies. Using Karneleth's staff, Malice sent the monsters after his friends, crowding them, keeping them back with swords and infected teeth. Zombia nearly freed herself by decapitating one of the zombies, but two more filled the spot, severing her from her best friend. Tristan's hope deflated.

"Don't touch me!" Tibia shouted from afar. She fired at the zombies and when some got too close, she rammed into them with the crossbow's barrel.

Malice crouched down to Tristan's level, grabbed his satchel, and pulled out the Grimoire. Tucking it under her arm, she said, "I'll be taking that."

A bottle flew through the air striking Malice in the face. She screamed and staggered backward, clawing at her face and dropping the Grimoire and Karneleth's staff. Her skin sizzled, complemented by the scent of burning flesh.

"Leave Tristan alone!" Zombia shouted. She swooped in and swiped the book; Emerson grabbed the staff and tossed it to Tibia, safe out of Malice's reach.

"Water from the Moon Goddess herself?" seethed Malice. "How *dare* you!"

To Tristan's surprise, his friends managed to break through the wall of zombies.

Crack! Another bottle smashed into the demon's back. Tiny tendrils of smoke wafted off her. She shrieked, doubling over as her skin smoldered. This was the first time Malice's face displayed agony. Zokar, now soaking wet from being in the stream, ducked behind Marcus.

With Malice weakened, the spell locking Tristan's limbs in place faded. Feeling better, he scrambled to his feet, collected his sword and swung for Malice. She ducked under Tristan's attack and went for Zombia. Still holding the Grimoire, she cast a spell and shoved the demon back. Her powers were improving.

Zokar's knife came flying at her. Zombia barely had time to dodge its serrated edge and she yelped as it grazed her arm before returning to the zombie king. Blood welled in the knife's wake.

Zokar took this opportunity: while Zombia was distracted by her pain, he wrestled the Apocalypse Grimoire out of her grasp and shoved her to the ground.

"Zombia!" Tristan cried.

Malice clambered to her feet and took the book from Zokar. She headed for the barren landscape ahead.

"What about the staff?" asked Marcus.

Malice waved him off, her face drenched with sweat and Goddess water. "We have the Apocalypse Grimoire. That's all we need."

Chapter Twenty-Two

Tristan kept his eyes on Malice as she fled into the desiccated landscape, taking the zombies and the Apocalypse Grimoire with her. When the light of their torches faded, it felt like the light in Tristan's heart faded as well, leaving nothing but scattered embers. He sighed, his heart and limbs weighed down with defeat.

The sun was well over the treetops, glinting off the armor of fallen zombies. Monsters littered the ground, each with a bleeding wound to the head; some lay without heads at all. The morning air should smell of dew, but it didn't. It reeked of decomposing flesh and blood.

"Your arm!" Tristan gasped. He took Zombia's hand, a hiss of pain escaping her. The cut wasn't deep, but blood pooled and dripped onto the grass.

"I'll wrap it for you," offered Tristan.

Zombia smiled and shook her head. "I'm a healer, remember." Murmuring a spell, little golden tendrils rose from her fingers, lacing over her wound and knitting the skin back together. The blood vanished by the time the light disappeared, leaving a narrow scar barely noticeable from a distance.

Tristan stared out into the desert through the trees, shoulders slumped. A painful lump settled in his throat. Zombia wrapped her arms around her friend, and instantly, for a moment, the king's troubles disappeared. He leaned into her, listening to her steady heartbeat that only demi-zombies had. But when she let go, his dilemmas returned with a vengeance.

Glaring back toward the desert, Tristan clenched his fists in defeat. He sank into the grass, knees pulled to his chest. He couldn't look at his friends. He'd let them down; he'd let the entire Haunted Lands down. If Malice released her army, keeping magic out of the world would be the least of their problems.

"I did not expect someone as dim-witted as the zombie king to get hold of magic," Emerson said with folded arms, trying to add some levity to the dire situation. Usually, Tristan would have laughed, but now it seemed ill-suited. Emerson, seeing that, followed up with, "The good news, we can use Zokar's stupidity against him."

"Malice has the Grimoire," Tristan mumbled, still not facing his companions. Guilt squeezed him like a python squeezing the life out of its prey. Tristan took a few deep, cleansing breaths deciding what to do next. There was only one thing to do.

Standing, Tristan collected his enchanted bow-turned-sword and his satchel, and strode for the desert lands. "If we hurry, we can catch Malice. Let's go," Tristan said flatly, not bothering to face his friends.

The friends walked in silence with Tristan taking the head of the formation, still unable to look at his companions. The trees became farther apart; lush grass and shrubs gave way to sunbaked dirt and sand. The ground was dry and uneven and while no shrubbery remained—only cracked, parched ground stretching for miles in every direction. Tristan's tongue felt like it was made from sandpaper.

Glancing to the ground, Tristan spotted tracks, dozens of them. *Malice went this way.* He took Blanchett's journal out and kept his gaze glued to the map. The group walked in silence for an hour.

"Tristan, it's not your fault."

Tristan recognized his sister's voice. It was unusual for her to be calm. A few footsteps later, Tristan found his sister by his side, walking in sync with his somber gait. Sweat glistened on her face, her black bangs plastered to her forehead. She walked with pride and confidence—two things Tristan didn't have now. His eyes drifted to Karneleth's staff in her right hand as his failure replayed itself.

The king kept his gaze forward, head down. "It is, Tibia. Don't act like it's not."

When Tristan walked faster, his sister did the same, catching up. "But you're not responsible. You need to stop blaming yourself for things out of your control."

Tristan's gaze hardened; tears stung his eyes. "It is my responsibility. A ruler is supposed to protect their people from all harm—demons included. I can't believe I let Malice get away with the Grimoire."

A frustrated growl freed itself from Tristan's throat. He still refused to meet his sister's gaze. The dry road ahead, leading through dead and charred trees looked a lot better at the moment. The rising temperature in this desert-like place felt better than facing any of his friends.

Tibia sighed through her nose. "Even a king can't be prepared for everything, let alone a freaking

Shadowblood. Malice is a powerful demon with even more powerful magic. And of course, Mom and Dad didn't prepare us properly."

"They couldn't, remember?" said Tristan. He finally mustered the courage to face his sister. "Magic is still against the law."

Tibia's lip curled. Her fingers tightened around Karneleth's staff. "Gods above, you're still worried about that?"

Tristan didn't answer. It was true: magic was against the law. A minute droned by before Tibia spoke again. "Let me ask you, Tristan: Is it the Cadre hindering you from accepting magic, or are you the one hindering yourself from accepting it?"

It was both, actually. They went hand in hand. Fear of the Cadre targeting Tristan and his friends hindered his own reasoning and will to accept magic.

"Did you ever stop to think the Cadre is maybe wrong?" said Tibia. Her voice softened again; her features loosened. "They claim magic is destructive. The truth is anything can be destructive. Magic is destructive, so is war, but the Cadre doesn't seem to have a problem with that. As long as there's no magic being used, Kieran doesn't care what goes on in the

Haunted Lands."

It startled Tristan how true Tibia's words were. He *had* noticed the Cadre solely stamped out magic. Rooted out every magic-wielder and burned them, but they didn't do anything to end the war between zombies and humans. They didn't even bother invading the elf realms. This was mainly because of the dragons, but the Cadre didn't seem to have any goal besides annihilating every magic-wielder in the world. And wasn't stopping Malice using magic more important than disobeying unjust laws? The more Tristan considered it, ending the Shadowblood's reign would not only save the Haunted Lands, it would also prove magic wasn't entirely dangerous and evil.

"You're right, Tib," Tristan said, his voice barely above a whisper. "I've wondered that for years. I've even wondered if the Cadre was responsible for our parents' deaths. I was honestly more shocked to discover Malice was responsible for their murder."

Tibia's hand drifted to her brother's shoulder, easing the tightness in Tristan's chest. While it was rare for Tibia to display this type of affection, Tristan liked when she did—it showed she wasn't always set in battle-mode and that she did have a side that cared for her loved ones and queendom of Skeleteria.

Tristan met Tibia's gaze, his eyes moist—she was also the only family he had left. He wiped his eyes with the back of his hand.

"Magic is part of our lives, Tristan, it always was. From the day we were born, magic was bound to you and me, and it's our job to fulfill Blanchett's prophecy, no matter what the Cadre says or thinks." Tibia sighed. "It's not easy for me either. I spend every day concealing my magic from my people too. I know what my duty as queen of Skeleteria is. It's the monarch's code: protect and serve. Build strong armies, formidable warriors, and keep the zombies out. But I didn't want to forget my magic roots either. So, in my free time, I studied the magic our parents never got the chance to teach us."

Her hand hadn't left Tristan's shoulder, which he liked. Offering comfort when her friends needed it was something Tibia did well. Underneath the impassive warrior was a stalwart sibling, proving the rigorous training that began at age seven hadn't hardened her soul. Tristan was grateful for that.

It felt as though a huge rock had been lifted from Tristan's shoulders, one that had long been tied to him. Though they handled it differently, he and his sister shared the same struggle: concealing and accepting their magic. Tristan glanced back at his friends. Zombia was talking to Cerys, probably asking more questions about her magic, and Emerson walked a few inches ahead, sword drawn, eyes scanning for threats. His brilliant blue armor stood out against the dusty, gray landscape.

"Our duty goes beyond our kingdoms, Tristan," Tibia said to her brother. "We're wizards—the only wizards who can stop Malice and end the Apocalypse. And we'll do it together."

Tibia nudged Tristan with her elbow and smiled. He suddenly found his posture straightening; shoulders back as confidence found him like a long-lost friend. His stomach fluttered with a renewed eagerness.

Tristan never considered looking at using his magic this way. Instead of fearing it, seeing it as a curse, he should have seen it as a blessing. He could use magic to protect Skeletonia. Magic could save the Haunted Lands rather than destroy them. Maybe then, showing the beneficial sides of magic would break the barrier of hate society built for the practice. Maybe the Haunted Lands could revert to the way it was in Blanchett's time where magic was accepted. Magic could be a safeguard against the zombies.

Lifting his chin, Tristan smiled at Tibia. "Sounds good to me.

Chapter Twenty-Three

Malice's boots crunched over what had to be the hundredth twig since arriving in this wasteland. There had been nothing but dead, gnarled trees and cracked, infertile ground for miles. Pieces of wood scattered on the ground, each bleached and desiccated. The earth was charred, mottled with brown here and there, but life was nowhere to be seen. No grass, no animals—not even desert animals. The land was entirely destroyed, forever imprisoned under layers of soot and ash.

Malice sniffed the air, taking in an acrid, smoky scent. Years ago, this wasteland was a forest of lush trees. After the Battle of Scales, the point in the Great War when dragons were introduced, this patch of land would never meet life again. Normal forest fires were damaging enough. Dragon fire was a whole other story.

Hotter than regular fire, dragon fire could burn for longer periods of time, due to their magical impact. Dragon fire was as hot as magma, maybe a little more so.

Lethal and disastrous. Malice could barely contain her twisted glee.

I'll have dragons soon enough.

The demon licked her sharp teeth, her eyes peeled for the Fortress of Portals—the last remaining gateway to the Underworld. During the war, Blanchett built a portal to the Underworld to gain aid of the Firebournes, a tribe of elves who dwelt in the fiery dimension.

The demon's spirits lifted when a rocky silhouette appeared through the gray haze. An army of zombies marched behind her. A few demons, not Shadowbloods, were mixed in, but there were way too many zombies for Malice's comfort. Each wielded a sword, spear, or ax, their scarlet eyes staring off into the distance, hungry for violence.

Marcus walked beside Malice. The demon looked at him with pride. *He'll make a great zombie king. Great prowess and not inane like Zokar.*

"You realize the Firebournes live in the Underworld, right?" Zokar said from behind Malice. The demon closed her eyes and took a long sigh.

"It doesn't matter. We can override them easily. We have the Grimoire now."

I can't wait to pay those elves a visit, thought

Malice. Once in the Underworld, the Hall of Black Mirrors was straight through Firebourne territory. Why not kill two birds with one stone: destroy the tribe and free the Shadowblood demons?

Zokar strode ahead, shoved Marcus aside and reached for the book. Malice snapped her fingers and shocked the zombie king with a bolt of blue lightning. He retraced with a small yelp and shook his hand as a burn appeared on his green skin. Malice growled at him.

"This book isn't for the inept minds of zombies. It's only for the most skilled wizards and magic-wielders."

"Didn't you give me magic so I could control the Grimoire's power?" Zokar protested, rubbing his hand. "It's my right to study it." The zombie king stuck his chest out confidently.

Malice rolled her eyes, sickened by Zokar's overinflated ego. "You idiot, you're still a mindless zombie. You could never fathom the Grimoire's magic."

"We'll see about that!" shouted Zokar. He clenched his fists.

The Shadowblood ignored his griping and focused on the path ahead. The sun hovered high over the land, quickly raising temperatures from warm to boiling. Malice's energy pulsed and hummed, magic from the Fortress of Portals pulling at her own energy.

The sandstone fortress almost melted into the mix of beige and ashen grays of the ruined forest. It was a small fortress, more like a keep, but a portal didn't need too large of a house. It was fully intact, guarded from erosion by the enchantments placed on the sandstone itself.

When the army neared, Malice noticed strips of ivy creeping up the walls and in between the bricks, still alive and flourishing in the midst of this arid climate. Malice knew these enchantments keeping the fortress intact were done with light magic. Though Malice preferred dark magic, she had to admit light magic worked wonders.

The parapets stretched high into the air, filled with archer slots. Frogs croaked, hopping around the moat. Malice approached the drawbridge overlooking a murky moat that reeked of must and stagnant water. Dark green shapes of crocodiles swarmed beneath the grayish water, hungry and leering at the army with their yellow eyes. Between the crocodiles swam large brown trout.

One of the frogs hopped in Malice's path. With

a growl, she kicked the poor amphibian into the water. Several crocodiles piled on top of it. Though no one was here to feed them, the magic kept the reptiles alive by providing an endless supply of frogs and fish. But that didn't mean the crocodiles would pass up devouring anyone unlucky enough to tumble in.

Zokar, seeing the crocodiles, used Marcus as a shield.

"Get off me, you dolt!" snarled Marcus.

He shoved the zombie king; Zokar nearly fell into the moat. His arms flailed as he tried gathering his balance. The reptiles snapped their powerful jaws and lashed their tails, spraying water onto Zokar, adding to his embarrassment. The scene made Malice chuckle.

The Shadowblood led her army over the drawbridge and entered a vast corridor that led to a circular room with a staircase leading down to a black marble floor of the same shape. Malice blew black strands of hair off her forehead, glad to be in some shade. The sighs of relief from the army suggested they agreed.

The room was ornate compared to the fortress's exterior. The ceiling was a dome with a skylight, spilling sunlight on the center of the floor. Two sitting dragon statues flanked the staircase, each with a brazier at their clawed feet. Behind the statues, pillars constructed from black granite supported the ceiling. The High Wizard's heraldry sat in the center of the marble, inlaid with gold—two dragon heads facing each other with a garnet between them.

Malice waved her staff, and all the braziers burst to life with a *whoosh*.

"Now what?" Zokar asked with an impatient edge in his voice.

Malice placed the Grimoire in her bag. "We're going to open the portal. This is the only portal to the Underworld."

"How do we activate it?" asked Zokar.

Fury lit Malice's eyes. "Quit asking a million questions and listen for once!"

The zombie king stomped his foot. "We'd have Skeleton's head by now if you'd stop dithering!"

Baring her teeth, Malice turned to the second-in-command. "Fine, if you don't want to help, then Marcus will." He stood straight, ready for her order. "Bring Zokar to me."

Marcus nodded and marched over to the zombie king.

X Zombie

"What the—" Zokar demanded as his own second-in-command dragged him to the Shadowblood.

Smiling, Malice pulled one of Zokar's knives from his belt.

Sweat formed on his brow; his gaze bounced between the blade and Malice. "W-what are you doing?"

"Hold him still," the demon said to Marcus.

With a curt nod, the captain tightened his hold, his grip like a solid rock against ocean waves. The army of zombies and demons gasped, their eyes widening in horror, some in anticipation.

"What do you think you're doing?" demanded Zokar, his voice trembling. He struggled in Marcus's grip, but to no avail. "Marcus, I am your *king*. You don't have the right to do this to me!"

"Now you know how I felt when you took my eye," Marcus retorted through gritted teeth.

Malice tapped her claw on the tip of Zokar's dagger. "If you had let me finish what I was saying earlier, you'd have heard that we need blood to activate the portal." She pointed the dagger at Zokar. "When you walked away from me, you volunteered. As punishment for constantly interrupting me, your blood is going to open the portal."

Zokar's face blanched. "No!" he shouted, squirming in Marcus's grasp. His grip held like iron.

Malice's hand wrapped around Zokar's wrist, her claws digging into his flesh. For a teasing moment, she poised the blade for the zombie king's throat, but then she lowered it to his palm, slicing a thin line. Blood welled in the cut, slowly spilling over his fingers like running water.

The tenseness in Zokar's posture relaxed, his eyes turning to the slice in his hand. His eyes crinkled with pain, but his lips parted with relief.

"I thought you were going to kill me," Zokar said, voice tightened.

Malice took her index finger and dipped it into Zokar's blood. Then, she knelt by Blanchett's crest and wrote a letter. She kept dabbing her finger into the zombie king's palm, writing until a single word lay at her feet, written in red: *Aperire.*

Malice stood, flashing Zokar a grin. "Thank you for your help." She wasn't really thanking Zokar; she was more thanking Marcus. But taunting the zombie king was too good of an opportunity to pass up. Marcus simpered at her, suggesting she and the second-in-command were on the same page.

"You're so dim-witted," Malice said to Zokar. "I said I needed your blood. That doesn't automatically translate to 'I'm going to kill you.' Though, killing you would mean one less foolish zombie to deal with." The demon looked at Marcus. *And I could crown a new zombie king.*

Zokar grumbled and yanked away from the second-in-command. The letters on the floor began glowing a bright yellow orange. Malice's crimson eyes flitted to raven black—devoid of any emotion. Suddenly, the glow turned to fire.

It swirled, growing brighter. The army stepped back—Marcus and Zokar included—as the orange light fell over their faces, emphasizing every scar. They watched with eyes wide, brows arched as they witnessed Malice's powers at work.

The fire circled the floor, leaving a blazing trail along the lines of Blanchett's crest. Malice grabbed the zombie king's hand and squeezed his open wound over the fire; more crimson fell into it. The flames transformed to a scarlet red as the floor began to sink like a trap door and open. Inside was a land covered in brimstone, lava, and smoke.

Zokar flashed Malice an apprehensive glance. "We're going through *that*?"

Even Marcus stepped back, his face paling a little.

It made Malice laugh. Zombies were such cowards compared to demons.

I'll remember that next time I decide to spawn someone to serve me.

The army reluctantly jumped through the portal. Just before Marcus jumped through, the pallor faded from his green face, replaced with a gallant smile. *He's proving himself to me. He knows I don't tolerate fear or failure. Well played.* Winking at Zokar, the captain hopped through the portal.

Zokar balled his hands into fists, wincing at the pain as more blood seeped through his wounded hand. The entire army was through now, leaving him and Malice.

"If you wish to stay here, I hope you realize doing so would mark you as a traitor to your queen. If you want so badly to serve me again and gain my trust, I suggest you follow my command."

Zokar bristled. "No one talks to me that way."

"Look at all the help I've given you. You and the zombies would be nothing without my magic. You'd still be in your squalid kingdom. So, do you want to conquer the Haunted Lands or not?"

Before Zokar could respond, Malice snatched

his arm and threw him in, head-first. Demons were far stronger than zombies, allowing the Shadowblood to throw Zokar through, though he was a head taller than her. Listening to the zombie king's screams, she laughed, flashing her sharp teeth.

"Wise choice."

Holding a helpless Zokar in his grasp was one of the most satisfying things Marcus ever did. He almost laughed when Zokar tried not to tremble in his clutches, trying to pose a brave face to his soldiers. The zombie king's struggle, his shaking form entrapped in the second-in-command's grip made Marcus smile.

For that moment, Marcus felt powerful. Instead of him being the one tormented and ordered around, Zokar was at the receiving end. Fear, uncertainty, and best of all, shock, were written on the zombie king's face. His look of helplessness made Marcus want to laugh. Those were all the same emotions Marcus—along with the other zombies in Zombieshire—felt under Zokar's rule.

Malice reprimanding Zokar and using his blood to open the portal evoked a certain emotion in Marcus—

revenge. He could still feel the hot poker carving into his eye, burning like all the fire of the Underworld was imbued into a small pointed tip. Years back, Marcus knew planning a coup to overthrow Zokar was risky, but if Zombieshire was going to thrive and succeed, they needed a new leader. A leader who'd unite them, not starve and oppress them.

Marcus had gathered a steady number of loyal soldiers—at least he thought they were all loyal. Being too trusting cost Marcus his success. He'd never forget when that one soldier, who was actually one of Zokar's spies, reported him after ages spent growing close to Marcus and becoming his friend. Later the same day, Marcus was dragged before Zokar where his entire plan fell apart. The next thing he knew, a hot iron poker was headed for his eye, with Zokar claiming how this was more merciful than flat-out killing the captain for treason to the crown.

Marcus woke up a day later in the apothecary's room where she sewed his left eye closed and gave him a black eye patch. The rest was history. Since then Marcus never tried a coup again—that was until he met Malice. A powerful demon who hated Zokar, her own spawn, just as much as he did planted a new seed of hope within

The Forgotten Prophecy

Marcus.

Another chance of a coup presented itself; he'd earn the Shadowblood's trust, then together, they'd dethrone Zokar. Zombieshire would thrive.

When the portal was opened, the sweltering heat of the Underworld shrouded Marcus like a cocoon. The fear emanating off Zokar was palpable. Marcus's insides vibrated with ambition as he winked at Malice and jumped through.

Chapter Twenty-Four

"What happened here?" Zombia asked Cerys.

The dead, burnt trees told Tristan this used to be part of the forest. What happened to it? A common forest fire, or something more sinister? The sun and temperature rose higher, beating down on the group. Sweat quickly formed on Tristan's brow, tempting him to morph into skeleton form, but needing to reserve his magic, he opted against it. The air smelled of ash and soot; the particles clung to the back of Tristan's throat as he and his friends sidestepped fallen branches.

Cerys bent down and retrieved some of the twigs from the ground. The wood was black and flaky, rubbing off on her hands as charcoal. She placed the twigs in her bag and turned to Zombia.

"What took place here was one of the most destructive battles in the Great War, resulting in mass casualties," the mage began, her voice weighed down with sorrow. "It was the first battle that involved dragons. It was because of the dragons that we won the first time." Cerys cast her eyes to the ground.

Tristan's gut twisted. *War is abhorrent.*

"Is everything okay, Cerys?" Zombia asked, placing a hand on the mage's back.

Cerys sniffled. "I lost one of my best friends in combat. It was my first time fighting in battle on dragonback. Blanchett taught all her mages to ride dragons and we used them alongside the Dragonblood elves. One of Malice's soldiers shot her dragon out of the sky. Both rider and the dragon crashed to the ground below in a burst of flames. Dragon fire caused this destruction, leaving an indelible mark on the earth."

The mage gestured to the charred forest. She stared for a long moment, avoiding contact with any of her new friends. Tristan's heart ached. Returning to a place that held such tragic memories must have been difficult for Cerys.

Zombia wrapped her arm around the mage as she paused in her tracks and quietly sobbed into Zombia's shoulder. Tristan offered his support as well. A lump formed in his throat, a boulder in a narrow river. Cerys's loss reminded the king of what it would feel like to lose his friends—to war, the Cadre, or the zombies.

The ruined land didn't lighten Tristan's mood either. He knew about dragon fire. It was strong and fueled with magic; anything it touched would be completely destroyed. He recalled a time when Faye invited the king and his friends to the Dragon Isles for the Winter Solstice. Zombie had brought over some chrysanthemums for the centerpiece, fresh from his garden. When her dragon, Shadowstalker, sniffed the flowers, he sneezed. Fire spurted from his nose, devouring the plants in an instant. The dragon had been a dragonling, but not any less powerful. Baron Xerin and Emerson raced to put the fire out, but even after it was extinguished, nothing remained—not even the vase.

"Yes, dragon fire is very destructive."

Cerys pulled away from Zombia and Tristan's arms and wiped her eyes with her sleeve. "Once we defeat Malice, the destruction will end. Peace can thrive at last."

"Fire is great!" Tibia shouted with glee, clearly done with her more sensitive side. "I'd love to become a dragon-rider. Cameron would never mess with me again."

"This isn't funny, Tibia." Tristan snapped his gaze

to his sister. Why couldn't her sensitive side last longer? "War is serious. It's not supposed to be fun."

"Besides, what did Cameron do to you?" queried Emerson. "He hasn't pulled jokes on you in a while."

Tibia huffed and kept walking. "He pranked my troll, Empeck. It wasn't fair. He didn't even apologize."

Emerson shrugged and brushed some of the soot off his polished armor. "It wasn't that bad."

Tibia's cold gaze was suddenly on him. Her words came in a terse manner. "Try being stranded on a shelf that's ten times your height. Then we'll see if you like it."

Emerson's face reddened. He opened his mouth to protest, but nothing came out. "Hmm. I see your point."

Tristan rolled his eyes at their prattling. Sure enough, as the map indicated, a silhouette of a fortress emerged from the smoky air. "There it is, the Fortress of Portals."

With renewed energy, the group sprinted for the fortress. Crocodiles lashed and snapped in the moat. Tristan wondered how the reptiles survived.

I presume it was magic.

That was a question for another time. The drawbridge was already down, so they darted across it, emerging in a vast, dank corridor. The fortress wasn't as large as a castle, it was more of a keep. One large circular keep. A staircase led down to a circular floor made of black marble and bearing Blanchett's crest. He recognized it from his studies. At least Tristan's parents taught him and Tibia that much.

There was a scuttling sound of something traversing the floor. Fine cobwebs decorated the stones and corners, white against dark gray. Emerson began to shake, and Tibia laughed.

"Stop it, Tib," said Emerson. "You know I hate spiders."

The Skeleteria queen doubled over in a fit of giggles. "That's why I'm laughing. You've faced dragons and hordes of zombies. By the Moon Goddess, you'll jump over a ravine, yet you're so afraid of something that isn't even the size of your finger."

Tristan, Zombia, and Cerys snickered behind their hands.

"It's not funny!"

The knight's brows rose, then he turned and stomped down the staircase, standing next to Blanchett's crest. His crystal boots clicked against the cold marble with an almost hypnotic sound. The braziers were already lit, sitting at stone dragons' feet, blending with the sunlight from the skylight.

"Welcome to the only portal to the Underworld," Cerys said. Her voice had returned to its uplifting tone. Descending the stairs, Tristan noticed his magic, that had started as a distant buzz, had amplified to a full hum, drumming through his veins. Being in magic places sent his magic into a frenzy. He looked to Zombia and Tibia; they nodded, feeling the same electric hum.

"How do we open it?" said Tibia in a bitter tone. "Malice has the Apocalypse Grimoire."

Tristan pulled Blanchett's journal from his satchel. For a moment, he wondered if Blanchett had bothered to write the specifics of opening an Underworld portal. He nearly yielded to his sister's pessimism. Instead, Tristan took the leap of faith and opened the journal. A tense feeling in his throat abated when he saw instructions.

"It says to write *Aperire* beneath the heraldry," said Tristan. He read further and blanched. "It says to use blood, charcoal, or chalk."

Zombia wrinkled her nose. "That's gross. Please tell me someone has chalk or charcoal."

Cerys held out her palm. In it were the few burnt twigs she collected earlier. They were crushed now, covering her hands in black smears.

"Thank the gods," Tibia said, blowing out a breath.

Cerys's face darkened. "Blood magic is perilous. It's usually only for dark magic. If the spell is too big, it can drain every pint from the wielder's body, killing them."

Tristan shivered, his stomach churning.

"Yuck," said Emerson, sticking out his tongue.

"I have no doubt Malice used her own blood to open the portal," said Zombia.

"Or someone else's," Emerson responded. "Sacrificed one of her zombies perhaps?" The knight shook his head. "Despicable."

Tristan couldn't imagine sacrificing one of his people for a spell—or for anything. Even sending Emerson on knightly quests disquieted the king.

Tibia folded her arms. "I hope it was Zokar. Or Marcus."

Tristan shook his head, fixing his sister with his eyes. "Tib, really? That's morbid, even for you."

"The Haunted Lands would be a better place without those two, wouldn't it?"

Tristan took the charcoal and wrote *Aperire* on

the floor. He motioned for Zombia and Tibia to come to his side. The letters began glowing, the orange-gold light spread from the word to the crest, outlining the entire illustration. Tristan felt energy being drained from his body as the portal opened. His vision spotted. The magic hum in the back of his head grew to a full roar as fire sparked from the *Aperire* rune and danced around the crest's outline.

The word alone ignited the portal, but opening it required energy—wizard energy. And the portal fed off Tristan's magic like a blood-sucking mosquito. Slowly, the fire crept and burned as the floor within the crest sank into the ground. Pain lashed through Tristan's muscles like a rabid animal fighting to escape its cage. The gemstone in the king's crown flared bright, blinding purple as his magic worked.

Quickly after, a cooling sensation flooded Tristan. The spell was complete. Composing himself, shaking off the dizziness and feeling of pins beneath his skin, he peered through the portal. Dark red brimstone met his gaze. Rivers of lava flowed everywhere, mirroring the surface world. Heat pressed into his face, making Tristan lurch back.

Taking a deep breath and solidifying his courage,

Tristan grabbed Zombia and Tibia's hands, jumping through.

Chapter Twenty-Five

Tristan, Cerys, Tibia, and Zombia made it through, landing on their feet. Emerson didn't even try performing any crazy stunts. Even he knew being brazen in an unfamiliar land wasn't a bright idea.

"We have to go," Tristan said, adjusting his two bows comfortably on his back. He stared out into the landscape.

This was it: the Underworld. The place Tristan had only seen in books and nightmares. The portal deposited the group in what appeared to be a hill, overlooking a city. Behind it were black mountains, seemingly forged from obsidian. Reds, yellows, oranges, and blacks stretched in all directions. The Underworld reflected the surface world in many aspects. Rivers were filled with lava instead of water, there were no trees, and the sky wasn't blue and had no sun. It was just dark gray, like being inside a looming cave.

The scent of smoke and sulfur hit Tristan like a

slap to the face. *How could anyone live down here?* Tristan remembered hearing and reading rumors of a race of elves that lived down here with their own dragons and all. The Cadre hoped to exterminate them, as they, like all elves, practiced magic

The race of elves was just a myth though, right? Though the soil was volcanic soil, without water, there was no room for agriculture. No food. No, only demons could dwell under these conditions. Tristan had only heard about the Firebournes once, and that was in a debasing manner from the Cadre. Kieran had said Underworld dwellers were all demons, the elves included. The Underworld was a place to be avoided and shamed.

"Did you ever stop to think the Cadre may be wrong?" Tibia's words spun around in Tristan's head. *Who lived in that city? Shadowbloods?*

The group started walking. To Tristan's surprise, Blanchett's journal no longer displayed a map of the Haunted Lands. It had switched to one of the Underworld.

Blanchett must have made it so the map changes in different dimensions. Fascinating.

The Hall of Black Mirrors was just past the city

and wedged in the side of the obsidian mountains. If they didn't encounter any demons, then the trip would be quick.

Saying the Underworld was hot would be an understatement. Cerys removed her cloak and stuffed it into the strap of her satchel. Sweat beaded on her forehead, plastering brunette strands to her face. Lakes and rivulets dotted the rocky terrain, bubbling with molten lava—pretty to the eye, lethal to the touch. Tristan coughed as he inhaled the sulfuric scent. A sandpaper feeling settled across his tongue.

The king looked at the city. A black castle rose out of the masses of brimstone buildings. "What's in that city?" Tristan asked.

"That's Nova, home of the Firebourne elves," answered Cerys.

Tristan's muscles went numb. "So they *are* real?"

It was Cerys's turn to raise an eyebrow, regarding Tristan as though he'd sprouted horns and a tail. "Of course they're real."

"Shouldn't there be four elf tribes then?" Tibia said, holding up four fingers for emphasis.

"There are," answered Cerys. "But there's only three in the surface world: the Icebloods, Moonbloods,

The Forgotten Prophecy

and Dragonbloods."

Tristan's face slackened at her words. *The Cadre was wrong again! What other lies have they been feeding the Haunted Lands?*

A shrill screech pierced the air, followed by wingbeats—tons of them. Tristan's gaze darted to the sky. Several creatures circled above like vultures over prey. Tristan squinted; the animals resembled dragons. This was highly unusual.

Dragons dwelt within their corresponding tribes. They were not known for venturing into other dimensions. But, if elves lived down here, then it would only make sense for them to have their own dragons.

One dragon dove for Tristan; its whip-like tail knocked the enchanted bow from his hands.

Zombia drew her glaive and swiped at the dragon's underbelly, cutting a thin red line. Its screech reverberated around them, and it swerved away. Zombia moved to swing again, but more dragons descended and swarmed her. Another tail swooped in, wrapping around her glaive and tearing it away from her hands.

Dragons with prehensile tails?

The barrage of teeth and tails continued until all of Tristan's friends were disarmed. The beasts landed all at once, shaking the ground and encircling the newcomers. With the dragons closer, Tristan surveyed them.

Could you call them dragons? They were like dragons: two horns, talons, and wings, except they had two legs instead of four. Their shoulders, rather than connecting to arms, linked to their wings. They were smaller than a regular dragon, with scales in various shades of browns and muted oranges. One of the beasts neared Tristan, making his body stiff. Hot breath that smelled of death clogged his nose. Zombia gave an audible cry of disgust.

Each dragon had a rider mounted in a fancy leather saddle. Tristan stole a glance at Cerys. Her hands were up, palms out peacefully. Keeping her body facing the riders, the mage said out of the corner of her mouth, "Wyverns. These are wyverns."

Tristan had never heard of them before. Then again, some people in Skeletonia believed in dragons with three heads, so anything was possible. *How many species of dragons existed before the war?*

"In the name of the Hearthstone Queendom, halt!" one of the riders said—a female voice. "State your business here."

Tristan showed them his empty palms. "Please, we mean no harm. We are here to stop the queen of the Shadowbloods, Malice Sanguine."

Tristan's muscles slackened when the soldiers suddenly lowered their weapons and forced their wyverns to step aside.

Two riders came forward, still atop their winged mounts. Instead of spears, they wielded poleaxes crafted from sharp onyx—black as night and pulsing with foreign power. The duo dismounted and stopped in front of Tristan.

The soldier to the left removed her helmet, revealing a young girl. She had ginger hair tied into two braids, dangling over her shoulders. A set of copper goggles rested on her head, complementing her golden eyes. Her pointed ears marked her as elven, but unlike most elves, she was short, only meeting Tristan's shoulders.

Two white tentacles, thin as ribbons, trailed down her back. The appendages slithered up and writhed around the new wizard, taking in his scent like a dog sniffing an unfamiliar hand, curious about someone new. His body tensed. The tentacles were like snakes, hovering in the air. One of the tentacles neared Tristan's face. He poked it. It was scaly like snake-skin—white snake skin. They continued swirling around Tristan until they had taken in every smell possible discerning his character.

The girl's eyes widened with wonder as she assessed Tristan. Then, she bowed.

"You're a king from the surface world," the girl said. Her voice was perky, surprising for someone in the Underworld. Tristan expected these elves to sound more melancholy—especially living in a place like this. But if this was their home, they must've liked it.

Tibia stood behind her brother, rolling her sapphire eyes. "Thanks for pointing out the obvious."

Tristan nudged her in the shoulder.

"Please ignore my sister, she can be a little . . .

forthright. So, you know Malice Sanguine?"

The girl tucked her helmet under her arm. "She's been an enemy of the Firebournes for years. The Shadowbloods were expanding their land, in turn swallowing ours. They want control of the entire Underworld."

Tristan chimed in. "And everything else."

The girl nodded. Lava light feathered against her ginger braids. "We want them gone as much as you do. Malice and her army just swept through Nova, raiding our city and heading for the Hall of Black Mirrors."

Malice destroyed Nova the way she did those poor villages in the surface world. Her thirst for revenge was unquenchable—no amount of people killed would suffice. Tristan felt sick just thinking about it.

The girl extended a hand to Tristan. "Apologies for the barbarous greeting, we thought you were more of her army. I am Ghist Hearthstone, Queen Regent of the Underworld." She turned to the Firebourne still atop his wyvern. He removed his helmet, revealing a boy with bright ginger hair, short and spiky. His eyes were gold, but a few shades lighter than Ghist's. "And this is my brother, Blaster, king of the Underworld."

Ghist paused and looked to the giddy Firebourne behind her. "Well, king-to-be. He's a prince right now."

A quirky grin adorned Blaster's face, reminding Tristan of Cameron.

Ghist replaced her helmet and remounted her wyvern. "Malice's army is moments away from storming the Hall of Black Mirrors and summoning her demons. Our soldiers are tracking her, but we're running out of time. Hop on a wyvern."

"Thank you, but we can continue on our own," Tibia snarled. "Can we trust you?"

Ghist glanced down from her wyvern, scowling at

the Skeleteria queen.

"Heed this: the Underworld and surface world are in equal danger. Malice has been amassing her armies for decades, manipulating, and exploiting. You'll need help whether you like it or not. Hostility between kingdoms and factions isn't important now. It's light magic versus black magic, humans against the dead, and good combating evil. We're stronger together than apart."

Tibia ground her teeth and looked at Tristan.

"We need all the help we can get," he said in a steady tone. "We can't afford to make more enemies."

Emerson leaned close. "I can't say I trust them either, but we don't have time, Tibia."

Closing her eyes, Tibia sighed. "Fine."

Ghist didn't smile, she just lifted her chin. "You'll thank us later. Now, hop on."

Tristan and his friends gathered their strewn weapons and each chose a mount. Blaster offered a place in the saddle for Tristan. The boy extended a hand to the king, lifting him onto the wyvern. The beast's skin was rough and textured, its scales scintillating in lava light. Zombia mounted the wyvern next to Blaster's. She sat calm and composed, her glaive strapped to her back. Orange light backed her brunette hair, giving her a halo. Tristan swooned, his world tilting momentarily.

Tibia rode with Ghist. Her crossbow was laid in her lap in a threatening manner as she glared at the girl from behind. Emerson did the same as he mounted. His hand gripped his crystal sword, knuckles white.

Ghist replaced her helmet and gripped the reins. "Hang on!"

The wyverns roared and shot into the air.

Chapter Twenty-Six

Halfway through the ride, Tristan realized riding a wyvern wasn't an effortless task. Even in the saddle, the motion was turbulent. To his surprise, no bile rose in his throat in response. Clutching tight to Blaster's waist, Tristan prayed he didn't fall. A smile of awe grew on the king's face as he observed the view below.

Everything shrunk to insect size; the crimson landscape merged together, divided by thin strips of molten lava. Soon, they flew over patches of fertile volcanic soil. Little brown and gold-orange dots were wyverns lounging by the lava rivers, some swimming in the molten liquid. Tristan raised an eyebrow. There wasn't a drop of water in sight. This wasn't at all how he pictured the Underworld. Lava, fire, brimstone, and more lava was what Tristan had read—and how the Cadre described it. Uninhabitable and deadly.

His parents never talked about the Underworld. Though they mentioned Firebournes briefly, they weren't mentioned often enough for Tristan to care or truly believe they existed. That combined with the horrifying drawings depicted in his school books was enough to quell his interest in the dimension. He knew the Underworld existed, but it was a place of demons and fire. But the Cadre was wrong and the textbooks Tristan's mentors gave him were fabricated lies. There was a whole world down here.

Still hovering above the volcanic soil, Tristan shouted into Blaster's ear, "How do you live down here?" His voice was ripped away by the wind, but luckily, the boy seemed to hear him.

"The volcanic soil is great for growing food," said Blaster. The wind nearly shredded his voice. "There's a single fountain in the heart of Nova where we get water. It's protected by a magic shield. So no evaporation. We can't drink lava, but the wyverns can. Their scales are built for fire and heat."

Tristan narrowed his eyes, curious. "What do they eat?"

Blaster shrugged. "Cattle and deer, all built for fiery climates. Believe it or not, the Underworld mirrors the surface world, except everything here can withstand the temperatures—animals included."

Tristan's brows furrowed then eased. The Cadre *was* wrong.

I wonder what else they're lying about.

Tristan watched the black soil patches fade as the wyverns flew over Nova. Blaster steered his wyvern by the horns, getting it to lower a bit. The turmoil below was nearly as deafening as the wind. Tristan scanned the ground for Malice's army, but they weren't there—only a trail of destruction remained.

Dead bodies lay in the streets. Wyverns keened over their fallen riders. Their lamenting was high pitched, a shrill, sorrowful sound. Tristan's heart broke. The bond between a dragon and their rider was inseparable; even after death, the dragon or rider would forever mourn the loss of the other. This was one of the first things his parents told Tristan about dragons; later on, he learned more about them from Faye.

Surviving commanders barked orders, deciding how to protect the city from another attack. Ghist was telling the truth; she was patrolling the land for more of Malice's army.

One of the soldiers shouted something to Ghist, his words eaten by the wind. Ghist nodded and the soldier steered his wyvern into the chaos. Tristan assumed she was giving the rider orders to recruit the rest of the Firebourne army.

"Malice has been here," Blaster said with a low growl. With his heels, he nudged his wyvern to fly higher again.

The wyvern carrying Zombia flew adjacent to Tristan. Her face said it all. Her eyes glanced down at the carnage, her green skin pallid, lips pressed into a thin line; her disgust matched his.

The semi-good news was that these elves wouldn't reanimate as zombies, even if bitten. Tristan hadn't found any evidence of the virus transmitting to dragons or elves. Their magic and systems worked differently, blocking the virus from even taking hold and highjacking their cells. At least the fallen Firebournes could rest in peace.

As Nova disappeared in the distance, the obsidian walls of the Hall of Black Mirrors panned into view. It was a large fortress, nestled into the mountain-side, nearly blending into the rock. It was more opulent than the castle in Nova, decorated with sharp spires and towers. The wyvern banked and dove for their destination. The sudden change of direction made Tristan tighten his grip on Blaster.

"Don't grab so hard," the Firebourne prince shouted. "You'll break my ribs."

"Sorry, I've never . . . flown before." Tristan blushed and loosened his grip a bit.

All dove for the front terrace. Tristan closed his eyes as wind slammed into him. The ground rushed to meet them; inches before smashing into the brimstone, the wyvern pulled back, allowing air to fill its wings. The landing was smooth. Blaster swung a leg over the saddle, dismounted, then helped Tristan down. The wyvern shook out its wings and nudged Blaster in the back, presumably begging for food. Reaching into his bag, he pulled out a handful of orange and brown geckos. The wyvern sniffed Blaster's hand and gobbled them up.

Zombia slid off her wyvern with shaky legs. Tristan raced to her side to steady her.

She smiled at him, her hand lingered in his. "Thanks, Tristan. Riding wyverns is something I'll have to get used to." Releasing her friend's hand, she adjusted the glaive across her back.

Cerys, Tibia, and Emerson hopped off their mounts with ease. The king's sister kept her crossbow down, but her body turned toward Ghist, ready to fire if the Firebourne tried to backstab them.

The mage patted the beast's scaly snout. "Riding a wyvern actually was something on my list of stuff to do."

"Wow, that was so fun!" shouted Emerson. His hair was a mess, tangled and knotted by the wind. By the knight's stance, he seemed proud of it. "Can we do it again? I've never had that much excitement on a quest."

"We can on our way back," said Zombia.

"That's if there is a coming back," Tibia grunted.

"Don't be so cynical, Tibia," the knight said.

"Challenges are fun. They're one of the reasons I wanted to become a knight."

Tristan knew Tibia had a point. They might not survive. Breathing deeply, Tristan whispered his shapeshifting spell. Once again, his skin melted away, leaving him as a skeleton. He took his bow and pulled back the string, a shimmery arrow forming in place.

"Come on."

The hallways of the fortress were arched and dark, save for the torches lining the walls. Instead of sconces, torches were held in the mouths of stone wyverns. Silver runes were written in the obsidian walls. Tristan could only assume they were for dark magic spells. A chill skittered down Tristan's spine. The sulfuric scent penetrated the walls, clogging the king's nose and making him sneeze.

Tristan and his friends rounded a corner to see a set of massive ebony doors. He ran for them and threw them open. Smoky air hammered his senses as he stood on a balcony overlooking a wide courtyard. Fountains spurting lava lit the place, revealing s single dais with three rectangular mirrors leaning against the wall behind it. Their frames were decorative, crafted from the finest silver.

Malice was nowhere to be seen. No zombies or demons either.

"Did we beat Malice here?" Zombia asked, voice hopeful. Her fingers loosened on her glaive.

Cerys stood over the balcony, her eyes scrutinizing the mirrors, her shoulders tightening. "Something's not right." The mage moved down the stairs, to the ground floor. Tristan watched her make her way to the mirrors, listening to her boots scuffing against stone.

This seemed too easy. Malice took the Grimoire and got a head start to the hall. How could Tristan and his friends have beat her here?

Tristan swallowed nervously. *Cerys is right. Something's amiss.*

The king and his companions descended the steps and joined Cerys by the mirrors. The mage's posture was rigid and motionless.

"What is it, Cerys?" the king asked. She didn't answer.

Tristan spun her around. "Please, tell me what's wrong." Tristan's voice was louder, firmer. He looked to the mirrors to see them glowing a sickly green color.

"They're activated," Cerys said under her breath. Her emerald eyes were cast to the floor. "Malice has already opened the mirrors and released the demons." Her voice was plaintive and solemn.

It felt like the wind had been knocked from Tristan's chest. He turned to his friends. They shared the same expressions—horror and defeat.

"Where is she?" Zombia asked. Her grip tightened on her glaive, holding it up, ready for combat.

A footfall echoed. Not just one set of footsteps, but many. The air chilled as a rotting scent filled the room.

"Ah, Tristan Skeleton, glad to see you made it."

Tristan recognized Malice's voice immediately. Eerie and soft, with threatening undertones. Taking a deep breath, Tristan forced himself to turn and face her. Cold settled over his exposed bones. Zokar and Marcus flanked Malice, but that wasn't what made Tristan's body tense. Demons, in spiked armor, fanned out behind the Shadowblood queen. Each had varying numbers of horns. Most had four like her, save the few who had two. Zombies were dispersed in between the demons, adding to her army. Malice's crimson eyes flitted to Tristan.

He heard Tibia's bow creak, preparing to shoot one of the monsters. Her bravery didn't dampen his fear. He admired his sister's valor, but it worried him sometimes. If they were going to win this battle, the wizards would have to think and use their magic rationally.

"I've been waiting for you," the demon crooned. Malice looked at Ghist and Blaster, who were making their way down the steps, bringing their own group of Firebournes with them. It wasn't enough. Malice's army still outnumbered them.

Malice looked Blaster and Ghist up and down with a mocking gaze. "You lesser elves can only escape Shadowblood rule for so long. After this, you'll be our subordinates."

A tumult of laughter erupted from Malice's army, echoing around the courtyard.

"You're not getting the Firebourne kingdom," growled Ghist. Her face flushed with anger, lips thinned. Malice practically laughed at the poleax gripped in her hand.

"You wizards are mighty idiotic, thinking these elves can help you win the war," Malice said coolly.

"Watch your tongue," seethed Tibia as she took aim.

Malice opened her arms, chin high. "Go ahead."

Tibia released the bolt. Before it touched Malice, she reached out and grabbed the projectile, gripping it tightly. Smoke wafted off her fingers as the metal melted through her palm. Tristan gasped, glancing at the ground in dismay. All that remained of the bolt was a pool of silver liquid.

Malice chuckled and drummed her fingers on her staff. "You're new wizards, I pity you. So here's a lesson for you; black magic overpowers light magic. Too bad society is afraid of magic, maybe you wouldn't be so unprepared. Isn't that right, Tristan? Your parents didn't prepare you?"

Tristan's rage skimmed the surface, set to boil over. *You killed them, you heartless monster.* All the zombies behind her appeared to be wearing peasant garb under their armor. Tristan's heart sank.

That's why Malice was invading villages. She wasn't just amassing supplies, she was making more zombies.

Disgust consumed Tristan.

The demon shrugged. "I prefer it this way; makes my job easier." She neared the king. Evil magic radiated off her, feeling like powerful dragon claws closing around him, wringing him dry. "I'll start with your companions here. After you watch them die, I'll kill you."

Tristan stood straight and protectively in front of his friends. "That's not going to happen. We have Blanchett's weapons and we've trained. The Haunted Lands will never be yours."

"They already are." Malice's lip curled into a sneer, staff raised above her head. "KILL THEM ALL!"

Chapter Twenty-Seven

Clashing metal and the screams of the wounds and dying quickly filled the air. Zokar didn't hesitate as he lunged for Tristan. Emerson tackled the zombie king, pushing him to the ground. The king spun around and sprinted to his friend's side. Emerson and Zokar scuffled; the zombie king tried to knife the knight in the eyes. Tristan took aim; however, he couldn't get a clear shot.

"Defeat Malice!" said Emerson, glancing over his shoulder momentarily. "Don't worry about me."

"No, I'm not leaving you! Once I get a clear shot, I can—"

"Leave me, Tristan." Emerson swerved to the side, avoiding Zokar's knife. "As your knight, I vowed to give my life for you. Allow me to fulfill that oath." Emerson's eyes shone. "Please. "

Tristan faltered. He couldn't live knowing he survived and Emerson didn't. He didn't want to have

Cameron ask why the king returned home without his best friend.

Tristan opened his mouth to protest when something walloped him from behind. He crashed to the ground, his bow flying from his hands. Pain ripped through Tristan's chest as he landed forward on the solid ground.

Bones aching, Tristan scrambled for his bow and stood. He found Malice standing behind him, her staff smoking. His breath came short.

"Don't make this harder than it has to be," the demon seethed. "I've waited for my revenge long enough."

Wingbeats echoed overhead, drawing Malice and Tristan's attention to the sky. Hundreds of wyverns with Firebourne riders swarmed the courtyard, spewing fire down on the zombies and demons. Screams shot into the air as Tristan's nose quickly smelled burning flesh. Firebourne infantry burst through the doors to the hall, pouring down the stairs in droves and tearing into Malice's ranks.

Ghist hovered above Tristan and waved with a wink. She and her wyvern dove into the fray, clashing with the green and pale-skinned masses. He watched as she, Blaster, and Cerys directed the army, giving orders. Tristan couldn't help but give a grateful laugh. Ghist had ordered reinforcements. Without them, Tristan and his friends wouldn't have a chance.

Malice's face pinched, her cheeks flushing. Staff aimed high, a translucent chain of magic shot from the pointed tip, wrapping around a wyvern who got too close. The chain snaked up the reptile's body, causing it to scream and flap its wings frantically. Malice pulled the magic links closer, dragging the wyvern and rider to her until she and the beast were nose and nose. Next, she whispered a spell, drawing a rune with her free hand. The symbol Tristan had never seen before touched the wyvern's head and both it and the rider exploded in a mess of gore.

Tristan fought the urge to vomit.

Malice nonchalantly wiped her victims' blood from her cheek; her sharp teeth curved into a twisted smile.

"I told you those pathetic elves and dragons aren't going to help you!"

Tibia and Zombia carved their way through the rotting masses, making their way to Tristan. The trio faced Malice.

The Shadowblood snapped her fingers, and three demons raced straight for the wizards. Tristan gathered his powers and lifted one of the demons off the ground, tossing him to the far side of the chamber. Zombia swung her glaive, severing the head of the other. Two bolts shot from Tibia's crossbow. She used her magic to guide the projectiles, sending them spinning around the demon. His red eyes followed the bolts' trajectory until he went dizzy with confusion. When the demon least expected it, the bolts plunged themselves deep in his chest.

Malice's eyes widened. Not horror necessarily, but more perplexed.

"We're more prepared than you think," Tristan said with a confident smirk.

Veins feathered in the demon's neck; her jaw clenched. "I've been told that a lot. Everyone who'd gotten overconfident before fighting me always died first. Told you not to underestimate the power of dark magic."

More demons appeared and dove for Tibia and Zombia. The girls, using tips Cerys had taught, built a golden force field, blocking the demons' attacks. While they were distracted, Tibia drew lava from the nearby fountains and dumped the molten rock over her adversaries. Screams and sizzling flesh clotted the atmosphere. When a handful of zombies approached her, Tibia unleashed the power in Karneleth's staff, hypnotizing the green monsters and turning them against the demons, growing into a pile of claws and teeth.

With a flick of her wrist, the Shadowblood waved more demons the wizards' way. "Take care of the king's friends," commanded Malice. "Tristan is mine."

The king flipped his bow into a sword as a sickly green flare of magic spun his way. He blocked the attack, deflecting it over Malice's shoulder. Two Firebournes approached Malice from behind. Without looking behind her, the demon whispered another spell. Two bolts of magic flew through the air. At the last moment, the energy took the shape of swords and pierced both elves. They plummeted, adding to the growing casualties.

Tristan's lip curled. He swung his sword into her staff; his bony arms reverberated as the blade sliced into ebony wood.

Malice cracked a smile. "You've got a lot of nerve to attack me directly. I admire your valor. Too bad it won't save you."

Tristan's magic flared, propelling his arms forward, striking Malice in the face with her own staff as she held on. She yelped as black blood trickled from her nose like an overfilled inkwell.

Tristan drew fire energy from the lava fountains and poured it through his hands, heating Malice's staff. His brow creased with pain as the blinding hot power coursed through his hands like liquid fire. The demon gritted her teeth as she, too, felt the burning sensation.

Malice released her grip, cursing and shaking her hands. Her palms were red; blisters already speckled her skin.

Tristan cast Malice a mocking smirk, holding the Shadowblood's staff in one hand and his sword in the other. "Looks like you're not getting your revenge after all."

Incensed, Malice wiped the inky blood from her nose and extended her hand. Her lips moved as she drew her staff from Tristan's grip. The king held on with all his might, whispering a reverse spell to combat her magic.

SNAP!

Malice's staff clattered to the ground, broken in two. Tristan scowled seeing the sapphire orb remained intact. He'd hoped to shatter the sphere, stopping the Shadowblood's powers.

An enraged scream tore from Malice's throat, shaking the courtyard and threatening to crack the mirrors. "You're dead, wizard!"

She jumped forward, retrieved the top half of her staff and loomed over Tristan. Her eyes faded from their crimson color to pitch-black holes. Dark veins branched down her alabaster skin. The king froze. Her beautiful features melted away, revealing Malice's true form.

Tristan didn't have time to react. A lurid green light sprang from Malice's staff, her voice too low for him to hear her incantation. Magic wrapped around Tristan, weaving between his bones. Sickness quickly shrouded him. The magic seeped into his joints, locking them in place. He poised his sword for another swing, but froze as though each part of his body transformed to stone. He dropped his sword and collapsed onto his back, unable to move. Tristan couldn't even twitch his fingers, their joints locked up, paralyzed. Pain ricocheted through his body. It was like a giant was pressing a foot on the king's chest.

At the same time, a sudden weakness took over, making Tristan feel even more fatigued, like every ounce of energy and blood was drained from his being. His vision swirled. Purple light rippled over his body, and Tristan reverted to human form. Cold stone pressed against his bruised skin.

The Shadowblood closed the space between her and Tristan. Malice chortled as she reached down and swiped Tristan's crown. "One thing dark magic-wielders can do is counteract their opponent's magic. I can take and feed off your powers. Something that would take years for a light magic-wielder to master. You'll never get the chance."

Out of the corner of his eyes, he saw Zombia behind Malice. She screamed his name and darted toward her friend. Cerys spoke behind her, both hers and Zombia's voices inaudible.

Tristan's vision blurred. He was going to die. He felt his strength flee in droves, growing weaker. Soon, he'd be under Malice's reign. The Haunted Lands would be hers. The king's vision warped then faded black.

Chapter Twenty-Eight

Emerson felt like this was his first time fighting Zokar. The zombie king moved with supernatural speed, knocking Emerson to the ground. Miraculously, the knight maintained a grip on his sword. Zokar's knife whistled past his ear, embedding itself into the stones. Emerson took this opportunity to knee the zombie in the stomach. Pain registered, giving the knight time to roll away from his attacker and spring to his feet.

Zokar was up in a matter of seconds. He spun, swinging for Emerson's head. His blade clashed with Zokar's; Emerson's small arms shook at the zombie's unnatural strength. Light-blue waves rippled over the obsidian edges.

Zokar swung relentlessly, but Emerson deflected each attack with parries. Emerson knew magic wasn't on his side; he'd have to rely on his combat skills alone. Hopefully, that would be enough. Orange light flickered in the distance. And an idea popped into Emerson's head.

If I can get him close to the lava fountains, I can push him in.

With his new idea in mind, Emerson redirected his position and backed toward the deadly fountains. He effortlessly wove through the maze of bodies—both dead and alive. Suddenly, Emerson sensed a presence behind him. He spun and slashed a demon that sneaked up on him. The monster didn't get a chance as Emerson plunged his blade through the demon's chest. Inky blood poured and his enemy collapsed. Gods, it looked like someone spilled several ink wells onto the fortress floor.

A foot came and smashed into Emerson's cheek. Agony laced through his face as he tasted copper. He flew backward, landing dangerously close to one of the lava fountains. This time, he didn't maintain grip on his sword; it skidded across the floor, tapping the base of the fountain.

Zokar came into view, approaching Emerson. Grunting, the knight twisted and dove for his sword. He barely had time to dodge one of his knives. A thin, red line materialized on his cheek. The knife hit the wall behind him. Zokar clenched his fist, and his weapons returned to his hand like an obedient dog. Emerson's heart hammered in his chest, trying to flee his ribcage.

When Emerson grappled for his sword again, Zokar chanted a spell. A rune flashed before his open hand and flew at Emerson's feet. Incandescent gold chains of pure magic wrapped around the knight's ankles, pinioning his legs together. He fought against the enchanted bindings, but to no avail.

Zokar's scarred face hovered over Emerson. His face split into a grin, showing his yellow, serrated teeth.

"I never thought I'd see the best knight in Skeletonia overpowered by a zombie," Zokar taunted.

It was true. In every battle Emerson could remember, he fought ten zombies at a time. However, that was before magic resurfaced in them.

Feet tied, Emerson twisted his torso to rise on his elbows when Zokar delivered a swift kick to the jaw. Fire shot through his teeth and mandible. Zokar straddled Emerson's chest and held his knives in an X over Emerson's throat, ready to decapitate him. Something glowing sliced through the air, colliding with Zokar.

It sent him back a few feet. Turning his head, Emerson found his savior. Blaster sat on his wyvern, hovering in the air above the courtyard. He winked at Emerson, and pulled on the reins, lowering his wyvern a bit. The Underworld prince cast a spell of his own. A gold bolt of elven magic shot from Blaster's hand and directly sliced through Emerson's bindings perfectly.

Scrambling to his feet, Emerson retrieved his sword from the fountain's base and waved at Blaster. The prince disappeared once more into the fray.

"You put up a better fight than I expected," Zokar said from behind Emerson, seething with rage. His green skin was mottled with burns, his clothing charred at the hem. Small scrapes covered his face, adding to the jagged scar that ran over his right eye.

Finding renewed strength, Emerson deflected Zokar's knife as it cut through the atmosphere. The dagger bounced off Emerson's sword and into the lava. The weapon sank into the molten masses in a gurgle of bubbles, leaving Zokar with one knife. The zombie king stared into the lava and back at the knight, his teeth bared.

Emerson laughed at the zombie king's rage. "Ready to give up?" he asked with a smirk. Was laughing in the face of a magic zombie a bad idea? Probably, but the knight didn't care.

"No matter," said Zokar. "I only need one to kill you."

He whispered another spell. More translucent, blue chains shot from the zombie's palm, this time snaking around Emerson's legs rather than just his ankles. The knight fell to the ground in a heap. Still holding the end of the chains, Zokar pulled Emerson close. With one hand, the zombie king tore the knight's sword from his grasp, sending it sliding across the stones, out of reach. Straddling his torso, Zokar tried to do something zombies did best: bite.

Emerson twisted and turned, trying to avoid Zokar's infected teeth. Sharp points clamped down on his armor plates, but the zombie didn't relent as he tried biting through solid crystal. Green hands gripped Emerson's collar as Zokar went for his jugular. He fought tooth and nail, pushing against Zokar's shoulders to keep him away.

Emerson tried not to shudder. He knew what would happen if he was bitten. There was no going back. In Blanchett's absence, no one knew the cure to the zombie virus. Maybe Cerys knew a cure, perhaps it was in the Apocalypse Grimoire. Still, Emerson wasn't about to take that chance.

Zokar's strength came as a shock. Zombies' movements were clumsy and cumbersome. However, the zombie king fought with the prowess of a soldier. Finding inner strength, the knight brought both knees—still bound—into Zokar's stomach again, then slammed his gauntlet into his temple. Zokar's grip loosened for a second; that was all Emerson needed.

Scrambling for his sword, he plunged the blade through Zokar's chest. Emerson knew it wouldn't kill him. Weakening his enemy was all he wanted at this point.

Blood seeped through between the blade and Zokar's armor. With his feet still tied together, Emerson pushed against his enemy's chest and dislodged his sword. The bindings around Emerson's legs dissipated. It seemed stabbing the zombie king had severed his hold on the enchanted chains. The knight closed his eyes for a brief second, blowing out a relieved breath. When he opened them, Emerson saw Zokar had disappeared. Emerson assumed he retreated like the coward he was.

That was fine; he had avoided getting bit.

Chapter Twenty-Nine

Tristan expected to see the golden light of the afterlife greet him, but it never came. First came the shouting and metal clanging, wyverns flapping their wings. Then, he heard three female voices. The blinding scorching magic had loosened its grip on Tristan's body. Breathing became easier. His eyes cracked open to see Malice was no longer facing him. In her left hand, she still held his crown, all while battling Zombia.

Her glaive came up to meet Malice's staff, the blade slicing into the wood. A flash of light threw Malice to the ground. Her satchel flew from her shoulder; the Apocalypse Grimoire fell out and skidded to a halt at Cerys's feet, whose wand was smoking from the spell she had cast. The mage picked up the book, clutching it to her chest. Tristan's crown clattered to the floor.

Tristan heard footsteps. Seconds later, hands pressed to his chest. Instantly, Malice's spell loosened its hold as Zombia knelt over the king. He felt his energy return. The leaden sensation weighing down his limbs lifted. He could breathe normally. Tristan sat up, staring into Zombia's shining eyes, a simper on her face.

How'd she do it? Reverse magic? I guess healers can cure magical afflictions as well as physical ones.

When Zombia's hand left his chest, Tristan's vision cleared, and he found the strength to stand. A demon roared behind Tristan but was swiftly silenced with a bolt from Tibia's crossbow. She ran through the crowd and wrapped her arms around her brother.

"Are you all right?" Tristan's sister asked.

Tristan nodded, hugging her back. Releasing her embrace, the Skeleteria queen bent down, retrieved her brother's crown and placed it back on his head with a grin.

Movement behind Tibia cut their sibling moment short. Malice stood from the ground, clutching her broken staff. Smoke wafted off her. Cracks slithered across her armor. Her navy robes were torn at the edges and covered in soot and blood. Her posture was slumped, fists clenched as her black eyes focused on Tristan.

Tibia, Cerys, Tristan, and Zombia encircled the Shadowblood, their weapons all aimed at her. She raised her staff, but another bolt, infused with lava, shot from Tibia's crossbow. It struck the royal blue orb, shattering it entirely; ebony wood splintered harmlessly to the ground. Malice looked down at her destroyed staff. Pieces of glass lay scattered, glowing a warm orange still hot from the lava-imbued bolt. Bending the elements had been helpful. If they weren't locked in battle, Tristan could have hugged Cerys.

A heartbeat later, Malice sprang forward, grabbing the mage in her grip, stopping her mid-incantation. Cerys yelped as the demon twisted her arm backward. Tristan flipped his sword back into a bow, directed at Malice's forehead. The demon pivoted so the arrowhead was pointed at Cerys's forehead instead of hers. Tristan let the string go slack.

"Let her go!" said Tibia, her voice low and threatening as always. She was in the same predicament; if she fired, she'd shoot Cerys. Not Malice.

"I wouldn't try anything if I were you," Malice said. "I don't need any weapon to get what I want." She pulled Cerys's arm tighter; there was a loud pop. The mage cried out again.

Tibia looked to Tristan. "It would be helpful if you could direct my bolts like you did when we were practicing."

The king shook his head. "It's too risky. You don't know what Malice could do." Malice pulled harder on the mage's arm—so hard, threatening to break it. With her other hand, she summoned a piece of shattered glass from her staff and held it to Cerys's throat. The edge pressed in, drawing blood.

Something smashed against the Shadowblood's back, followed by the sound of breaking glass. Malice's grip slipped, allowing Cerys to pry herself free. The demon crumpled to the ground, screaming as steam wafted off her back in tendrils.

Zombia ran to the mage's side, grabbing her hand. Her shoulder was twisted at a horrible angle. Any further and it would've been completely dislocated. Still holding the mage's hand, Zombia chanted. A golden sheen enveloped the girl's shoulder. Cerys stood and smiled, rolling her shoulder.

"Thank you," she said. "You're going to save many lives."

Zombia's eyes twinkled as she led Cerys back to the group. Tristan turned and found Emerson, standing over a hunched Malice, holding a vile of clear liquid. Blessed water. He remembered what Cerys had said about it—it could repel demons.

"I'm glad we got these," said Emerson, rolling a bottle in his palm. "Who knew an all-powerful demon would be bested by a bottle of water," the knight said with a mocking smile. Holding his satchel, Tristan shook it, hearing the bottles clank inside. He looked from the activated mirror back to Malice's hunched form. An idea formed in his head. He addressed Zombia, Cerys, and Tibia.

"Throw these at Malice," the king instructed. "Once she's weakened, I'll push her through the mirror then break the glass. Understand?"

The three nodded, reached into their bags, and produced bottles of blessed water.

Malice groaned as she pushed herself back up to standing. She staggered, momentarily weakened. "I'm not done with you," she said through gritted teeth. Pale green light encased Malice's fingers, forming a magic twine. The strings shot from her claws and wrapped around Tristan's bow, yanking the weapon from his hands.

Zombia severed the string with her glaive, but it was too late. Malice bent over and grabbed the bow, flashing her pointed teeth at the wizards.

"Ha, not only do I have your weapon, I'm going to use it against you," called Malice, her voice filled with pride.

"Now!" shouted Tristan. Together, the five friends tossed bottle after bottle of blessed water. Her skin sizzled and burned. Her fingers splayed, letting the king's bow fall from her grasp. Tristan watched her, making sure he and his friends backed her into the mirrors. Once he ran out of water, Tristan collected his bow and fired upon any zombies and demons blocking the path, but with each arrow, his magic energy weakened.

His stomach clenched, realizing he couldn't do this much longer.

"I don't have any more bottles!" Zombia called. Her final bottle smashed Malice in the face. More black blood dripped from her nose and forehead. Her clothes had black smears, like she'd rolled around in an ink puddle.

"I'm out as well," said Tibia. "I think my magic is getting low. My bow is having trouble reloading."

Malice stood upright, grinning at the wizards. "Looks like you're out of ideas."

The moment she said this, something streaked through the sky. A runaway fireball from one of the wyverns soared for the dais—directly at Zombia. The wyvern hadn't meant it. If a dragon breathed fire, the slightest movement could throw off the flame's trajectory.

Tristan ran for her, but the fireball was faster. Just as Tristan's hope fizzled out, a blur of green knocked Zombia to the ground, saving her. The fireball struck the ground, erupting rock everywhere; a large piece of the floor struck Malice in the temple, rendering her unconscious. When the dust cleared, Tristan saw who saved his friend. Breath lodged in the king's throat.

The person—zombie—who had saved Zombia was Marcus.

The amount of dragons and people dying in this battle made Marcus's stomach churn. In contrast, Marcus still wanted to rise in Malice's ranks, so he chose to fight. During combat, Marcus avoided the zombies and demons, Zokar especially, so they couldn't see that he wasn't actually killing Malice's enemies. His arrows bounced harmlessly off wyvern scales; Marcus took out many Firebournes—opting to wound rather than kill.

Marcus didn't know these elves. He didn't even know there was a *whole* race of elves and dragons in the Underworld. Part of him wanted to learn more about these elves, how they survived in an unbearably hot climate. When Malice took the tribe as slaves, perhaps then, Marcus could study them further. He hoped he'd be in charge of tending to the elves. If she placed them in Zokar's care, Marcus was sure they'd suffer.

Marcus caught a glimpse of the king's knight— Emerson was his name—fighting Zokar. Deep down, excitement surged inside the second-in-command. He hoped the knight would kill the zombie king. Then, he wouldn't have to kill Zokar himself. Nor would Malice have to do it either. Though Marcus had dreamt of putting an arrow in the zombie king's skull, it would be far more efficient if he just died in the battle.

A Firebourne ran at Marcus, but he didn't give the elf a chance. Rather than killing him, Marcus wounded the Firebourne by shooting him in the leg. The elf crumpled to the ground; red-orange blood blossomed on his already dark trousers. The arrow stopped his attack but didn't further the killing. Zokar had done enough of that. Ruthless and brutal. No, that wasn't what Marcus wanted.

Marcus was tired of the killing, actually. He wanted to focus on creating allies. Allies were better than enemies; it was the smarter option, and Malice would notice it. Zokar was such a fool. Using fear to gain allies was stupid. Being generous, but also formidable was how you built an army.

Scanning the courtyard, Marcus saw Malice on the dais, back against the mirrors. Tristan and his friends surrounded her, pelting her with what looked like bottles of water. He sprinted through the brawling bodies. Marcus didn't want to hurt anymore people if he could help it. If he could just stop Tristan from pushing her through the mirrors, that would be enough to earn the demon's trust.

A distressed screech echoed overhead, drawing Marcus's attention. A wyvern heated up a fireball, directed at an offending demon. Its adversary was smarter and launched a blast of black magic at the dragon. The magic struck the wyvern the same time it unleashed its fire, throwing off the wyvern's trajectory. The fire shot for the dais, poised for the queen of Skeletonia.

Marcus acted quickly—it became a race between him and the flaming sphere. Powering his legs, the captain collided with Zombia, knocking her to the ground, the pair landing on the hard floor. A second later, the ground reverberated with an ear-shattering crash.

Blinking, Marcus glanced at a bewildered Zombia. Her brows furrowed with confusion, her eyes darted between her glaive and the second-in-command. She squirmed out of Marcus's arms, weapon aimed at his face, eyes narrowed. Marcus rose to his feet, hands up, palms open. Tristan, Emerson, and Tibia closed around Zombia defensively.

"Get away from her, you fiend," seethed Tibia, rage in her eyes. Marcus heeded her warning and backed away. Over Tibia's shoulder, he noticed a large piece of stone resting beside an unconscious Malice.

"W-why?" was all Tristan could get out. Marcus glanced to the ground then back to the king. "You hate us. Why help now?"

Marcus knew the answer, but didn't say anything. It was simple: he didn't want to be like Zokar. Zokar would have let the fireball hit a young girl without a care. He'd notice, then forget about her five minutes later.

Did Malice still want Zokar killed? Would she still want Marcus as the zombie king when she found out he had the chance to help her and he didn't? Or that he saved one of the demon's enemies?

Still not having answered, Marcus fled the dais.

Tristan's eyes remained glued to Marcus until he disappeared into the battle. He turned to Zombia and wrapped his arms around her, the tension in his shoulders easing. She was alive. But only because of Marcus.

What made Zokar's second-in-command do such a thing? Tristan knew Marcus and Zokar always butted heads; he'd hear them argue in battle all the time. He could see the contempt for Zokar on Marcus's face when the cowardly zombie king remained at the back of the army, safe, while his soldiers died on the front lines. Was Marcus learning morals, or did he have an ulterior motive?

It would be nice if Marcus turned good and repented. One less zombie to fight and one more person on our side.

"It's going to take more than a stupid fireball to kill me, wizard," Malice said from behind Tristan. She rose on wobbly legs. Inky blood cascaded down her temple, a nasty bruise formed around the wound, the purple-blue skin puckered, caked in black from where the chunk of rock hit her. Lightning crackled in her fingers, but the Shadowblood was weak.

Thank the gods.

Tristan remembered he could generate magic from his crown's gem. So, he did. He drew a portion of his magic and transferred it to his sister. When she lifted her bow again, the bolts became easier to reload. She took out two zombies sprinting her way. She winked at her brother.

Tristan smirked as newfound confidence swelled inside. "Tib, prepare to fire again, draw more magic from the lava." Putting his fingers to his mouth, he whistled. Ghist flew down from the sky, astride her wyvern. She hovered just above the dais.

Simultaneously, Tibia, Tristan, and Ghist launched their projectiles. Her wyvern's fireball caught Tristan's arrow, forming a ball of enchanted fire.

Time seemed to slow as the flame careened through the air, striking Malice in the chest. Her eyes widened with an emotion Tristan never saw the demon express: fear. A pained shriek tore from her as she was pushed back, forced through the mirror.

Instinctively, Tristan slammed the hilt of his bow-turned-sword into the glass as hard as he could. Sharp edges exploded outward, skittering across the floor. The king repeated the same action until there was nothing left of the mirrors save for the filigreed frame.

Chapter Thirty

Tristan stepped back, breathing heavily. A few scrapes covered his arms from the flying shards, but it didn't matter. Malice was through the mirror, trapped in the Otherworld. The Haunted Lands could sleep in peace, for now. A leaden feeling weighed down Tristan's limbs, his magic energy nearly depleted. If he tried another spell, he was sure to overheat and combust.

Still on the dais, Tristan surveyed the courtyard. The casualties were too many to count. Firebournes, zombies, and demons littered the ground. The keening from the wyverns started up again, piercing Tristan's eardrums. Pools of crimson covered the stones, flowing in between the cracks. Any zombies left, Tibia guided away using Karneleth's staff. Seeing Malice, their leader, was gone, the demons scattered, fleeing the hall.

Tristan sighed. At least not all lives were lost, but still, one life lost is too many.

Tristan turned to his friends, warmth filling

his chest, replacing the sorrow. Words didn't form immediately. Sadness melted into happiness when a huge cacophony of cheers rose into the sky. The Firebournes, including Ghist and Blaster, swirled around in elated circles. The wyverns beat their wings, chirping with glee. Zombia threw her arms around Tristan and kissed him on the cheek. Heat rose to his face as he blushed.

Emerson, Cerys, and Tibia wrapped their arms around Zombia and Tristan, adding to the victorious excitement. When they parted, Tristan beckoned Ghist. The queen regent brought her wyvern to the ground and dismounted, her brother on her tail.

Tristan extended a hand. "Thank you for all your help. We couldn't have done this without you."

Ghist shrugged as her golden eyes looked off into the distance, as though this were trivial. She smirked, but her eyes sparkled with genuine acceptance.

"No problem. Like I said; you'll need our help whether you like it or not. Turns out, you did." Ghist smirked.

"And for that, we're eternally grateful," said Cerys. The mage nodded to Ghist.

Tristan faced Tibia, who refused to look at Ghist. He nudged his sister in the side. She frowned at him, but her brows were creased with an unsaid apology.

"I think you owe her an apology," Zombia said, arms crossed and eyebrows furrowed.

Tibia let out an exasperated sigh. "For what?" Her words faltered; the question wasn't genuine. She knew what she was sorry for. Tristan saw it in her eyes.

"How you treated Ghist and Blaster when you first met them," Tristan said, elbowing his sister again. "You weren't very accepting."

The Skeleteria queen sighed, her gaze softening. Forcing a smile, she extended a hand to Ghist. "I'm sorry. Thank you for your help. I should've been nicer."

Ghist grinned and returned the handshake. "I see . . . being open isn't your strong suit. I can get used to that. I will admit you have a way with weapons. You'll have to show me sometime."

Tibia's face lit up. "It would be my pleasure."

Tristan laughed. "I'm so glad we met you, Ghist. We are forever in your debt."

Blaster waved his hand. "Don't worry about that." He looked at Emerson. "Just take me to Skeletonia one day."

"Will do. I'll introduce you to my friend Cameron. He'll like you. Maybe the three of us can ride wyverns together!"

"I'd love that. We'll race!"

Ghist took her brother by the elbow. "We should head back to Nova. We have to help rebuild and continue your regal studies."

When Blaster made a mock pouty face, Ghist stared him down like a disappointed mother.

"Fine," the Underworld prince retorted. Ghist smiled and turned to Tristan.

"Please keep in contact." She bowed to the king. "Feel free to visit the Underworld anytime."

Ghist and Blaster both mounted their wyverns and whistled. All at once, the two-legged dragons shot into the sky; the air filled with the sound of beating wings. The king scanned the wreckage again, tears pricking his eyes at the sight of strewn bodies. Sighing, he and his friends made for the exit.

"Thank you," Tristan said to Cerys. "Without your help, we wouldn't have been able to defeat Malice."

The mage blushed and looked to the floor, kicking aside a glass shard with her boot. "All I did was give you advice. You did the real work. You dared to learn. You worked arduously; Blanchett would be so proud of you three. A wizard is strongest when they cooperate with their fellow wizards. Light magic is strongest when combined, growing strong enough to combat evil forces."

The mage paused at the top of the stairs and peered over her shoulder at Tristan. "Stick together, and you'll be unstoppable."

Tristan glanced down at his wrist; Blanchett's marking was still covered by the gold cuff his father gave him. At the start of the journey, Tristan felt that his magic was a curse and should be hidden. Now they had vanquished Malice's army. He had a newfound respect for light magic. Magic could be used for good.

"What are you going to do when we return to the surface world?" Zombia asked Cerys.

"Help you train, of course," the mage said with a grin.

"I'm so glad to hear that! You've been so much fun to be around." Zombia jumped for joy and threw her arms around her new friend.

Releasing her embrace, Zombia looked from the mage to Tristan. "We should head back to Skeletonia. Hopefully Faye will have reached peace between the elf tribes."

"And she'll give us the dragon-claw dagger," said

Tibia. "Malice isn't dead, so she's still a threat."

Tristan nodded. As they exited the courtyard, Tristan forced himself to traverse the sea of bodies, searching for Marcus or Zokar. The king took a shaky breath seeing Malice's closest zombies weren't among the casualties.

They're still alive. I have no doubt they're already returning to the surface world and planning how to release Malice from the Otherworld. We have to get that dagger quickly.

Tristan swallowed nervously and left the courtyard.

Emerson lingered at the rear of the formation, watching for threats. The bodies of their enemies and comrades littered the courtyard. Small fires ignited by the wyverns lingered on the mirrors' wooden frames. The place was as silent as death, yet Emerson's spine tingled in alarm.

There was a scuffing of boots on stone. Emerson spun, bringing up his sword to defend himself, but it was too late. Zokar sprinted from the darkness with unnatural speed. Red was smeared over his armor, surrounding the thin stab wound delivered by

Emerson's blade. The zombie king dove for the knight, gripped his right arm, and sank his teeth into his bicep.

Pain, sharper than any sword or arrow, blasted down the length of his arm and out his fingertips. Blood ran down Emerson's tanned skin, staining his blue shirt and splattering his face. A scream welled in Emerson's throat, but never came out. Thinking fast, Emerson swung his sword, cutting into Zokar's cheek.

The zombie king reeled back, losing his grip on Emerson, then fled back into the darkness like the coward he was. Only a few drops of crimson flecked the floor where he stood. Chest heaving, Emerson caught his breath and practically collapsed against the wall, legs shaking as he inspected his wound. A ring of tooth marks covered his bicep, close to his shoulder. His breath hitched as he realized what this meant. Tears prickled his eyes—both from the pain and deciding what to do next.

Emerson looked at his sword. He knew soldiers with infected battle wounds would have their limbs amputated to stop the spread of gangrene. But the zombie infection was different. Amputation wouldn't work here. The zombie virus worked by entering the bloodstream, traveling up to the brain. It was too late from the moment Zokar's teeth punctured Emerson's skin.

No, Emerson couldn't tell his friends, for he knew what they would do. They'd ostracize him, then kill him.

An image of Tristan putting an arrow through the knight's skull through tearstained eyes flashed in Emerson's head. Sweat trailed down his neck and back.

Blinking away his tears, Emerson spared a glance at his wound. With each ticking second, the virus crawled through his blood, invading his system.

First, a fever would begin, followed by partial paralysis and numbness of the joints. A coma would follow, leading to eventual heart stoppage. Next came reanimation.

Emerson closed his eyes briefly, letting warm tears roll down his cheeks. His fate was sealed. Swallowing the lump in his throat, Emerson covered his wound with his armor's pauldron, and exited the courtyard.

Tristan stepped out onto the terrace. There, he met a ring of five wyverns, two of them carrying Blaster and Ghist.

"We thought you might need a ride back," said Ghist, bringing her wyvern close, his legs bending, allowing for anyone to board.

Zombia looked at him with that do-we-have-to face. The king had to agree riding on the back of a wyvern was terrifying. But it would be faster than walking.

"Yeah, that would be great!" said Tristan with a cordial smile.

"Hey, where's Emerson?" asked Zombia, grabbing Ghist's hand, climbing into the saddle.

"Here," Emerson called from behind Tibia and Cerys.

"There you are, come on, Blaster and Ghist are offering us a ride back to the portal," Tristan said with a smile, but it quickly wavered. The knight looked distressed—pale and shaken.

The king tilted his head, locking eyes with Emerson. What happened in the past few minutes?

"Are you okay?" asked Tristan.

Emerson nodded vigorously. "Oh, I'm just great." The knight tilted his right arm out of sight.

Strange. Why's he acting like this? Was he wounded? I'll have to see when we return to the surface world.

Tristan smiled when Blaster offered a hand, helping the king into the saddle. Cerys, Emerson, and Tibia climbed on the other three wyverns. A split second later, the dragons launched into the air. The ground grew smaller as the wyverns climbed into the sky. Warm wind whistled past Tristan's ears, his soul and heart feeling light. They'd accomplished their mission, though it was temporary. Malice was gone, for now.

But without the dragon-claw dagger, Tristan knew Malice would soon return.

Acknowledgements

Huge thank you to my friends and family for standing by my side and supporting me through my writing journey. You've all been so helpful as I work through endless writing sessions and revisions. Your encouragements and kind words have kept me motivated. I am eternally grateful.

I'd also like to thank my editors, Isobelle and Carly. Here's to everyone who helped with formatting, cover design, and proofreading. Thank you for your wonderful editing and kind support.

Finally, I'd like to express gratitude to my readers, beta readers, and everyone who reviewed my book. All your excitement for my characters and story has been so wonderful and encouraging. I'm truly grateful that you supported me on my road to publication. Without you, my book would still be just an idea in my head. Thank you.